The Author

MAVIS GALLANT was born in Montreal in 1922. She spent her childhood years in Quebec, Ontario, and the eastern United States. After completing high school in New York City, she returned to Montreal, where, among other jobs, she worked at the National Film Board. At the age of twenty-one, she became a reporter for the Montreal *Standard* and stayed with the newspaper for six years. In 1950 she left Canada for Europe, living at various times in Austria, Italy, Spain, and the south of France before settling in Paris.

One of the most acclaimed writers of fiction of our time, Gallant invests the characters of her novels and short stories with a sense of their ambiguous and haunting past, their dilemmas often reflecting more public expressions of postwar anxiety and dislocation. She leavens her vision with a deft irony which reaches at once towards the comic and the tragic.

Gallant is a Companion of the Order of Canada, Fellow of the Royal Society of Literature, and Honorary Foreign Member of the American Academy of Arts and Letters.

Mavis Gallant resides in Paris, France.

THE NEW CANADIAN LIBRARY

General Editor: David Staines

Mavis Gallant

THE MOSLEM
WIFE
AND OTHER STORIES

*Selected and
with an Afterword by Mordecai Richler*

M&S

Canadian Cataloguing in Publication Data

Gallant, Mavis, 1922-
The Moslem wife and other stories

(New Canadian library)
Includes bibliographical references.
ISBN 0-7710-9891-X

I. Richler, Mordecai. II. Title. III. Series.

PS8513.A593M65 1993   C813'.54   C93-093798-8
PR9199.3.G35M68 1993

The publishers acknowledge the support of the Canada Council and
the Ontario Arts Council for their publishing program.

Cover design by Andrew Skuja
Typesetting by M&S, Toronto
The support of the Government of Ontario through the
Ministry of Culture and Communications is acknowledged.

Printed and bound in Canada

McClelland & Stewart Inc.
The Canadian Publishers
481 University Avenue
Toronto, Ontario
M5G 2E9

1 2 3 4 5   98 97 96 95 94

Contents

Acknowledgements

The year printed at the end of each story indicates its original date of publication. In this collection I have reprinted the text of each story as it appeared in the author's most recent published version: "About Geneva" (*The Other Paris* 1956); "When We Were Nearly Young" (*In Transit* 1988); "My Heart Is Broken" and "The Ice Wagon Going Down the Street" (*My Heart Is Broken* 1964); "An Autobiography" (*The Pegnitz Junction* 1973); "Saturday" and "In Youth Is Pleasure" (*Home Truths* 1981); "The Latehomecomer" and "The Moslem Wife" (*From the Fifteenth District* 1979); "Grippes and Poche" and "Overhead in a Balloon" (*Overhead in a Balloon* 1985).

D.S.

The Moslem Wife and Other Stories

About Geneva

Granny was waiting at the door of the apartment. She looked small, lonely, and patient, and at the sight of her the children and their mother felt instantly guilty. Instead of driving straight home from the airport, they had stopped outside Nice for ice cream. They might have known how much those extra twenty minutes would mean to Granny. Colin, too young to know what he felt, or why, began instinctively to misbehave, dragging his feet, scratching the waxed parquet. Ursula bit her nails, taking refuge in a dream, while the children's mother, Granny's only daughter, felt compelled to cry in a high, cheery voice, "Well, Granny, here they are, safe and sound!"

"Darlings," said Granny, very low. "Home again." She stretched out her arms to Ursula, but then, seeing the taxi driver, who had carried the children's bags up the stairs, she drew back. After he had gone she repeated the gesture, turning this time to Colin, as if Ursula's cue had been irrevocably missed. Colin was wearing a beret. "Wherever did that come from?" Granny said. She pulled it off and stood still, stricken. "My darling little boy," she said, at last. "What have they done to you? They have cut your hair. Your lovely golden hair. I cannot believe it. I don't want to believe it."

"It was high time," the children's mother said. She stood in the outer corridor, waiting for Granny's welcome to subside. "It was high time someone cut Colin's hair. The curls made such a baby of him. We should have seen that. Two women can't really bring up a boy."

Granny didn't look at all as if she agreed. "Who cut your hair?" she said, holding Colin.

"Barber," he said, struggling away.

"Less said the better," said Colin's mother. She came in at last, drew off her gloves, looked around, as if she, and not the children, had been away.

"He's not my child, of course," said Granny, releasing Colin. "If he were, I can just imagine the letter I should write. Of all the impudence! When you send a child off for a visit you expect at the very least to have him returned exactly as he left. And you," she said, extending to Ursula a plump, liver-spotted hand, "what changes am I to expect in you?"

"Oh, Granny, for Heaven's sake, it was only two weeks." She permitted her grandmother to kiss her, then went straight to the sitting room and hurled herself into a chair. The room was hung with dark engravings of cathedrals. There were flowers, red carnations, on the rickety painted tables, poked into stiff arrangements by a maid. It was the standard seasonal Nice *meublé*. Granny spent every winter in rented flats more or less like this one, and her daughter, since her divorce, shared them with her.

Granny followed Ursula into the room and sat down, erect, on an uncomfortable chair, while her daughter, trailing behind, finally chose a footstool near the empty fireplace. She gave Granny a gentle, neutral look. Before starting out for the airport, earlier, she had repeated her warning: There were to be no direct questions, no remarks. It was all to appear as natural and normal as possible. What, indeed, could be more natural for the children than a visit with their father?

"What, indeed," said Granny in a voice rich with meaning.

It was only fair, said the children's mother. A belief in fair play was so embedded in her nature that she could say the words without coloring deeply. Besides, it was the first time he had asked.

"And won't be the last," Granny said. "But, of course, it is up to you."

Ursula lay rather than sat in her chair. Her face was narrow and freckled: She resembled her mother who, at thirty-four, had settled into a permanent, anxious-looking, semi-youthfulness. Colin, blond and fat, rolled on the floor. He pulled his mouth out at the corners, then pulled down his eyes to show the hideous red underlids. He looked at his grandmother and growled like a lion.

"Colin has come back sillier than ever," Granny said. He lay prone, noisily snuffing the carpet. The others ignored him.

"Did you go boating, Ursula?" said Granny, not counting this as a direct question. "When I visited Geneva, as a girl, we went boating on the lake." She went on about white water birds, a parasol, a boat heaped with colored cushions.

"Oh, Granny, no," said Ursula. "There weren't even any big boats, let alone little ones. It was cold."

"I hope the house, at least, was warm."

But evidently Ursula had failed to notice the temperature of her father's house. She slumped on her spine (a habit Granny had just nicely caused her to get over before the departure for Geneva) and then said, unexpectedly, "She's not a good manager."

Granny and her daughter exchanged a look, eyebrows up.

"Oh?" said Ursula's mother, pink. She forgot about the direct questions and said, "Why?"

"It's not terribly polite to speak that way of one's hostess," said Granny, unable to resist the reproof but threatening Ursula's revelation at the source. Her daughter looked at her, murderous.

"Well," said Ursula, slowly, "once the laundry didn't come

back. It was her fault, he said. Our sheets had to be changed, he said. So she said Oh, all right. She took the sheets off Colin's bed and put them on my bed, and took the sheets off my bed and put them on Colin's. To make the change, she said."

"Dear God," said Granny.

"Colin's sheets were a mess. He had his supper in bed sometimes. They were just a mess."

"Not true," said Colin.

"Another time . . . ," said Ursula, and stopped, as if Granny had been right, after all, about criticizing one's hostess.

"Gave us chocolate," came from Colin, his face muffled in carpet.

"Not every day, I trust," Granny said.

"For the plane."

"It might very well have made you both airsick," said Granny.

"Well," said Ursula, "it didn't." Her eyes went often to the luggage in the hall. She squirmed upright, stood up, and sat down again. She rubbed her nose with the back of her hand.

"Ursula, do you want a handkerchief?" said Granny.

"No," said Ursula. "Only it so happens I'm writing a play. It's in the suitcase."

Granny and the children's mother looked at each other again. "I *am* pleased," Granny said, and her daughter nodded, agreeing, for, if impertinence and slumping on one's spine were unfortunate inherited tendencies, this was something else. It was only fair that Ursula's father should have bequeathed her *something* to compensate for the rest. "What is it about?" said Granny.

Ursula looked at her feet. After a short silence she said, "Russia. That's all I want to tell. It was her idea. She lived there once."

Quietly, controlled, the children's mother took a cigarette from the box on the table. Granny looked brave.

"Would you tell us the title, at least?" said Granny.

"No," said Ursula. But then, as if the desire to share the splendid thing she had created were too strong, she said, "I'll tell you one line, because they said it was the best thing they'd ever heard anywhere." She took a breath. Her audience was gratifyingly attentive, straining, nearly, with attention and control. "It goes like this," Ursula said. "'The Grand Duke enters and sees Tatiana all in gold.'"

"Well?" said Granny.

"Well, what?" said Ursula. "That's it. That's the line." She looked at her mother and grandmother and said, "*They* liked it. They want me to send it to them, and everything else, too. She even told me the name Tatiana."

"It's lovely, dear," said Ursula's mother. She put the cigarette back in the box. "It sounds like a lovely play. Just when did she live in Russia?"

"I don't know. Ages ago. She's pretty old."

"Perhaps one day we shall see the play after all," said Granny. "Particularly if it is to be sent all over the Continent."

"You mean they might act in it?" said Ursula. Thinking of this, she felt sorry for herself. Ever since she had started "The Grand Duke" she could not think of her own person without being sorry. For no reason at all, now, her eyes filled with tears of self-pity. Drooping, she looked out at the darkening street, to the leafless trees and the stone façade of a public library.

But the children's mother, as if Granny's remark had for her an entirely different meaning, not nearly so generous, said, "I shall give you the writing desk from my bedroom, Ursula. It has a key."

"Where will you keep your things?" said Granny, protesting. She could not very well say that the desk was her own, not to be moved: Like everything else – the dark cathedrals, the shaky painted tables – it had come with the flat.

"I don't need a key," said the children's mother, lacing her fingers tightly around her knees. "I'm not writing a play, or anything else I want kept secret. Not any more."

"They used to take Colin for walks," said Ursula, yawning, only vaguely taking in the importance of the desk. "That was when I started to write this thing. Once they stayed out the whole afternoon. They never said where they'd been."

"I wonder," said her mother, thoughtful. She started to say something to Ursula, something not quite a question, but the child was too preoccupied with herself. Everything about the trip, in the end, would crystallize around Tatiana and the Grand Duke. Already, Ursula was Tatiana. The children's mother looked at Ursula's long bare legs, her heavy shoes, her pleated skirt, and she thought, I must do something about her clothes, something to make her pretty.

"Colin, dear," said Granny in her special inner-meaning voice, "do you remember your walks?"

"No."

"I wonder why they wanted to take him alone," said Colin's mother. "It seems odd, all the same."

"Under seven," said Granny, cryptic. "Couldn't influence girl. Too old. Boy different. Give me first seven years, you can have rest."

"But it wasn't seven years. He hasn't been alive that long. It was only two weeks."

"Two very impressionable weeks," Granny said.

"I understand everything you're saying," Ursula said, "even when you talk that way. They spoke French when they didn't want us to hear, but we understood that, too."

"I fed the swans," Colin suddenly shouted.

There, he had told about Geneva. He sat up and kicked his heels on the carpet as if the noise would drown out the consequence of what he had revealed. As he said it, the image became static: a gray sky, a gray lake, and a swan wonderfully turning upside down with the black rubber feet showing above the water. His father was not in the picture at all; neither was *she*. But Geneva was fixed for the rest of his life: gray, lake, swan.

Having delivered his secret he had nothing more to tell. He began to invent. "I was sick on the plane," he said, but Ursula at once said that this was a lie, and he lay down again, humiliated. At last, feeling sleepy, he began to cry.

"He never once cried in Geneva," Ursula said. But by the one simple act of creating Tatiana and the Grand Duke, she had removed herself from the ranks of reliable witnesses.

"How would you know?" said Granny bitterly. "You weren't always with him. If you had paid more attention, if you had taken care of your little brother, he wouldn't have come back to us with his hair cut."

"Never mind," said the children's mother. Rising, she helped Colin to his feet and led him away to bed.

She stood behind him as he cleaned his teeth. He looked male and self-assured with his newly cropped head, and she thought of her husband, and how odd it was that only a few hours before Colin had been with him. She touched the tender back of his neck. "Don't," he said. Frowning, concentrating, he hung up his toothbrush. "I told about Geneva."

"Yes, you did." He had fed swans. She saw sunshine, a blue lake, and the boats Granny had described, heaped with colored cushions. She saw her husband and someone else (probably in white, she thought, ridiculously bouffant, the origin of Tatiana) and Colin with his curls shorn, revealing ears surprisingly large. There was nothing to be had from Ursula – not, at least, until the Grand Duke had died down. But Colin seemed to carry the story of the visit with him, and she felt the faintest stirrings of envy, the resentfulness of the spectator, the loved one left behind.

"Were you really sick on the plane?" she said.

"Yes," said Colin.

"Were they lovely, the swans?"

But the question bore no relation to anything he had seen. He said nothing. He played with toothpaste, dawdling.

"Isn't that child in bed yet?" called Granny. "Does he want his supper?"

"No," said Colin.

"No," said his mother. "He was sick on the plane."

"I thought so," Granny said. "That, at least, is a fact."

They heard the voice of Ursula, protesting.

But how can they be trusted, the children's mother thought. Which of them can one believe? "Perhaps," she said to Colin, "one day, you can tell me more about Geneva?"

"Yes," he said perplexed.

But, really, she doubted it; nothing had come back from the trip but her own feelings of longing and envy, the longing and envy she felt at night, seeing, at a crossroad or over a bridge, the lighted windows of a train sweep by. Her children had nothing to tell her. Perhaps, as she had said, one day Colin would say something, produce the image of Geneva, tell her about the lake, the boats, the swans, and why her husband had left her. Perhaps he could tell her, but, really, she doubted it. And, already, so did he.

1955

When We Were Nearly Young

IN MADRID, nine years ago, we lived on the thought of money. Our friendships were nourished with talk of money we expected to have, and what we intended to do when it came. There were four of us – two men and two girls. The men, Pablo and Carlos, were cousins. Pilar was a relation of theirs. I was not Spanish and not a relation, and a friend almost by mistake. The thing we had in common was that we were all waiting for money.

Every day I went to the Central Post Office, and I made the rounds of the banks and the travel agencies, where letters and money could come. I was not certain how much it might be, or where it was going to arrive, but I saw it riding down a long arc like a rainbow. In those days I was always looking for signs. I saw signs in cigarette smoke, in the way ash fell and in the cards. I laid the cards out three times a week, on Monday, Wednesday and Friday. Tuesday, Thursday and Saturday were no good, because the cards were mute or evasive; and on Sundays they lied. I thought these signs – the ash, the smoke and so on – would tell me what direction my life was going to take and what might happen from now on. I had unbounded belief in free will, which most of the people I knew despised, but I was superstitious, too. I saw inside my eyelids at night the nine of clubs, which is an excellent card, and the ten of hearts, which is better, morally speaking, since it implies gain through effort. I saw the aces of clubs and diamonds, and the jack of diamonds, who is the postman. Although Pablo and Pilar and Carlos were not waiting for anything in particular – indeed, had nothing to wait for, except a fortune – they were anxious about the postman, and relieved when he turned up. They never supposed that the postman would not arrive, or that his coming might have no significance.

Carlos and Pablo came from a town outside Madrid. They had no near relatives in the city, and they shared a room in a flat on Calle Hortaleza. I lived in a room along the hall; that was how we came to know each other. Pilar, who was twenty-two, the youngest of the four of us, lived in a small flat of her own. She had been married to Carlos's stepbrother at seventeen, and had been a widow three years. She was eager to marry again but feared she was already too old. Carlos was twenty-nine, the oldest. Pablo and I came in between.

Carlos worked in a bank. His salary was so small that he could barely subsist on it, and he was everywhere in debt. Pablo studied law at the University of Madrid. When he had nothing to do, he went with me on my rounds. These rounds took up most of the day, and had become important, for, after a time, the fact of waiting became more valid than the thing I was waiting for. I knew that I would feel let down when the waiting was over. I went to the post office, to three or four banks, to Cook's and American Express. At each place, I stood and waited in a queue. I have never seen so many queues, or so many patient people. I also gave time and thought to selling my clothes. I sold them to the gypsies in the flea market. Once I got a dollar-fifty for a coat and a skirt, but it was stolen from my pocket when I stopped to buy a newspaper. I thought I had jostled the thief, and when I said "Sorry" he nodded his head and walked quickly away. He was a man of about thirty. I can still see his turned-up collar and the back of his head. When I put my hand in my pocket to pay for the paper, the money was gone. When I was not standing in queues or getting rid of clothes, I went to see Pilar. We sat out on her balcony when it was fine, and next to her kitchen stove when it was cold. We were not ashamed to go to the confectioner's across the street and bargain in fractions of pennies for fifty grams of chocolate, which we scrupulously shared. Pilar was idle, but restful. Pablo was idle, but heavy about it. He was the most heavily idle person I have ever known. He was also the only one of us who had any money. His father sent him money for his room and his meals, and he had an extra allowance from his godfather, who owned a hotel on one of the coasts. Pablo was dark, curly-haired and stocky, with the large head and opaque eyes you saw on the streets of Madrid. He was one of the New Spaniards – part of the first generation grown to maturity under Franco. He was the generation they were so proud of in the newspapers. But he must be – he *is* – well over thirty now, and no longer New. He had already calculated, with paper and pencil, what the future held, and decided it was worth only half a try.

We stood in endless queues together in banks, avoiding the bank where Carlos worked, because we were afraid of giggling and embarrassing him. We shelled peanuts and gossiped and held hands in the blank, amiable waiting state that had become the essence of life. When we had heard the ritual "No" everywhere, we went home.

Home was a dark, long flat filled with the sound of clocks and dripping faucets. It was a pension, of a sort, but secret. In order to escape paying taxes, the owners had never declared it to the police, and lived in perpetual dread. A girl had given me the address on a train, warning me to say nothing about it to anyone. There was one other foreign person – a crazy old Englishwoman. She never spoke a word to me and, I think, hated me on sight. But she did not like Spaniards any better; one could hear her saying so when she talked to herself. At first we were given meals, but after a time, because the proprietors were afraid about the licensing and the police, that stopped, and so we bought food and took it to Pilar's, or cooked in my room on an alcohol stove. We ate rationed bread with lumps of flour under the crust, and horrible ersatz jam. We were always vaguely hungry. Our craving for sweet things was limitless; we bought cardboard pastries that seemed exquisite because of the lingering sugary taste they left in the mouth. Sometimes we went to a restaurant we called "the ten-peseta place" because you could get a three-course meal with wine and bread for ten pesetas – about twenty-three cents then. There was also the twelve-peseta place, where the smell was less nauseating, although the food was nearly as rank. The décor in both restaurants was distinctly unEuropean. The cheaper the restaurant, the more cheaply Oriental it became. I remember being served calves' brains in an open skull.

One of the customers in the ten-peseta restaurant was a true madman, with claw hands, sparse hair and dying skin. He looked like a monkey, and behaved like one I had known, who would accept grapes and bananas with pleasure, and then, shrieking with hate at some shadowy insult, would dance and gibber and try to bite. This man would not eat from his plate. He was beyond even saying the plate was poisoned; that had been settled long ago. He shovelled his food onto the table, or onto pieces of bread, and scratched his head with his fork, turning and muttering with smiles and scowls. Everyone sat still when he had his seizures – not in horror, even less with compassion, but still, suspended. I remember a coarse-faced sergeant slowly lowering his knife and fork and parting his heavy lips as he stared; and I remember the blankness in the room – the waiting. What will happen next? What does it mean? The atmosphere was full of cold, secret marvelling. But nobody moved or spoke.

We often came away depressed, saying that it was cheaper and pleasanter to eat at home; but the stove was slow, and we were often too hungry to linger, watching water come to the boil. But food was cheap enough; once, by returning three empty Valdepeñas wine bottles, I bought enough food for three. We ate a lot of onions and potatoes – things like that. Pilar lived on sweet things. I have seen her cook macaroni and sprinkle sugar on it and eat it up. She was a pretty girl, with a pointed face and blue-black hair. But she was an untidy, a dusty sort of girl, and you felt that in a few years something might go wrong; she might get swollen ankles or grow a moustache.

Her flat had two rooms, one of which was rented to a young couple. The other room she divided with a curtain. Behind the curtain was the bed she had brought as part of her dowry for the marriage with Carlos's stepbrother. There was a picture of María Felix, the Mexican actress, on the wall. I would like to tell a story about Pilar, but nobody will believe it. It is how she thought, or pretended to think, that the Museo Romantico was her home. This was an extraordinary museum – a set of rooms furnished with all the trappings of the romantic period. Someone had planned it with love and care, but hardly any visitors came. If any did wander in when we were around, we stared them out. The cousins played the game with Pilar because they had no money and nothing better to do. I see Pilar sitting in an armchair, being elegant, and the boys standing or lounging against a mantelpiece; I say "boys" because I never thought of them as men. I am by the window, with my back turned. I disapprove, and it shows. I feel like a prig. I tip the painted blind, just to see the street and be reassured by a tram going by. It *is* the twentieth century. And Pilar cries, in unaffected anguish, "Oh, make her stop. She is spoiling everything."

I can hear myself saying grandly, "I don't want your silly fairy-tales. I'm trying to get rid of my own."

Carlos says, "I've known people like you before. You think you can get rid of all the baggage – religion, politics, ideas, everything. Well, you won't."

The other two yawn, quite rightly. Carlos and I are bores.

Of them all, I understood Carlos best, but we quarrelled about anything. We could have quarrelled about a piece of string. He was pessimistic, and I detested this temperament; worse, I detested his face. He resembled a certain kind of Swiss or South African or New Zealander. He was suspicious and faintly Anglo-Saxon looking. It was not the English bun-face, or the Swiss canary, or the lizard, or the hawk; it was the unfinished, the undecided, face that accompanies the rotary sprinkler, the wet Martini, pussyfooting in love and friendship, expense-account foolery, the fear of the open heart. He made me think of a lawyer who had once told me, in all sincerity, "Bad things don't happen to nice people." It was certainly not Carlos's fault; I might have helped my prejudices, which I had dragged to Spain with my passport, but he could not help the way he looked. Pablo was stupid, but cheerful. Pilar was demented, but sweet. What was needed – we agreed to this many times – was a person who was a composite of all our best qualities, which we were not too modest to name. Home from the Romantic Museum, they made me turn out the cards. I did the Petit Jeu, the Square, the Fan, and the Thirteen, and the Fifteen. There was happy news for everyone except Carlos, but, as it was Sunday, none of it counted.

Were they typical Spaniards? I don't know what a typical Spaniard is. They didn't dance or play the guitar. Truth and death and pyromania did not lurk in their dark eyes; at least I never saw it. They were grindingly hard up. The difference between them and any three broke people anywhere else was in a certain passiveness, as though everything had been dealt in advance. Barring catastrophe, death and revolution, nothing could happen any more. When we walked together, their steps slowed in rhythm, as if they had all three been struck with the same reluctance to go on. But they did go on, laughing and chattering and saying what they would do when the money came.

We began keeping diaries at about the same time. I don't remember who started it. Carlos's was secret. Pilar asked how to spell words. Pablo told everything before he wrote it down. It was a strange occupation, considering the ages we were, but we hadn't enough to think about. Poverty is not a goad but a paralysis. I have never been back to Madrid. My memories are of squares and monuments, of things that are free or cheap. I see us huddled in coats, gloved and scarfed, fighting the icy wind, pushing along to the ten-peseta place. In another memory it is so hot that we can scarcely force ourselves to the park, where we will sit under elm trees and look at newspapers. Newspapers are the solace of the worried; one absorbs them without having to read. I sometimes went to the libraries – the British Institute and the American one – but I could not for the life of me have put my nose in a book. The very sight of poetry made me sick, and I could not make sense of a novel, or even remember the characters' names.

Oddly enough, we were not afraid. What was the worst that could happen? No one seemed to know. The only fear I remember was an anxiety we had caught from Carlos. He had rounded twenty-nine and saw down a corridor we had not yet reached. He made us so afraid of being thirty that even poor Pilar was alarmed, although she had eight years of grace. I was frightened of it, too. I was not by any means in first youth, and I could not say that the shape of my life was a mystery. But I felt I had done all I could with free will, and that circumstances, the imponderables, should now take a hand. I was giving them every opportunity. I was in a city where I knew not a soul, save the few I had come to know by chance. It was a city where the mentality, the sound of the language, the hopes and possibilities, even the appearance of the people in the streets, were as strange as anything I might have invented. My choice in coming here had been deliberate: I had a plan. My own character seemed to me ill-defined; I believed that this was unfortunate and unique. I thought that if I set myself against a background into which I could not possibly merge that some outline would present itself. But it hadn't succeeded, because I adapted too quickly. In no time at all, I had the speech and the movements and very expression on my face of seedy Madrid.

I was with Pablo more than anyone, but I remember Carlos best. I regret now how much we quarrelled. I think of the timorous, the symbolic, stalemate of our chess games. I was not clever enough to beat him, but he was not brave enough to win. The slowing down of our respective positions on the board led to immobility of thought. I sat nervously smoking, and Carlos sat with his head in his hands. Thought suspended, fear emerged. Carlos's terror that he would soon be thirty and that the affective part of his life had ended with so little to show haunted him and stunned his mind. He would never be anything but the person he was now. I remember the dim light, the racket in the street, the silence inside the flat, the ticking of the Roman-numbered clock in the hall. Time was like water dropping – Madrid time. And I would catch his fear, and I was afraid of the movement of time, at once too quick and too slow. After that came a revolt and impatience. In his company I felt something I had never felt before – actively northern. Seeing him passive, head on hands, I wanted to urge and exhort and beg him to do something: act, talk, sing, dance, finish the game of chess – anything at all. At no period was I as conscious of the movement and meaning of time; and I had chosen the very city where time dropped, a drop from the roof of a cave, one drop at a time.

We came to a financial crisis at about the same moment. Pablo's godfather stopped sending money to him – that was a blow. Pilar's lodgers left. I had nothing more to sell. There was Carlos's little salary, but there were also his debts, and he could not be expected to help his friends. He looked more vaguely Anglo-Saxon, more unfinished and decent than ever. I wished there was something to kick over, something to fight. There was the Spanish situation, of course, and I had certainly given a lot of thought to it before coming to Spain, but now that I was here and down and out I scarcely noticed it. I would think, "*I* am free," but what of it? I was also hungry. I dreamed of food. Pilar dreamed of things chasing her, and Pablo dreamed of me, and Carlos dreamed he was on top of a mountain preaching to multitudes, but I dreamed of baked ham and Madeira sauce. I suspected that my being here and in this situation was all folly, and that I had been trying to improve myself – my moral condition, that is. My financial condition spoke for itself. It was like Orwell, in Paris, revelling in his bedbugs. If that was so, then it was all very plain, and very Protestant, but I could not say more for it than that.

One day I laid out forty-eight cards – the Grand Jeu. The cards predicted treachery, ruin, illness, accidents, letters bringing bad news, disaster and pain.

I made my rounds. In one of the places, the money had come, and I was saved. I went out to the University, where the fighting had been, eleven or twelve years before. It looked like a raw suburban housing development, with its mud, its white buildings and puny trees. I waited in the café where Pablo took his bitter coffee, and when he came in I told him the news. We rode into the heart of Madrid on a swaying tram. Pablo was silent – I thought because he was delighted and overwhelmed; actually, he must have been digesting the astonishing fact that I had been expecting something and that my hanging around in banks was not a harmless mania, like Pilar in the Romantic Museum.

My conception of life (free will plus imponderables) seemed justified again. The imponderables were in my pocket, and free will began to roll. I decided, during the tram ride, to go to Mallorca, hire a villa, invite the three for a long holiday and buy a dog I had seen. We got down from the tram and bought white, tender, delicious, unrationed bread, weighed out by the pound; and three roasted chickens, plus a pound of sweet butter and two three-litre bottles of white Valdepeñas. We bought some nougat and chestnut paste. I forget the rest.

Toward the end of our dinner, and before the end of the wine, Carlos made one bitter remark: "The difference between you and us is that in the end something will always come for you. Nothing will ever come from anywhere for any of us. You must have known it all along."

No one likes to be accused of posturing. I was as irritated as I could be, and quickly turned the remark to his discredit. He was displaying self-pity. Self-pity was the core of his character. It was in the cards; all I could ever turn out for him were plaintive combinations of twos and threes – an abject fear of anonymous threats, and worry that his friends would betray him. This attack silenced him, but it showed that my character was in no way improved by my misfortunes. I defended myself against the charge of pretending. My existence had been poised on waiting, and I had always said I was waiting for something tangible. But they had thought I was waiting in their sense of the word – waiting for summer and then for winter, for Monday and then for Tuesday, waiting, waiting for time to drop into the pool.

We did not talk about what we could do with money now. I was thinking about Mallorca. I knew that if I invited them they would never come. They were polite. They understood that my new fortune cast me out. There was no evasion, but they were nice about it. They had no plans, and simply closed their ranks. We talked of a longer future, remembering Carlos and his fear. We talked of our thirties as if we were sliding toward an icy subterranean water; as if we were to be submerged and frozen just as we were: first Carlos, then Pablo and me, finally little Pilar. She had eight years to wait, but eight would be seven, and seven six, and she knew it.

I don't know what became of them, or what they were like when their thirtieth year came. I left Madrid. I wrote, for a time, but they never answered. Eventually they were caught, for me, not by time but by the freezing of memory. And when I looked in the diary I had kept during that period, all I could find was descriptions of the weather.

1960

My Heart Is Broken

"WHEN THAT Jean Harlow died," Mrs. Thompson said to Jeannie, "I was on the 83 streetcar with a big, heavy paper parcel in my arms. I hadn't been married for very long, and when I used to visit my mother she'd give me a lot of canned stuff and preserves. I was standing up in the streetcar because nobody'd given me a seat. All the men were unemployed in those days, and they just sat down wherever they happened to be. You wouldn't remember what Montreal was like then. *You* weren't even on earth. To resume what I was saying to you, one of these men sitting down had an American paper – the *Daily News*, I guess it was – and I was sort of leaning over him, and I saw in big print 'JEAN HARLOW DEAD.' You can believe me or not, just as you want to, but that was the most terrible shock I ever had in my life. I never got over it."

Jeannie had nothing to say to that. She lay flat on her back across the bed, with her head toward Mrs. Thompson and her heels just touching the crate that did as a bedside table. Balanced on her flat stomach was an open bottle of coral-pink Cutex nail polish. She held her hands up over her head and with some difficulty applied the brush to the nails of her right hand. Her legs were brown and thin. She wore nothing but shorts and one of her husband's shirts. Her feet were bare.

Mrs. Thompson was the wife of the paymaster in a road-construction camp in northern Quebec. Jeannie's husband was an engineer working on the same project. The road was being pushed through country where nothing had existed until now except rocks and lakes and muskeg. The camp was established between a wild lake and the line of raw dirt that was the road. There were no towns between the camp and the railway spur, sixty miles distant.

Mrs. Thompson, a good deal older than Jeannie, had become her best friend. She was a nice, plain, fat, consoling sort of person, with varicosed legs, shoes unlaced and slit for comfort, blue flannel dressing gown worn at all hours, pudding-bowl haircut, and coarse gray hair. She might have been Jeannie's own mother, or her Auntie Pearl. She rocked her fat self in the rocking chair and went on with what she had to say: "What I was starting off to tell you is you remind me of her, of Jean Harlow. You've got the same teeny mouth, Jeannie, and I think your hair was a whole lot prettier before you started fooling around with it. That peroxide's no good. It splits the ends. I know you're going to tell me it isn't peroxide but something more modern, but the result is the same."

Vern's shirt was spotted with coral-pink that had dropped off the brush. Vern wouldn't mind; at least, he wouldn't say that he minded. If he hadn't objected to anything Jeannie did until now, he wouldn't start off by complaining about a shirt. The campsite outside the uncurtained window was silent and dark. The waning moon would not appear until dawn. A passage of thought made Mrs. Thompson say, "Winter soon."

Jeannie moved sharply and caught the bottle of polish before it spilled. Mrs. Thompson was crazy; it wasn't even September.

"Pretty soon," Mrs. Thompson admitted. "Pretty soon. That's a long season up here, but I'm one person doesn't complain. I've been up here or around here every winter of my married life, except for that one winter Pops was occupying Germany."

"I've been up here seventy-two days," said Jeannie, in her soft voice. "Tomorrow makes seventy-three."

"Is that right?" said Mrs. Thompson, jerking the rocker forward, suddenly snappish. "Is that a fact? Well, who asked you to come up here? Who asked you to come and start counting days like you was in some kind of jail? When you got married to Vern, you must of known where he'd be taking you. He told you, didn't he, that he liked road jobs, construction jobs, and that? Did he tell you, or didn't he?"

"Oh, he told me," said Jeannie.

"You know what, Jeannie?" said Mrs. Thompson. "If you'd of just listened to me, none of this would have happened. I told you that first day, the day you arrived here in your high-heeled shoes, I said, 'I know this cabin doesn't look much, but all the married men have the same sort of place.' You remember I said that? I said, 'You just get some curtains up and some carpets down and it'll be home.' I took you over and showed you my place, and you said you'd never seen anything so lovely."

"I meant it," said Jeannie. "Your cabin is just lovely. I don't know why, but I never managed to make this place look like yours."

Mrs. Thompson said, "That's plain enough." She looked at the cold grease spattered behind the stove, and the rag of towel over by the sink. "It's partly the experience," she said kindly. She and her husband knew exactly what to take with them when they went on a job, they had been doing it for so many years. They brought boxes for artificial flowers, a brass door knocker, a portable bar decorated with sea shells, a cardboard fireplace that looked real, and an electric fire that sent waves of light rippling over the ceiling and walls. A concealed gramophone played the records they loved and cherished – the good old tunes. They had comic records that dated back to the year 1, and sad soprano records about shipwrecks and broken promises and babies' graves. The first time Jeannie heard one of the funny records, she was scared to death. She was paying a formal call, sitting straight in her chair, with her skirt pulled around her knees. Vern and Pops Thompson were talking about the Army.

"I wish to God I was back," said old Pops.

"Don't I?" said Vern. He was fifteen years older than Jeannie and had been through a lot.

At first there were only scratching and whispering noises, and then a mosquito orchestra started to play, and a dwarf's voice came into the room. "Little Johnnie Green, little Sallie Brown," squealed the dwarf, higher and faster than any human ever could. "Spooning in the park with the grass all around."

"Where is he?" Jeannie cried, while the Thompsons screamed with laughter and Vern smiled. The dwarf sang on: "And each little bird in the treetop high/Sang 'Oh you kid!' and winked his eye."

It was a record that had belonged to Pops Thompson's mother. He had been laughing at it all his life. The Thompsons loved living up north and didn't miss cities or company. Their cabin smelled of cocoa and toast. Over their beds were oval photographs of each other as children, and they had some Teddy bears and about a dozen dolls.

Jeannie capped the bottle of polish, taking care not to press it against her wet nails. She sat up with a single movement and set the bottle down on the bedside crate. Then she turned to face Mrs. Thompson. She sat cross-legged, with her hands outspread before her. Her face was serene.

"Not an ounce of fat on you," said Mrs. Thompson. "You know something? I'm sorry you're going. I really am. Tomorrow you'll be gone. You know that, don't you? You've been counting days, but you won't have to any more. I guess Vern'll take you back to Montreal. What do you think?"

Jeannie dropped her gaze, and began smoothing wrinkles on the bedspread. She muttered something Mrs. Thompson could not understand.

"Tomorrow you'll be gone," Mrs. Thompson continued. "I know it for a fact. Vern is at this moment getting his pay, and borrowing a jeep from Mr. Sherman, and a Polack driver to take you to the train. He sure is loyal to *you.* You know what I heard Mr. Sherman say? He said to Vern, 'If you want to send her off, Vern, you can always stay,' and Vern said, 'I can't very well do that, Mr. Sherman.' And Mr. Sherman said, 'This is the second time you've had to leave a job on account of her, isn't it?,' and then Mr. Sherman said, 'In my opinion, no man by his own self can rape a girl, so there were either two men or else she's invented the whole story.' Then he said, 'Vern, you're either a saint or a damn fool.' That was all I heard. I came straight over here, Jeannie, because I thought you might be needing me." Mrs. Thompson waited to hear she was needed. She stopped rocking and sat with her feet flat and wide apart. She struck her knees with her open palms and cried, "I *told* you to keep away from the men. I told you it would make trouble, all that being cute and dancing around. I said to you, I remember saying it, I said nothing makes trouble faster in a place like this than a grown woman behaving like a little girl. Don't you remember?"

"I only went out for a walk," said Jeannie. "Nobody'll believe me, but that's all. I went down the road for a walk."

"In high heels?" said Mrs. Thompson. "With a purse on your arm, and a hat on your head? You don't go taking a walk in the bush that way. There's no place to walk *to.* Where'd you think you were going? I could smell Evening in Paris a quarter mile away."

"There's no place to go," said Jeannie, "but what else is there to do? I just felt like dressing up and going out."

"You could have cleaned up your home a bit," said Mrs. Thompson. "There was always that to do. Just look at that sink. That basket of ironing's been under the bed since July. I know it gets boring around here, but you had the best of it. You had the summer. In winter it gets dark around three o'clock. Then the wives have a right to go crazy. I knew one used to sleep the clock around. When her Nembutal ran out, she took about a hundred aspirin. I knew another learned to distill her own liquor, just to kill time. Sometimes the men get so's they don't like the life, and that's death for the wives. But here you had a nice summer, and Vern liked the life."

"He likes it better than anything," said Jeannie. "He liked the Army, but this was his favorite life after that."

"There," said Mrs. Thompson. "You had every reason to be happy. What'd you do if he sent you off alone, now, like Mr. Sherman advised? You'd be alone and you'd have to work. Women don't know when they're well off. Here you've got a good, sensible husband working for you and you don't appreciate it. You have to go and do a terrible thing."

"I only went for a walk," said Jeannie. "That's all I did."

"It's possible," said Mrs. Thompson, "but it's a terrible thing. It's about the worst thing that's ever happened around here. I don't know why you let it happen. A woman can always defend what's precious, even if she's attacked. I hope you remembered to think about bacteria."

"What d'you mean?"

"I mean Javel, or something."

Jeannie looked uncomprehending and then shook her head.

"I wonder what it must be like," said Mrs. Thompson after a time, looking at the dark window. "I mean, think of Berlin and them Russians and all. Think of some disgusting fellow you don't know. Never said hello to, even. Some girls ask for it, though. You can't always blame the man. The man loses his job, his wife if he's got one, everything, all because of a silly girl."

Jeannie frowned, absently. She pressed her nails together, testing the polish. She licked her lips and said, "I was more beaten up, Mrs. Thompson. It wasn't exactly what you think. It was only afterwards I thought to myself, Why, I was raped and everything."

Mrs. Thompson gasped, hearing the word from Jeannie. She said, "Have you got any marks?"

"On my arms. That's why I'm wearing this shirt. The first thing I did was change my clothes."

Mrs. Thompson thought this over, and went on to another thing: "Do you ever think about your mother?"

"Sure."

"Do you pray? If this goes on at nineteen —"

"I'm twenty."

"— what'll you be by the time you're thirty? You've already got a terrible, terrible memory to haunt you all your life."

"I already can't remember it," said Jeannie. "Afterwards I started walking back to camp, but I was walking the wrong way. I met Mr. Sherman. The back of his car was full of coffee, flour, all that. I guess he'd been picking up supplies. He said, 'Well, get in.' He didn't ask any questions at first. I couldn't talk anyway."

"Shock," said Mrs. Thompson wisely.

"You know, I'd have to see it happening to know what happened. All I remember is that first we were only talking . . ."

"You and Mr. Sherman?"

"No, no, before. When I was taking my walk."

"Don't say who it was," said Mrs. Thompson. "We don't any of us need to know."

"We were just talking, and he got sore all of a sudden and grabbed my arm."

"Don't say the name!" Mrs. Thompson cried.

"Like when I was little, there was this Lana Turner movie. She had two twins. She was just there and then a nurse brought her in the two twins. I hadn't been married or anything, and I didn't know anything, and I used to think if I just kept on seeing the movie I'd know how she got the two twins, you know, and I went, oh, I must have seen it six times, the movie, but in the end I never knew any more. They just brought her the two twins."

Mrs. Thompson sat quite still, trying to make sense of this. "Taking advantage of a woman is a criminal offense," she observed. "I heard Mr. Sherman say another thing, Jeannie. He said, 'If your wife wants to press a charge and talk to some lawyer, let me tell you,' he said, 'you'll never work again anywhere,' he said. Vern said, 'I know that, Mr. Sherman.' And Mr. Sherman said, 'Let me tell you, if any reporters or any investigators start coming around here, they'll get their . . . they'll never . . .' Oh, he was mad. And Vern said, 'I came over to tell you I was quitting, Mr. Sherman.' " Mrs. Thompson had been acting this with spirit, using a quiet voice when she spoke for Vern and a blustering tone for Mr. Sherman. In her own voice, she said, "If you're wondering how I came to hear all this, I was strolling by Mr. Sherman's office window – his bungalow, that is. I had Maureen out in her pram." Maureen was the Thompsons' youngest doll.

Jeannie might not have been listening. She started to tell something else: "You know, where we were before, on Vern's last job, we weren't in a camp. He was away a lot, and he left me in Amos, in a hotel. I liked it. Amos isn't all that big, but it's better than here. There was this German in the hotel. He was selling cars. He'd drive me around if I wanted to go to a movie or anything. Vern didn't like him, so we left. It wasn't anybody's fault."

"So he's given up two jobs," said Mrs. Thompson. "One because he couldn't leave you alone, and now this one. Two jobs, and you haven't been married five months. Why should another man be thrown out of work? We don't need to know a thing. I'll be sorry if it was Jimmy Quinn," she went on, slowly. "I like that boy. Don't say the name, dear. There's Evans. Susini. Palmer. But it might have been anybody, because you had them all on the boil. So it might have been Jimmy Quinn – let's say – and it could have been anyone else, too. Well, now let's hope they can get their minds back on the job."

"I thought they all liked me," said Jeannie sadly. "I get along with people. Vern never fights with me."

"Vern never fights with anyone. But he ought to have thrashed *you*."

"If he . . . you know. I won't say the name. If he'd liked me, I wouldn't have minded. If he'd been friendly. I really mean that. I wouldn't have gone wandering up the road, making all this fuss."

"Jeannie," said Mrs. Thompson, "you don't even know what you're saying."

"He could at least have liked me," said Jeannie. "He wasn't even friendly. It's the first time in my life somebody hasn't liked me. My heart is broken, Mrs. Thompson. My heart is just broken."

She has to cry, Mrs. Thompson thought. She has to have it out. She rocked slowly, tapping her foot, trying to remember how she'd felt about things when she was twenty, wondering if her heart had ever been broken, too.

1961

The Ice Wagon Going Down the Street

Now that they are out of world affairs and back where they started, Peter Frazier's wife says, "Everybody else did well in the international thing except us."

"You have to be crooked," he tells her.

"Or smart. Pity we weren't."

It is Sunday morning. They sit in the kitchen, drinking their coffee, slowly, remembering the past. They say the names of people as if they were magic. Peter thinks, *Agnes Brusen*, but there are hundreds of other names. As a private married joke, Peter and Sheilah wear the silk dressing gowns they bought in Hong Kong. Each thinks the other a peacock, rather splendid, but they pretend the dressing gowns are silly and worn in fun.

Peter and Sheilah and their two daughters, Sandra and Jennifer, are visiting Peter's unmarried sister, Lucille. They have been Lucille's guests seventeen weeks, ever since they returned to Toronto from the Far East. Their big old steamer trunk blocks a corner of the kitchen, making a problem of the refrigerator door; but even Lucille says the trunk may as well stay where it is, for the present. The Fraziers' future is so unsettled; everything is still in the air.

Lucille has given her bedroom to her two nieces, and sleeps on a camp cot in the hall. The parents have the living-room divan. They have no privileges here; they sleep after Lucille has seen the last television show that interests her. In the hall closet their clothes are crushed by winter overcoats. They know they are being judged for the first time. Sandra and Jennifer are waiting for Sheilah and Peter to decide. They are waiting to learn where these exotic parents will fly to next. What sort of climate will Sheilah consider? What job will Peter consent to accept? When the parents are ready, the children will make a decision of their own. It is just possible that Sandra and Jennifer will choose to stay with their aunt.

The peacock parents are watched by wrens. Lucille and her nieces are much the same – sandy-colored, proudly plain. Neither of the girls has the father's insouciance or the mother's appearance – her height, her carriage, her thick hair, and sky-blue eyes. The children are more cautious than their parents; more Canadian. When they saw their aunt's apartment they had been away from Canada nine years, ever since they were two and four; and Jennifer, the elder, said, "Well, now we're home." Her voice is nasal and flat. Where did she learn that voice? And why should this be home? Peter's answer to anything about his mystifying children is, "It must be in the blood."

On Sunday morning Lucille takes her nieces to church. It seems to be the only condition she imposes on her relations: the children must be decent. The girls go willingly, with their new hats and purses and gloves and coral bracelets and strings of pearls. The parents, ramshackle, sleepy, dim in the brain because it is Sunday, sit down to their coffee and privacy and talk of the past.

"We weren't crooked," says Peter. "We weren't even smart."

Sheilah's head bobs up; she is no drowner. It is wrong to say they have nothing to show for time. Sheilah has the Balenciaga. It is a black afternoon dress, stiff and boned at the waist, long for the fashions of now, but neither Sheilah nor Peter would change a thread. The Balenciaga is their talisman, their treasure; and after they remember it they touch hands and think that the years are not behind them but hazy and marvelous and still to be lived.

The first place they went to was Paris. In the early 'fifties the pick of the international jobs was there. Peter had inherited the last scrap of money he knew he was ever likely to see, and it was enough to get them over: Sheilah and Peter and the babies and the steamer trunk. To their joy and astonishment they had money in the bank. They said to each other, "It should last a year." Peter was fastidious about the new job; he hadn't come all this distance to accept just anything. In Paris he met Hugh Taylor, who was earning enough smuggling gasoline to keep his wife in Paris and a girl in Rome. That impressed Peter, because he remembered Taylor as a sour scholarship student without the slightest talent for life. Taylor had a job, of course. He hadn't said to himself, I'll go over to Europe and smuggle gasoline. It gave Peter an idea; he saw the shape of things. First you catch your fish. Later, at an international party, he met Johnny Hertzberg, who told him Germany was the place. Hertzberg said that anyone who came out of Germany broke now was too stupid to be here, and deserved to be back home at a desk. Peter nodded, as if he had already thought of that. He began to think about Germany. Paris was fine for a holiday, but it had been picked clean. Yes, Germany. His money was running low. He thought about Germany quite a lot.

That winter was moist and delicate; so fragile that they daren't speak of it now. There seemed to be plenty of everything and plenty of time. They were living the dream of a marriage, the fabric uncut, nothing slashed or spoiled. All winter they spent their money, and went to parties, and talked about Peter's future job. It lasted four months. They spent their money, lived in the future, and were never as happy again.

After four months they were suddenly moved away from Paris, but not to Germany — to Geneva. Peter thinks it was because of the incident at the Trudeau wedding at the Ritz. Paul Trudeau was a French-Canadian Peter had known at school and in the Navy. Trudeau had turned into a snob, proud of his career and his Paris connections. He tried to make the difference felt, but Peter thought the difference was only for strangers. At the wedding reception Peter lay down on the floor and said he was dead. He held a white azalea in a brass pot on his chest, and sang, "Oh, hear us when we cry to Thee for those in peril on the sea." Sheilah bent over him and said, "Pete, darling, get up. Pete, listen, every single person who can do something for you is in this room. If you love me, you'll get up."

"I do love you," he said, ready to engage in a serious conversation. "She's so beautiful," he told a second face. "She's nearly as tall as I am. She was a model in London. I met her over in London in the war. I met her there in the war." He lay on his back with the azalea on his chest, explaining their history. A waiter took the brass pot away, and after Peter had been hauled to his feet he knocked the waiter down. Trudeau's bride, who was freshly out of an Ursuline convent, became hysterical; and even though Paul Trudeau and Peter were old acquaintances, Trudeau never spoke to him again. Peter says now that French-Canadians always have that bit of spite. He says Trudeau asked the Embassy to interfere. Luckily, back home there were still a few people to whom the name "Frazier" meant something, and it was to these people that Peter appealed. He wrote letters saying that a French-Canadian combine was preventing his getting a decent job, and could anything be done? No one answered directly, but it was clear that what they settled for was exile to Geneva: a season of meditation and remorse, as he explained to Sheilah, and it was managed tactfully, through Lucille. Lucille wrote that a friend of hers, May Fergus, now a secretary in Geneva, had heard about a job. The job was filing pictures in the information service of an international agency in the Palais des Nations. The pay was so-so, but Lucille thought Peter must be getting fed up doing nothing.

Peter often asks his sister now who put her up to it – what important person told her to write that letter suggesting Peter go to Geneva?

"Nobody," says Lucille. "I mean, nobody in the way *you* mean. I really did have this girl friend working there, and I knew you must be running through your money pretty fast in Paris."

"It must have been somebody pretty high up," Peter says. He looks at his sister admiringly, as he has often looked at his wife.

Peter's wife had loved him in Paris. Whatever she wanted in marriage she found that winter, there. In Geneva, where Peter was a file clerk and they lived in a furnished flat, she pretended they were in Paris and life was still the same. Often, when the children were at supper, she changed as though she and Peter were dining out. She wore the Balenciaga, and put candles on the card table where she and Peter ate their meal. The neckline of the dress was soiled with make-up. Peter remembers her dabbing on the make-up with a wet sponge. He remembers her in the kitchen, in the soiled Balenciaga, patting on the make-up with a filthy sponge. Behind her, at the kitchen table, Sandra and Jennifer, in buttonless pajamas and bunny slippers, ate their supper of marmalade sandwiches and milk. When the children were asleep, the parents dined solemnly, ritually, Sheilah sitting straight as a queen.

It was a mysterious period of exile, and he had to wait for signs, or signals, to know when he was free to leave. He never saw the job any other way. He forgot he had applied for it. He thought he had been sent to Geneva because of a misdemeanor and had to wait to be released. Nobody pressed him at work. His immediate boss had resigned, and he was alone for months in a room with two desks. He read the *Herald-Tribune*, and tried to discover how things were here – how the others ran their lives on the pay they were officially getting.

But it was a closed conspiracy. He was not dealing with adventurers now but civil servants waiting for pension day. No one ever answered his questions. They pretended to think his questions were a form of wit. His only solace in exile was the few happy weekends he had in the late spring and early summer. He had met another old acquaintance, Mike Burleigh. Mike was a serious liberal who had married a serious heiress. The Burleighs had two guest lists. The first was composed of stuffy people they felt obliged to entertain, while the second was made up of their real friends, the friends they wanted. The real friends strove hard to become stuffy and dull and thus achieve the first guest list, but few succeeded. Peter went on the first list straight away. Possibly Mike didn't understand, at the beginning, why Peter was pretending to be a file clerk. Peter had such an air – he might have been sent by a universal inspector to see how things in Geneva were being run.

Every Friday in May and June and part of July, the Fraziers rented a sky-blue Fiat and drove forty miles east of Geneva to the Burleighs' summer house. They brought the children, a suitcase, the children's tattered picture books, and a token bottle of gin. This, in memory, is a period of water and water birds; swans, roses, and singing birds. The children were small and still belonged to them. If they remember too much, their mouths water, their stomachs hurt. Peter says, "It was fine while it lasted." Enough. While it lasted Sheilah and Madge Burleigh were close. They abandoned their husbands and spent long summer afternoons comparing their mothers and praising each other's skin and hair. To Madge, and not to Peter, Sheilah opened her Liverpool childhood with the words "rat poor." Peter heard about it later, from Mike. The women's friendship seemed to Peter a bad beginning. He trusted women but not with each other. It lasted ten weeks. One Sunday, Madge said she needed the two bedrooms the Fraziers usually occupied for a party of sociologists from Pakistan, and that was the end. In November, the Fraziers heard that the summer house had been closed, and that the Burleighs were in Geneva, in their winter flat; they gave no sign. There was no help for it, and no appeal.

Now Peter began firing letters to anyone who had ever known his late father. He was living in a mild yellow autumn. Why does he remember the streets of the city dark, and the windows everywhere black with rain? He remembers being with Sheilah and the children as if they clung together while just outside their small shelter it rained and rained. The children slept in the bedroom of the flat because the window gave on the street and they could breathe air. Peter and Sheilah had the living-room couch. Their window was not a real window but a square on a wall of cement. The flat seemed damp as a cave. Peter remembers steam in the kitchen, pools under the sink, sweat on the pipes. Water streamed on him from the children's clothes, washed and dripping overhead. The trunk, up-ended in the children's room, was not quite unpacked. Sheilah had not signed her name to this life; she had not given in. Once Peter heard her drop her aitches. "You kids are lucky," she said to the girls. "I never 'ad so much as a sit-down meal. I ate chips out of a paper or I 'ad a butty out on the stairs." He never asked her what a butty was. He thinks it means bread and cheese.

The day he heard "You kids are lucky" he understood they were becoming in fact something they had only *appeared* to be until now – the shabby civil servant and his brood. If he had been European he would have ridden to work on a bicycle, in the uniform of his class and condition. He would have worn a tight coat, a turned collar, and a dirty tie. He wondered then if coming here had been a mistake, and if he should not, after all, still be in a place where his name meant something. Surely Peter Frazier should live where "Frazier" counts? In Ontario even now when he says "Frazier" an absent look comes over his hearer's face, as if its owner were consulting an interior guide. What is Frazier? What does it mean? Oil? Power? Politics? Wheat? Real estate? The creditors had the house sealed when Peter's father died. His aunt collapsed with a heart attack in somebody's bachelor apartment, leaving three sons and a widower to surmise they had never known her. Her will was a disappointment. None of that generation left enough. One made it: the granite Presbyterian immigrants from Scotland. Their children, a generation of daunted women and maiden men, held still. Peter's father's crowd spent: they were not afraid of their fathers, and their grandfathers were old. Peter and his sister and his cousins lived on the remains. They were left the rinds of income, of notions, and the memories of ideas rather than ideas intact. If Peter can choose his reincarnation, let him be the oppressed son of a Scottish parson. Let Peter grow up on cuffs and iron principles. Let him make the fortune! Let him flee the manse! When he was small his patrimony was squandered under his nose. He remembers people dancing in his father's house. He remembers seeing and nearly understanding adultery in a guest room, among a pile of wraps. He thought he had seen a murder; he never told. He remembers licking glasses wherever he found them – on window sills, on stairs, in the pantry. In his room he listened while Lucille read Beatrix Potter. The bad rabbit stole the carrot from the good rabbit without saying please, and downstairs was the noise of the party – the roar of the crouched lion. When his father died he saw the chairs upside down and the bailiff's chalk marks. Then the doors were sealed.

He has often tried to tell Sheilah why he cannot be defeated. He remembers his father saying, "Nothing can touch us," and Peter believed it and still does. It has prevented his taking his troubles too seriously. "Nothing can be as bad as this," he will tell himself. "It is happening to me." Even in Geneva, where his status was file clerk, where he sank and stopped on the level of the men who never emigrated, the men on the bicycles – even there he had a manner of strolling to work as if his office were a pastime, and his real life a secret so splendid he could share it with no one except himself.

In Geneva Peter worked for a woman – a girl. She was a Norwegian from a small town in Saskatchewan. He supposed they had been put together because they were Canadians; but they were as strange to each other as if "Canadian" meant any number of things, or had no real meaning. Soon after Agnes Brusen came to the office she hung her framed university degree on the wall. It was one of the gritty, prideful gestures that stand for push, toil, and family sacrifice. He thought, then, that she must be one of a family of immigrants for whom education is everything. Hugh Taylor had told him that in some families the older children never marry until the youngest have finished school. Sometimes every second child is sacrificed and made to work for the education of the next born. Those who finish college spend years paying back. They are white-hot Protestants, and they live with a load of work and debt and obligation. Peter placed his new colleague on scraps of information. He had never been in the West.

She came to the office on a Monday morning in October. The office was overheated and painted cream. It contained two desks, the filing cabinets, a map of the world as it had been in 1945, and the Charter of the United Nations left behind by Agnes Brusen's predecessor. (She took down the Charter without asking Peter if he minded, with the impudence of gesture you find in women who wouldn't say boo to a goose; and then she hung her college degree on the nail where the Charter had been.) Three people brought her in – a whole committee. One of them said, "Agnes, this is Pete Frazier. Pete, Agnes Brusen. Pete's Canadian, too, Agnes. He knows all about the office, so ask him anything."

Of course he knew all about the office: he knew the exact spot where the cord of the venetian blind was frayed, obliging one to give an extra tug to the right.

The girl might have been twenty-three: no more. She wore a brown tweed suit with bone buttons, and a new silk scarf and new shoes. She clutched an unscratched brown purse. She seemed dressed in going-away presents. She said, "Oh, I never smoke" with a convulsive movement of her hand, when Peter offered his case. He was courteous, hiding his disappointment. The people he worked with had told him a Scandinavian girl was arriving, and he had expected a stunner. Agnes was a mole: she was small and brown, and round-shouldered as if she had always carried parcels or younger children in her arms. A mole's profile was turned when she said goodbye to her committee. If she had been foreign, ill-favored though she was, he might have flirted a little, just to show that he was friendly; but their being Canadian, and suddenly left together, was a sexual damper. He sat down and lit his own cigarette. She smiled at him, questioningly, he thought, and sat as if she had never seen a chair before. He wondered if his smoking was annoying her. He wondered if she was fidgety about drafts, or allergic to anything, and whether she would want the blind up or down. His social compass was out of order because the others couldn't tell Peter and Agnes apart. There was a world of difference between them, yet it was she who had been brought in to sit at the larger of the two desks.

While he was thinking this she got up and walked around the office, almost on tiptoe, opening the doors of closets and pulling out the filing trays. She looked inside everything except the drawers of Peter's desk. (In any case, Peter's desk was locked. His desk is locked wherever he works. In Geneva he went into Personnel one morning, early, and pinched his application form. He had stated on the form that he had seven years' experience in public relations and could speak French, German, Spanish, and Italian. He has always collected anything important about himself – anything useful. But he can never get on with the final act, which is getting rid of the information. He has kept papers about for years, a constant source of worry.)

"I know this looks funny, Mr. Ferris," said the girl. "I'm not really snooping or anything. I just can't feel easy in a new place unless I know where everything is. In a new place everything seems so hidden."

If she had called him "Ferris" and pretended not to know he was Frazier, it could only be because they had sent her here to spy on him and see if he had repented and was fit for a better place in life. "You'll be all right here," he said. "Nothing's hidden. Most of us haven't got brains enough to have secrets. This is Rainbow Valley." Depressed by the thought that they were having him watched now, he passed his hand over his hair and looked outside to the lawn and the parking lot and the peacocks someone gave the Palais des Nations years ago. The peacocks love no one. They wander about the parked cars looking elderly, bad-tempered, mournful, and lost.

Agnes had settled down again. She folded her silk scarf and placed it just so, with her gloves beside it. She opened her new purse and took out a notebook and a shiny gold pencil. She may have written

> Duster for desk
> Kleenex
> Glass jar for flowers
> Air-Wick because he smokes
> Paper for lining drawers

because the next day she brought each of these articles to work. She also brought a large black Bible, which she unwrapped lovingly and placed on the left-hand corner of her desk. The flower vase – empty – stood in the middle, and the Kleenex made a counterpoise for the Bible on the right.

When he saw the Bible he knew she had not been sent to spy on his work. The conspiracy was deeper. She might have been dispatched by ghosts. He knew everything about her, all in a moment: he saw the ambition, the terror, the dry pride. She was the true heir of the men from Scotland; she was at the start. She had been sent to tell him, "You can begin, but not begin again." She never opened the Bible, but she dusted it as she dusted her desk, her chair, and any surface the cleaning staff had overlooked. And Peter, the first days, watching her timid movements, her insignificant little face, felt, as you feel the approach of a storm, the charge of moral certainty round her, the belief in work, the faith in undertakings, the bread of the Black Sunday. He recognized and tasted all of it: ashes in the mouth.

After five days their working relations were settled. Of course, there was the Bible and all that went with it, but his tongue had never held the taste of ashes long. She was an inferior girl of poor quality. She had nothing in her favor except the degree on the wall. In the real world, he would not have invited her to his house except to mind the children. That was what he said to Sheilah. He said that Agnes was a mole, and a virgin, and that her tics and mannerisms were sending him round the bend. She had an infuriating habit of covering her mouth when she talked. Even at the telephone she put up her hand as if afraid of losing anything, even a word. Her voice was nasal and flat. She had two working costumes, both dull as the wall. One was the brown suit, the other a navy-blue dress with changeable collars. She dressed for no one; she dressed for her desk, her jar of flowers, her Bible, and her box of Kleenex. One day she crossed the space between the two desks and stood over Peter, who was reading a newspaper. She could have spoken to him from her desk, but she may have felt that being on her feet gave her authority. She had plenty of courage, but authority was something else.

"I thought – I mean, they told me you were the person . . ." She got on with it bravely: "If you don't want to do the filing or any work, all right, Mr. Frazier. I'm not saying anything about that. You might have poor health or your personal reasons. But it's got to be done, so if you'll kindly show me about the filing I'll do it. I've worked in Information before, but it was a different office, and every office is different."

"My dear girl," said Peter. He pushed back his chair and looked at her, astonished. "You've been sitting there fretting, worrying. How insensitive of me. How trying for you. Usually I file on the last Wednesday of the month, so you see, you just haven't been around long enough to see a last Wednesday. Not another word, please. And let us not waste another minute." He emptied the heaped baskets of photographs so swiftly, pushing "Iran – Smallpox Control" into "Irish Red Cross" (close enough), that the girl looked frightened, as if she had raised a whirlwind. She said slowly, "If you'll only show me, Mr. Frazier, instead of doing it so fast, I'll gladly look after it, because you might want to be doing other things, and I feel the filing should be done every day." But Peter was too busy to answer, and so she sat down, holding the edge of her desk.

"There," he said, beaming. "All done." His smile, his sunburst, was wasted, for the girl was staring round the room as if she feared she had not inspected everything the first day after all; some drawer, some cupboard, hid a monster. That evening Peter unlocked one of the drawers of his desk and took away the application form he had stolen from Personnel. The girl had not finished her search.

"How could you *not* know?" wailed Sheilah. "You sit looking at her every day. You must talk about *something*. She must have told you."

"She did tell me," said Peter, "and I've just told you."

It was this: Agnes Brusen was on the Burleighs' guest list. How had the Burleighs met her? What did they see in her? Peter could not reply. He knew that Agnes lived in a bedsitting room with a Swiss family and had her meals with them. She had been in Geneva three months, but no one had ever seen her outside the office. "You *should* know," said Sheilah. "She must have something, more than you can see. Is she pretty? Is she brilliant? What is it?"

"We don't really talk," Peter said. They talked in a way:

Peter teased her and she took no notice. Agnes was not a sulker. She had taken her defeat like a sport. She did her work and a good deal of his. She sat behind her Bible, her flowers, and her Kleenex, and answered when Peter spoke. That was how he learned about the Burleighs – just by teasing and being bored. It was a January afternoon. He said, "*Miss* Brusen. Talk to me. Tell me everything. Pretend we have perfect rapport. Do you like Geneva?"

"It's a nice clean town," she said. He can see to this day the red and blue anemones in the glass jar, and her bent head, and her small untended hands.

"Are you learning beautiful French with your Swiss family?"

"They speak English."

"Why don't you take an apartment of your own?" he said. Peter was not usually impertinent. He was bored. "You'd be independent then."

"I am independent," she said. "I earn my living. I don't think it proves anything if you live by yourself. Mrs. Burleigh wants me to live alone, too. She's looking for something for me. It mustn't be dear. I send money home."

Here was the extraordinary thing about Agnes Brusen: she refused the use of Christian names and never spoke to Peter unless he spoke first, but she would tell anything, as if to say, "Don't waste time fishing. Here it is."

He learned all in one minute that she sent her salary home, and that she was a friend of the Burleighs. The first he had expected; the second knocked him flat.

"She's got to come to dinner," Sheilah said. "We should have had her right from the beginning. If only I'd known! But *you* were the one. You said she looked like – oh, I don't even remember. A Norwegian mole."

She came to dinner one Saturday night in January, in her navy-blue dress, to which she had pinned an organdy gardenia. She sat upright on the edge of the sofa. Sheilah had ordered the meal from a restaurant. There was lobster, good wine, and a *pièce-montée* full of kirsch and cream. Agnes refused the lobster; she had never eaten anything from the sea unless it had been sterilized and tinned, and said so. She was afraid of skin poisoning. Someone in her family had skin poisoning after having eaten oysters. She touched her cheeks and neck to show where the poisoning had erupted. She sniffed her wine and put the glass down without tasting it. She could not eat the cake because of the alcohol it contained. She ate an egg, bread and butter, a sliced tomato, and drank a glass of ginger ale. She seemed unaware she was creating disaster and pain. She did not help clear away the dinner plates. She sat, adequately nourished, decently dressed, and waited to learn why she had been invited here – that was the feeling Peter had. He folded the card table on which they had dined, and opened the window to air the room.

"It's not the same cold as Canada, but you feel it more," he said, for something to say.

"Your blood has gotten thin," said Agnes.

Sheilah returned from the kitchen and let herself fall into an armchair. With her eyes closed she held out her hand for a cigarette. She was performing the haughty-lady act that was a family joke. She flung her head back and looked at Agnes through half-closed lids; then she suddenly brought her head forward, widening her eyes.

"Are you skiing madly?" she said.

"Well, in the first place there hasn't been any snow," said Agnes. "So nobody's doing any skiing so far as I know. All I hear is people complaining because there's no snow. Personally, I don't ski. There isn't much skiing in the part of Canada I come from. Besides, my family never had that kind of leisure."

"Heavens," said Sheilah, as if her family had every kind.

I'll bet they had, thought Peter. On the dole.

Sheilah was wasting her act. He had a suspicion that Agnes knew it was an act but did not know it was also a joke. If so, it made Sheilah seem a fool, and he loved Sheilah too much to enjoy it.

"The Burleighs have been wonderful to me," said Agnes. She seemed to have divined why she was here, and decided to give them all the information they wanted, so that she could put on her coat and go home to bed. "They had me out to their place on the lake every weekend until the weather got cold and they moved back to town. They've rented a chalet for the winter, and they want me to come there, too. But I don't know if I will or not. I don't ski, and, oh, I don't know – I don't drink, either, and I don't always see the point. Their friends are too rich and I'm too Canadian."

She had delivered everything Sheilah wanted and more: Agnes was on the first guest list and didn't care. No, Peter corrected; doesn't know. Doesn't care and doesn't know.

"I thought with you Norwegians it was in the blood, skiing. And drinking," Sheilah murmured.

"Drinking, maybe," said Agnes. She covered her mouth and said behind her spread fingers, "In our family we were religious. We didn't drink or smoke. My brother was in Norway in the war. He saw some cousins. Oh," she said, unexpectedly loud, "Harry said it was just terrible. They were so poor. They had flies in their kitchen. They gave him something to eat a fly had been on. They didn't have a real toilet, and they'd been in the same house about two hundred years. We've only recently built our own home, and we have a bathroom and two toilets. I'm from Saskatchewan," she said. "I'm not from any other place."

Surely one winter here had been punishment enough? In the spring they would remember him and free him. He wrote Lucille, who said he was lucky to have a job at all. The Burleighs had sent the Fraziers a second-guest list Christmas card. It showed a Moslem refugee child weeping outside a tent. They treasured the card and left it standing long after the others had been given the children to cut up. Peter had discovered by now what had gone wrong in the friendship – Sheilah had charged a skirt at a dressmaker to Madge's account. Madge had told her she might, and then changed her mind. Poor Sheilah! She was new to this part of it – to the changing humors of independent friends. Paris was already a year in the past. At Mardi Gras, the Burleighs gave their annual party. They invited everyone, the damned and the dropped, with the prodigality of a child at prayers. The invitation said "in costume," but the Fraziers were too happy to wear a disguise. They might not be recognized. Like many of the guests they expected to meet at the party, they had been disgraced, forgotten, and rehabilitated. They would be anxious to see one another as they were.

On the night of the party, the Fraziers rented a car they had never seen before and drove through the first snowstorm of the year. Peter had not driven since last summer's blissful trips in the Fiat. He could not find the switch for the windshield wiper in this car. He leaned over the wheel. "Can you see on your side?" he asked. "Can I make a left turn here? Does it look like a one-way?"

"I can't imagine why you took a car with a right-hand drive," said Sheilah.

He had trouble finding a place to park; they crawled up and down unknown streets whose curbs were packed with snow-covered cars. When they stood at last on the pavement, safe and sound, Peter said, "This is the first snow."

"I can see that," said Sheilah. "Hurry, darling. My hair."

"It's the first snow."

"You're repeating yourself," she said. "Please hurry, darling. Think of my poor shoes. My *hair*."

She was born in an ugly city, and so was Peter, but they have this difference: she does not know the importance of the first snow – the first clean thing in a dirty year. He would have told her then that this storm, which was wetting her feet and destroying her hair, was like the first day of the English spring, but she made a frightened gesture, trying to shield her head. The gesture told him he did not understand her beauty.

"Let me," she said. He was fumbling with the key, trying to lock the car. She took the key without impatience and locked the door on the driver's side; and then, to show Peter she treasured him and was not afraid of wasting her life or her beauty, she took his arm and they walked in the snow down a street and around a corner to the apartment house where the Burleighs lived. They were, and are, a united couple. They were afraid of the party, and each of them knew it. When they walk together, holding arms, they give each other whatever each can spare.

Only six people had arrived in costume. Madge Burleigh was disguised as Manet's "Lola de Valence," which everyone mistook for Carmen. Mike was an Impressionist painter, with a straw hat and a glued-on beard. "I am all of them," he said. He would rather have dressed as a dentist, he said, welcoming the Fraziers as if he had parted from them the day before, but Madge wanted him to look as if he had created her. "You know?" he said.

"Perfectly," said Sheilah. Her shoes were stained and the snow had softened her lacquered hair. She was not wasted; she was the most beautiful woman here.

About an hour after their arrival, Peter found himself with no one to talk to. He had told about the Trudeau wedding in Paris and the pot of azaleas, and after he mislaid his audience he began to look round for Sheilah. She was on a window seat, partly concealed by a green velvet curtain. Facing her, so that their profiles were neat and perfect against the night, was a man. Their conversation was private and enclosed, as if they had in minutes covered leagues of time and arrived at the place where everything was implied, understood. Peter began working his way across the room, toward his wife, when he saw Agnes. He was granted the sight of her drowning face. She had dressed with comic intention, obviously with care, and now she was a ragged hobo, half tramp, half clown. Her hair was tucked up under a bowler hat. The six costumed guests who had made the same mistake – the ghost, the gypsy, the Athenian maiden, the geisha, the Martian, and the apache – were delighted to find a seventh; but Agnes was not amused; she was gasping for life. When a waiter passed with a crowded tray, she took a glass without seeing it; then a wave of the party took her away.

Sheilah's new friend was named Simpson. After Simpson said he thought perhaps he'd better circulate, Peter sat down where he had been. "Now look, Sheilah," he began. Their most intimate conversations have taken place at parties. Once at a party she told him she was leaving him; she didn't, of course. Smiling, blue-eyed, she gazed lovingly at Peter and said rapidly, "Pete, shut up and listen. That man. The man you scared away. He's a big wheel in a company out in India or someplace like that. It's gorgeous out there. Pete, the *servants*. And it's warm. It never never snows. He says there's heaps of jobs. You pick them off the trees like . . . orchids. He says it's even easier now than when we owned all those places, because now the poor pets can't run anything and they'll pay *fortunes*. Pete, he says it's warm, it's heaven, and Pete, they pay."

A few minutes later, Peter was alone again and Sheilah part of a closed, laughing group. Holding her elbow was the man from the place where jobs grew like orchids. Peter edged into the group and laughed at a story he hadn't heard. He heard only the last line, which was, "Here comes another tunnel." Looking out from the tight laughing ring, he saw Agnes again, and he thought, I'd be like Agnes if I didn't have Sheilah. Agnes put her glass down on a table and lurched toward the doorway, head forward. Madge Burleigh, who never stopped moving around the room and smiling, was still smiling when she paused and said in Peter's ear, "Go with Agnes, Pete. See that she gets home. People will notice if Mike leaves."

"She probably just wants to walk around the block," said Peter. "She'll be back."

"Oh, stop thinking about yourself, for once, and see that that poor girl gets home," said Madge. "You've still got your Fiat, haven't you?"

He turned away as if he had been pushed. Any command is a release, in a way. He may not want to go in that particular direction, but at least he is going somewhere. And now Sheilah, who had moved inches nearer to hear what Madge and Peter were murmuring, said, "Yes, go, darling," as if he were leaving the gates of Troy.

Peter was to find Agnes and see that she reached home: this he repeated to himself as he stood on the landing, outside the Burleighs' flat, ringing for the elevator. Bored with waiting for it, he ran down the stairs, four flights, and saw that Agnes had stalled the lift by leaving the door open. She was crouched on the floor, propped on her fingertips. Her eyes were closed.

"Agnes," said Peter. "*Miss* Brusen, I mean. That's no way to leave a party. Don't you know you're supposed to curtsey and say thanks? My God, Agnes, anybody going by here just now might have seen you! Come on, be a good girl. Time to go home."

She got up without his help and, moving between invisible crevasses, shut the elevator door. Then she left the building and Peter followed, remembering he was to see that she got home. They walked along the snowy pavement, Peter a few steps behind her. When she turned right for no reason, he turned, too. He had no clear idea where they were going. Perhaps she lived close by. He had forgotten where the hired car was parked, or what it looked like; he could not remember its make or its color. In any case, Sheilah had the key. Agnes walked on steadily, as if she knew their destination, and he thought, Agnes Brusen is drunk in the street in Geneva and dressed like a tramp. He wanted to say, "This is the best thing that ever happened to you, Agnes; it will help you understand how things are for some of the rest of us." But she stopped and turned and, leaning over a low hedge, retched on a frozen lawn. He held her clammy forehead and rested his hand on her arched back, on muscles as tight as a fist. She straightened up and drew a breath but the cold air made her cough. "Don't breathe too deeply," he said. "It's the worst thing you can do. Have you got a handkerchief?" He passed his own handkerchief over her wet weeping face, upturned like the face of one of his little girls. "I'm out without a coat," he said, noticing it. "We're a pair."

"I never drink," said Agnes. "I'm just not used to it." Her voice was sweet and quiet. He had never seen her so peaceful, so composed. He thought she must surely be all right, now, and perhaps he might leave her here. The trust in her tilted face had perplexed him. He wanted to get back to Sheilah and have her explain something. He had forgotten what it was, but Sheilah would know. "Do you live around here?" he said. As he spoke, she let herself fall. He had wiped her face and now she trusted him to pick her up, set her on her feet, take her wherever she ought to be. He pulled her up and she stood, wordless, humble, as he brushed the snow from her tramp's clothes. Snow horizontally crossed the lamplight. The street was silent. Agnes had lost her hat. Snow, which he tasted, melted on her hands. His gesture of licking snow from her hands was formal as a handshake. He tasted snow on her hands and then they walked on.

"I never drink," she said. They stood on the edge of a broad avenue. The wrong turning now could lead them anywhere; it was the changeable avenue at the edge of towns that loses its houses and becomes a highway. She held his arm and spoke in a gentle voice. She said, "In our house we didn't smoke or drink. My mother was ambitious for me, more than for Harry and the others." She said, "I've never been alone before. When I was a kid I would get up in the summer before the others, and I'd see the ice wagon going down the street. I'm alone now. Mrs. Burleigh's found me an apartment. It's only one room. She likes it because it's in the old part of town. I don't like old houses. Old houses are dirty. You don't know who was there before."

"I should have a car somewhere," Peter said. "I'm not sure where we are."

He remembers that on this avenue they climbed into a taxi, but nothing about the drive. Perhaps he fell asleep. He does remember that when he paid the driver Agnes clutched his arm, trying to stop him. She pressed extra coins into the driver's palm. The driver was paid twice.

"I'll tell you one thing about us," said Peter. "We pay everything twice." This was part of a much longer theory concerning North American behavior, and it was not Peter's own. Mike Burleigh had held forth about it on summer afternoons.

Agnes pushed open a door between a stationer's shop and a grocery, and led the way up a narrow inside stair. They climbed one flight, frightening beetles. She had to search every pocket for the latchkey. She was shaking with cold. Her apartment seemed little warmer than the street. Without speaking to Peter she turned on all the lights. She looked inside the kitchen and the bathroom and then got down on her hands and knees and looked under the sofa. The room was neat and belonged to no one. She left him standing in this unclaimed room – she had forgotten him – and closed a door behind her. He looked for something to do – some useful action he could repeat to Madge. He turned on the electric radiator in the fireplace. Perhaps Agnes wouldn't thank him for it; perhaps she would rather undress in the cold. "I'll be on my way," he called to the bathroom door.

She had taken off the tramp's clothes and put on a dressing gown of orphanage wool. She came out of the bathroom and straight toward him. She pressed her face and rubbed her cheek on his shoulder as if hoping the contact would leave a scar. He saw her back and her profile and his own face in the mirror over the fireplace. He thought, This is how disasters happen. He saw floods of sea water moving with perfect punitive justice over reclaimed land; he saw lava covering vineyards and overtaking of dogs and stragglers. A bridge over an abyss snapped in two and the long express train, suddenly V-shaped, floated like snow. He thought amiably of every kind of disaster and thought, This is how they occur.

Her eyes were closed. She said, "I shouldn't be over here. In my family we didn't drink or smoke. My mother wanted a lot from me, more than from Harry and the others." But he knew all that; he had known from the day of the Bible, and because once, at the beginning, she had made him afraid. He was not afraid of her now.

She said, "It's no use staying here, is it?"

"If you mean what I think, no."

"It wouldn't be better anywhere."

She let him see full on her blotched face. He was not expected to do anything. He was not required to pick her up when she fell or wipe her tears. She was poor quality, really – he remembered having thought that once. She left him and went quietly into the bathroom and locked the door. He heard taps running and supposed it was a hot bath. He was pretty certain there would be no more tears. He looked at his watch: Sheilah must be home, now, wondering what had become of him. He descended the beetles' staircase and for forty minutes crossed the city under a windless fall of snow.

The neighbor's child who had stayed with Peter's children was asleep on the living-room sofa. Peter woke her and sent her, sleepwalking, to her own door. He sat down, wet to the bone, thinking, I'll call the Burleighs. In half an hour I'll call the police. He heard a car stop and the engine running and a confusion of two voices laughing and calling goodnight.

Presently Sheilah let herself in, rosy-faced, sniffing. She carried his trenchcoat over her arm. She said, "How's Agnes?"

"Where were you?" he said. "Whose car was that?"

Sheilah had gone into the children's room. He heard her shutting their window. She returned, undoing her dress, and said, "Was Agnes all right?"

"Agnes is all right. Sheilah, this is about the worst . . ."

She stepped out of the Balenciaga and threw it over a chair. She stopped and looked at him and said, "Poor old Pete, are you in love with Agnes?" And then, as if the answer were of so little importance she hadn't time for it, she locked her arms around him and said, "My love, we're going to Ceylon."

Two days later, when Peter strolled into his office, Agnes was at her desk. She wore the blue dress, with a spotless collar. White and yellow freesias were symmetrically arranged in the glass jar. The room was hot, and the spring snow, glued for a second when it touched the window, blurred the view of parked cars.

"Quite a party," Peter said.

She did not look up. He sighed, sat down, and thought if the snow held he would be skiing at the Burleighs' very soon. Impressed by his kindness to Agnes, Madge had invited the family for the first possible weekend.

Presently Agnes said, "I'll never drink again or go to a house where people are drinking. And I'll never bother anyone the way I bothered you."

"You didn't bother me," he said. "I took you home. You were alone and it was late. It's normal."

"Normal for you, maybe, but I'm used to getting home by myself. Please never tell what happened."

He stared at her. He can still remember the freesias and the Bible and the heat in the room. She looked as if the elements had no power. She felt neither heat nor cold. "Nothing happened," he said.

"I behaved in a silly way. I had no right to. I led you to think I might do something wrong."

"*I* might have tried something," he said gallantly. "But that would be my fault and not yours."

She put her knuckle to her mouth and he could scarcely hear. "It was because of you. I was afraid you might be blamed, or else you'd blame yourself."

"There's no question of any blame," he said. "Nothing happened. We'd both had a lot to drink. Forget about it. Nothing *happened*. You'd remember if it had."

She put down her hand. There was an expression on her face. Now she sees me, he thought. She had never looked at him after the first day. (He has since tried to put a name to the look on her face; but how can he, now, after so many voyages, after Ceylon, and Hong Kong, and Sheilah's nearly leaving him, and all their difficulties – the money owed, the rows with hotel managers, the lost and found steamer trunk, the children throwing up the foreign food?) She sees me now, he thought. What does she see?

She said, "I'm from a big family. I'm not used to being alone. I'm not a suicidal person, but I could have done something after that party, just not to see any more, or think or listen or expect anything. What can I think when I see these people? All my life I heard, Educated people don't do this, educated people don't do that. And now I'm here, and you're all educated people, and you're nothing but pigs. You're educated and you drink and do everything wrong and you know what you're doing, and that makes you worse than pigs. My family worked to make me an educated person, but they didn't know you. But what if I didn't see and hear and expect anything any more? It wouldn't change anything. You'd all be still the same. Only *you* might have thought it was your fault. You might have thought you were to blame. It could worry you all your life. It would have been wrong for me to worry you."

He remembered that the rented car was still along a snowy curb somewhere in Geneva. He wondered if Sheilah had the key in her purse and if she remembered where they'd parked.

"I told you about the ice wagon," Agnes said. "I don't remember everything, so you're wrong about remembering. But I remember telling you that. That was the best. It's the best you can hope to have. In a big family, if you want to be alone, you have to get up before the rest of them. You get up early in the morning in the summer and it's you, you, once in your life alone in the universe. You think you know everything that can happen . . . Nothing is ever like that again."

He looked at the smeared window and wondered if this day could end without disaster. In his mind he saw her falling in the snow wearing a tramp's costume, and he saw her coming to him in the orphanage dressing gown. He saw her drowning face at the party. He was afraid for himself. The story was still unfinished. It had to come to a climax, something threatening to him. But there was no climax. They talked that day, and afterward nothing else was said. They went on in the same office for a short time, until Peter left for Ceylon; until somebody read the right letter, passed it on for the right initials, and the Fraziers began the Oriental tour that should have made their fortune. Agnes and Peter were too tired to speak after that morning. They were like a married couple in danger, taking care.

But what were they talking about that day, so quietly, such old friends? They talked about dying, about being ambitious, about being religious, about different kinds of love. What did she see when she looked at him – taking her knuckle slowly away from her mouth, bringing her hand down to the desk, letting it rest there? They were both Canadians, so they had this much together – the knowledge of the little you dare admit. Death, near-death, the best thing, the wrong thing – God knows what they were telling each other. Anyway, nothing happened.

When, on Sunday mornings, Sheilah and Peter talk about those times, they take on the glamor of something still to come. It is then he remembers Agnes Brusen. He never says her name. Sheilah wouldn't remember Agnes. Agnes is the only secret Peter has from his wife, the only puzzle he pieces together without her help. He thinks about families in the West as they were fifteen, twenty years ago – the iron-cold ambition, and every member pushing the next one on. He thinks of his father's parties. When he thinks of his father he imagines him with Sheilah, in a crowd. Actually, Sheilah and Peter's father never met, but they might have liked each other. His father admired good-looking women. Peter wonders what they were doing over there in Geneva – not Sheilah and Peter, *Agnes* and Peter. It is almost as if they had once run away together, silly as children, irresponsible as lovers. Peter and Sheilah are back where they started. While they were out in world affairs picking up microbes and debts, always on the fringe of disaster, the fringe of a fortune, Agnes went on and did – what? They lost each other. He thinks of the ice wagon going down the street. He sees something he has never seen in his life – a Western town that belongs to Agnes. Here is Agnes – small, mole-faced, round-shouldered because she has always carried a younger child. She watches the ice wagon and the trail of ice water in a morning invented for her: hers. He sees the weak prairie trees and the shadows on the sidewalk. Nothing moves except the shadows and the ice wagon and the changing amber of the child's eyes. The child is Peter. He has seen the grain of the cement sidewalk and the grass in the cracks, and the dust, and the dandelions at the edge of the road. He is there. He has taken the morning that belongs to Agnes, he is up before the others, and he knows everything. There is nothing he doesn't know. He could keep the morning, if he wanted to, but what can Peter do with the start of a summer day? Sheilah is here, it is a true Sunday morning, with its dimness and headache and remorse and regrets, and this is life. He says, "We have the Balenciaga." He touches Sheilah's hand. The children have their aunt now, and he and Sheilah have each other. Everything works out, somehow or other. Let Agnes have the start of the day. Let Agnes think it was invented for her. Who wants to be alone in the universe? No, begin at the beginning: Peter lost Agnes. Agnes says to herself somewhere, Peter is lost.

1963

An Autobiography

I

I TEACH elementary botany to girls in a village half a day's journey by train from Montreux. Season by season our landscape is black on white, or green and blue, or, at the end of summer, olive and brown, with traces of snow on the mountains like scrubbed-out paint. The village is made up of concentric rings: a ring of hotels, a ring of chalets, another of private schools. Through the circles one straight street carries the tearooms and the sawmill and the stuccoed cinema with the minute screen on which they try to show things like *Ben-Hur*. Some of my pupils seem interested in what I have to say, but the most curious and alert are usually showing off. The dull girls, with their slow but capacious memories, are often a solace, a source of hope. Very often, after I have been on time for children raised to be unpunctual, or have counselled prudence, in vain, to these babies of heedless parents, I remind myself that they have not been sent here to listen to me. I must learn to become the substance their parents have paid for – a component of scenery, like a tree or a patch of grass. I must stop battering at the sand castles their parents have built. I might swear, at certain moments, that all the girls from Western Germany are lulled and spoiled, and all the French calculating, and the Italians insincere, and the English

65

impermeable, and so on, and on; but that would be at the end of a winter's day when they have worn me out.

At the start of the new term, two girls from Frankfurt came to me. They giggled and pushed up the sleeves of their sweaters so that I could see the reddish bruises. "Tomorrow is medical inspection," said Liselotte. "What can we say?" They should have been in tears, but they were biting their lips to keep from laughing too much, wondering what my reaction would be. They said they had been pinching each other to see who could stand the most pain. There are no demerits in our school; if there were, every girl would be removed at once. We are expected to create reserves of memory. The girls must remember their teachers as they remembered hot chocolate and after-skiing, all in the same warm fog. I disguised the bruises with iodine, and said that girls sometimes slipped and fell during my outdoor classes and sometimes scratched their arms. "*Merci, Mademoiselle*," said the two sillies. They could have said "*Fräulein*" and been both accurate and understood, but they are also here because of the French. Their parents certainly speak English, because it was needed a few years ago in Frankfurt, but the children may not remember. They are ignorant and new. Everything they see and touch at home is new. Home is built on the top layer of Ur. It is no good excavating; the fragments would be without meaning. Everything within the walls was inlaid or woven or cast or put together fifteen years ago at the very earliest. Every house is like the house of newly wed couples who have been disinherited or say they scorn their families' taste. It is easy to put an X over half your life (I am thinking about the parents now) when you have nothing out of the past before your eyes; when the egg spoon is plastic and the coffee cup newly fired porcelain; when the books have been lost and the silver, if salvaged, sold a long time ago. There are no dregs, except perhaps a carefully sorted collection of snapshots. You have survived and the food you eat is new – even that. There are bananas and avocado pears and plenty of butter. Not even an unpleasant taste in the mouth will remind you.

I have light hair, without a trace of gray, and hazel eyes. I am not fat, because, unlike my colleagues, I do not hide pastry and *petits fours* in my room to eat before breakfast. My calves, I think, are overdeveloped from years of walking and climbing in low-heeled shoes. I am a bit sensitive about it, and wear my tweed skirts longer than the fashion. Because I take my gloves off in all weather, my hands are rough; their untended appearance makes the French and Italian parents think I am not gently bred. I use the scents and creams my pupils present me with at Christmas. I have few likes and dislikes, but have lost the habit of eating whatever is put before me. I do not mind accepting gifts.

Everyone's father where I come from was a physician or a professor. You will never hear of a father who rinsed beer glasses in a hotel for his keep, or called at houses with a bottle of shampoo and a portable hair-drying machine. Such fathers may have existed, but we do not know about them. My father was a professor of Medieval German. He was an amateur botanist and taught me the names of flowers before I could write. He went from Munich to the university at Debrecen, in the Protestant part of Hungary, when I was nine. He did not care for contemporary history and took no notice of passing events. His objection to Munich was to its prevailing church, and the amount of noise in the streets. The year was 1937. In Debrecen, on a Protestant islet, he was higher and stonier and more Lutheran than anyone else, or thought so. Among the very few relics I have is *Wild Flowers of Germany: One Hundred Pictures Taken from Nature.* The cover shows a spray of Solomon's-seal – five white bells on a curving stem. It seems to have been taken against the night. Under each of the hundred pictures is the place and time we identified the flower. The plants are common, but I was allowed to think them rare. Beneath a photograph of lady's-slipper my father wrote, "By the large wood on the road going toward the vineyard at Durlach July 11 1936," in the same amount of space I needed to record, under snowdrops, "In the Black Forest last Sunday."

I have often wondered whether tears should rise as I leaf through the book; but no – it has nothing to do with me, or with anyone now. It would be a poor gesture to throw it away, an act of harshness or impiety, but if it were lost or stolen I would not complain.

I recall, in calm woods, my eyes on the ground, searching for poisonous mushrooms. He knocked them out of the soft ground with his walking stick, and I conscientiously trod them to pulp. I teach my pupils to do the same, explaining that they may in this way save countless lives; but while I am still talking the girls have wandered away along the sandy paths, chattering, collecting acorns. "Beware of mushrooms that grow around birch trees," I warn. It is part of the lesson.

I can teach in Hungarian, German, French, English, or Italian. I am grateful to Switzerland, where language is a matter of locality, not an imposition, and existence a question of choice. It is better to avoid dying unless the circumstances are clear. If I fall, by accident, out of the funicular tomorrow, it will only prove once again that the suicide rate is high in a peaceful society. In any case, I will see the shadow of the cable car sliding over trees. In a clearing, a woman sorting apples for cider will not look up, although her children may wave. There I shall be, gazing down in order to frighten my vertigo away (I have been trying this for years), in the cable car of my own will, hoping I shall not open the door without meaning to and fall out and become a reproach to a country that has been more than kind. Imagine gliding – floating down to them! Think of the silence, the turning trees! Sometimes I have thought of adopting a strict religion and living by codes and signs, but as I observe my pupils at their absent-minded rites I find they are all too lax and uncertain. These spoiled girls do not care whether they eat roast veal or fish in parsley sauce on

Fridays – it is all the same monotonous meal. Some say they have never been sure what they may eat Fridays, where the limits are. My father was a non-believer, and my mother followed, but without conviction. He led her into the desert. She died of tuberculosis, not daring to speak of God for fear of displeasing her husband. He never carried a house key, because he wanted his wife to answer the door whatever the hour; that is what he was like. My only living relation now is my mother's sister, who has disinherited me because I remind her of my father. She fetched me to Paris to tell me so – that old, fussy, artificial creature in a flat stuffed with showy trifles. "Proust's maternal grandfather lived on this street," she said severely. What of it? What am I supposed to make of that? She gave me a stiff dark photograph of my mother at her confirmation. My mother clasps her Bible to her breast and stares as if the camera were a house on fire.

What I wanted to comment on was children – children in Switzerland. I rent a large room in a chalet seven minutes from my school. Downstairs is the boisterous Canadian who married her ski instructor when she was a pupil here eleven years ago. She has a loud laugh and veined cheeks. He had to resign his post, and now works in the place near the sawmill where they make hand-carved picture frames. The house is full of animals. On rainy days their dining room smells of old clothes and boiled liver. When I am invited to tea (in mugs, without saucers) and sit in one of the armchairs covered with shredded chintz and scraps of blanket, I am obliged to borrow the vacuum cleaner later so as to get the animal hairs out of my skirt. One room is kept free for lodgers – skiers in winter, tourists in summer. In August there were five people in the room – a family of middle-aged parents, two boys, and a baby girl. Because of the rain the boys were restless and the baby screamed with anger and frustration. I took them all to the woods to gather mushrooms.

"If a mushroom has been eaten by a snail, that means it is not poisonous," said the father. Rain dripped through the pine trees. We wore boots and heavy coats. The mother was carrying the bad-tempered baby and could not bend down and search, but now and then she would call, "Here's one that must be safe, because it has been nibbled."

"How do you know the snail is not lying dead somewhere?" I asked.

"You must not make the boys lose confidence in their father," the mother said, trying to laugh, but really a little worried.

"Even if it kills them?" I wanted to say, but it would have spoiled the outing.

My mother said once, "You can tell when mushrooms are safe, because when you stir them the spoon won't tarnish. Poisonous mushrooms turn the spoon black."

"How do you know everyone has a silver spoon?" said my father. He looked at her seriously, with his light eyes. They were like the eyes of birds when he was putting a question. He was not trying to catch her out; he was simply putting the question. That was what I was trying to do. You can warn until your voice is extinguished, and still these people will pick anything and take it home and put their fingers in their mouths.

In Switzerland parents visit their children sometimes, but are always trying to get away. I would say that all parents of all children here are trying to get away. The baby girl, the screamer, was left for most of a day. The child of aging parents, she had their worried look, as if brooding on the lessons of the past. She was twenty-six months old. My landlady, who offered to keep her amused so that the parents and the two boys could go off on their own for once, had cause to regret it. They tricked the baby cruelly, taking her out to feed melon rinds to Coco, the donkey, in his enclosure at the bottom of the garden. When she came back, clutching the empty basket, her family had disappeared. The baby said something that sounded like "Mama-come-auto" and, writhing like a fish when she was held, slipped away and crawled up the stairs. She called upstairs and down, and the former ski instructor and his wife cried, "Yes, that's it! Mama-come-auto!" She reached overhead to door handles, but the rooms were empty. At noon they tried to make her eat the disgusting purée of carrots and potatoes the mother had left behind. "What if we spanked her?" said the former ski instructor, wiping purée from his sleeve. "Who, you?" shouted his wife. "You wouldn't have nerve enough to brain a mad dog." That shows how tough they thought the baby was. Sometimes during that year-long day, she forgot and let us distract her. We let her turn out our desks and pull our letters to bits. Then she would remember suddenly and look about her with elderly despair, and implore our help, in words no one understood. The weeping grew less frightened and more broken-hearted toward the end of the afternoon. It must have been plain to her then that they would never return. Downstairs they told each other that if she had not been lied to and deceived, then the mother would never have had a day's rest; she had been shut up in the rain in a chalet with this absolute tyrant of a child. The tyrant lay sleeping on the floor. The house was still except for her shuddering breath. Waking, she spoke unintelligible words. They had decided downstairs to pretend not to know; that is, they would not say "Yes, Mama-come-auto" or anything else. We must all three behave as if she had been living here forever and had never known anyone but us. How much memory can be stored in a mind that has not even been developed? What she understood was that we were too deaf to hear her cries and too blind to see her distress. She took the hand of the former ski instructor and dragged it to her face so that he could feel her tears. She was still and slightly feverish when the guilty parents and uneasy boys returned. Her curls were wet through and lay flat on her head. "She was perfect," the landlady said. "Just one little burst of tears after you left. She ate up all her lunch."

The mother smiled and nodded, as if giving thanks. "Children are always better away from their parents," she said, with regret. Later, the landlady repeated, to me, as if I had not been there, a strange but believable version of that day, in which the baby cried only once.

That was an exceptional case, where everyone behaved with the best intentions; but what I have wanted to say from the beginning is, do not confide your children to strangers. Watch the way the stranger holds a child by the wrist instead of by the hand, even when a hand has been offered. I am thinking of Véronique, running after the stranger she thought was making off with the imitation-leather bag that held her cardigan, mustard, salt, pepper, a postcard of the Pont-Neuf, a pink handkerchief, a peppermint, and a French centime. This was at the air terminal at Geneva. I thought I might help – interpret between generations, between the mute and the deaf, so to speak – but at that moment the woman rushing away with the bag stopped, shifted it from right hand to left, and grasped Véronique by the wrist.

I had just been disinherited by my aunt, and was extremely sensitive to all forms of injustice. I thought that Véronique's father and mother, because they were not here at the exact moment she feared her bag was being stolen, had lost all claim to her, and had I been dispensing justice, would have said so. It was late in June. My ancient aunt had made me a present of a Geneva–Paris round-trip tourist-class ticket for the purpose of telling me to my face why she had cut me out of her will: I resembled my father, and had somehow disappointed her. I needed a lesson. She did not say what the lesson would be, but spoke in the name of Life, saying that Life would teach me. She was my only relative, that old woman, my mother's eldest sister, who had had the foresight to marry a French officer in 1919 and spend the next forty years and more saying "Fie." She was never obliged to choose between duty and self-preservation, or somehow hope the two would coincide. He was a French officer and she made his sense of honor hers. He doted on her. She was one of the lucky women.

Véronique was brought aboard at Orly Airport after everyone else in the Caravelle had settled down. She was led by a pretty stewardess, who seemed bothered by her charge. "Do you mind having her beside you?" she asked. I at first did not see Véronique, who was behind the stewardess, held by the wrist. I placed her where she could look out, and the stewardess disappeared. This would be of more interest if Véronique were now revealed to be a baby ape or a tamed and lovable bear, but she was a child. The journey is a short one – fifty minutes. Some of the small girls in my school arrive alone from Teheran and Mexico City and are none the worse for the adventure. Mishaps occur when they think that pillows or blankets lent them were really presents, but any firm official can deal with that. The child is tossed from home to school, or from one acrobat parent to the other, and knows where it will land. I am frightened when I imagine the bright arc through space, the trusting flight without wings. Reflect on that slow drop from the cable car down the side of the mountain into the trees. The trees will not necessarily catch you like a net.

I fastened her seat belt, and she looked up at me to see what was going to happen next. She had been dressed for the trip in a blue-and-white cotton frock, white socks, and black shoes with a buttoned strap. Her hair was parted in the middle and contained countless shades of light brown, like a handful of autumn grass. There was a slight cast in one eye, but the gaze was steady. The buckle of the seat belt slid down and rested on one knee. She held on to a large bucket bag – held it tightly by its red handle. In the back of the seat before her, along with a map of the region over which we were to fly, were her return ticket and her luggage tags, and a letter that turned out to be a letter of instructions. She was to be met by a Mme. Bataille, who would accompany her to a *colonie de vacances* at Gsteig. I read the letter toward the end of the trip, when I realized that the air hostess had forgotten all about Véronique. I am against prying into children's affairs – even "How do you like your school?" is more inquisitive than one has a right to be. However, the important facts about Mme. Bataille and Gsteig were the only ones Véronique was unable to supply. She talked about herself and her family, in fits and starts, as if unaware of the limits of time – less than an hour, after all – and totally indifferent to the fact that she was unlikely ever to see me again. The place she had come from was "Orly," her destination was called "the mountains," and the person meeting her would be either "Béatrice" or "Catherine" or both. That came later; the first information she sweetly and generously offered was that she had twice been given injections in her right arm. I told her my name, profession, and the name of the village where I taught school. She said she was four but "not yet four and a half." She had been visiting, in Versailles, her mother and a baby brother, whose name she affected not to know – an admirable piece of dignified lying. After a sojourn in the mountains she would be met at Orly Airport by her father and taken to the sea. When would that be? "Tomorrow." On the promise of tomorrow, either he or the mother of the nameless brother had got her aboard the plane. The Ile-de-France receded and spread. She sucked her mint sweet, and accepted mine, wrapped, and was overjoyed when I said she might put it in her bag, as if a puzzle about the bag had now been solved. The stewardess snapped our trays into place and gave us identical meals of cold sausage, Russian salad in glue, savory pastry, canned pears, and tinned mineral water. Véronique gazed onto a plateau of food nearly at shoulder level, and picked up a knife and fork the size of gardening tools. "I can cut my meat," she said, meaning to say she could not. The voice that had welcomed us in Paris and had implored Véronique and me to put out our cigarettes now emerged, preceded by crackling sounds, as if the air were full of invisible fissures: "If you look to your right, you will see the city of Dijon." Véronique quite properly took no notice. "I am cold," she stated, knowing that an announcement of one's condition immediately brings on a change for the better. I opened the plastic bag and found a cardigan – hand-knit, light blue, with pearl buttons. I wondered when the change-over would come, when she would have to stop saying "I am cold" in order to grow up without being the kind of person who lets you know that there is a draft in the room, or the beach is too crowded, or the service in the restaurant has gone off. I have pupils who still cannot find their own cardigans, and my old aunt is something of a complainer, as her sister never was. Despite my disinheritance, I was carrying two relics – a compote spoon whose bowl was in the form of a strawberry leaf, and the confirmation photograph of my mother. They weighed heavily in my hand luggage. The weight of the picture was beyond description. I knew that they would be too heavy, yet I held out my hand greedily for more of the past; but my aunt's ration stopped there.

The well-mannered French girl beside me would not drink the water I had poured into her glass until advised she could. She held the glass in both hands and got it back in its slot without help. Specks of parsley now floated on the water. I said she might leave the remains of the cold sausage, which she was chewing courageously. Giddy with indiscipline, she had some of the salad and all of the pear, and asked, indicating the savory pastry, "Is that something to eat?"

"You can, but it's boring." She had never heard food referred to in that way, and hesitated. As I had left mine, she did not know what the correct attitude ought to be, and after one bite put her spoon down. I think she liked it but, not having understood "boring," was anxious to do the right thing. With her delicate fingers she touched the miniature salt and pepper containers and the doll's tube of mustard, asking what they were for. I remembered that some of the small girls in the school saved them as tokens of travel, and I said, "They are for children to keep."

"Why?"

"I don't know. Some children keep them."

I wondered if this was a mistake, and if she would begin taking things that did not belong to her. She curled her hand around the little mustard tube and said she would keep it for *Maman*. Now that she was wearing the cardigan, her purse was empty save for a mint sweet. I told her that a bag was to put things in, and she said she knew, looking comically worldly. I gave her a centime, a handkerchief, a postcard – searching my own purse to see what could be spared. The stewardess let us descend the ramp from the plane as if she had never seen Véronique before, and no one claimed her. I had great difficulty finding anyone at the terminal who knew anything about Mme. Bataille. When I caught sight of Véronique, later, hurrying desperately after a uniformed woman who did not slow her pace for a second, I feared that *was* Mme. Bataille; but fifteen minutes after that I saw Véronique in the bus that was to take us to the railway station. She was next to a mild, thin, harassed-looking person, who seemed exhausted at the thought of the journey to come.

Now, mark the change in Véronique: She shook out her hair and made it untidy, and stood on the seat and jumped up and down.

"You are a very lucky little girl, going to the mountains *and* the sea," said Mme. Bataille, in something of a whine. Véronique took no more notice of this than she had of Dijon, except to remark that she was going to the seashore tomorrow.

"Not tomorrow. You've only just arrived."

"Tomorrow!" The voice rose and trembled dangerously. "Papa is meeting me at Orly."

"Yes," said the stupid woman soothingly, "but not tomorrow. In August. This is June."

The seats between us were now filled. When I next heard Véronique, the corruption of memory had set in.

"It was the stewardess who cut up your meat," said Mme. Bataille.

"No, a lady."

"A lady in a uniform. The lady you were with when I met you."

"*No.*"

The reason I could hear them was that they were nearly shouting.

Presently, all but giving in, Mme. Bataille said, "Well, she was nice, the lady. I mean, the stewardess."

Two ideas collided: Véronique remembered the woman fairly well, even though the flight no longer existed, but Mme. Bataille knew it was the stewardess.

"I came all alone," said Véronique.

"Who cut your meat, then?"

"I did," said Véronique, and there was no shaking her.

II

Even if Peter Dobay had not instantly recognized me and called my name, my attention would have been drawn by the way he and his wife looked at the station of our village. They got out of the train from Montreux and stood as if dazed. One imagined them blinking behind their sunglasses. At that time of year, we saw only excursion parties – stout women with gray curls, or serious hikers who would stamp from the station through the village and up the slopes. Peter wore a dark suit and black shoes, his wife a black-and-white silk dress, a black silk coat, and fragile open sandals. Her blond hair had been waved that day. I wondered how she would walk in the village streets on her thin high heels.

When we were face to face, Peter and I said together, "What are *you* doing here?"

"I live here – I teach," I said.

"No!" Turning to his wife, he said excitedly, "You know who this is, don't you? It's Erika." Then, back to me, "We've come up to see my wife's twins. They're in a summer school here."

"Better than dragging them round with us," said his wife, in a low-pitched, foggy voice. "They're better off in the fresh air." She touched my arm as if she had always known me and said, "I just can't believe I've finally seen you. Poodlie, it's like a *dream*."

I was faced with two pandas – those glasses! Who was Poodlie? Peter, evidently, yet he called her "Poodlie," too: "Poodlie, it's wonderful," he said, as if she were denying it. His wife? Her voice was twenty years older than his.

He went off to see to their luggage and she stopped seeing me, abruptly, as if now that he was gone nothing was needed. She looked at the village – as much as she could see, which was the central street and the station and the shutters of the station buffet. All I could see was her mouth and the tight pinpoint muscles around it, and the flour dusting of face powder.

"Well?" she said when Peter returned.

"I can't believe it," he said to me, and laughed. "*Here!* What are you doing *here?*"

"I teach," I began again.

"No, here at the station, now, on Sunday."

"Oh, that. I was waiting for the train with the Sunday papers."

"I told you," he cried to his wife. "Remember it was one of the things I said. Even if Erika was starving, she'd buy newspapers. I never knew anyone to read so many papers."

"I haven't had to choose between starving and reading," I said, which was a lie. I watched with regret the bale of papers carted off to the kiosk. In half an hour, those I wanted would be gone.

"*We're* starving," he said. "You'll have lunch with us, won't you? Now?"

"It's early," I said, glancing at his wife.

"Call it breakfast, then." He began guiding us both toward the buffet, his arms around our shoulders in a peasant-like bonhomie that was not like anything I remembered of him.

"The luggage, Poodlie," said his wife.

"He'll take it to the hotel."

"What hotel?"

"The biggest."

"Then it's there," I said, and pointed to an Alpine fortified castle, circa 1912, of yellowish stone, propped behind the street as if on a ledge.

"Good," he said. "Now our lunch."

That was how, on a cool bright day, just before the start of term, I saw Peter again.

In the dark buffet, Peter and his wife kept their glasses on. It seemed part of their personal decorum. Although the clock had only just struck twelve, the restaurant was nearly filled, and we were given a table between the serving pantry and the door. I understood that this was Peter, even though he didn't look at all like the man I had known, and that I was sharing his table. I avoided looking at him. Across the room, over an ocean of heads, was an open window, geraniums, the mountains, and the sky.

"You have beautiful eyes," said Peter's wife. Her voice, like a ventriloquist's, seemed to come from the wrong place – from behind her sunglasses. "Poodlie never told me that. They look like topazes or something like that."

"Yes," said Peter. "Semiprecious stones from the snow-capped mountains of South America."

He sounded like a pompous old man. His English was smooth as cream now, and better than mine. I spoke it with too many people who had accents. Answering a question of his wife's, I heard myself making something thick and endless out of the letter "t": "It is crowded because it is Sunday. Tourists come for miles around. The food in the buffet is celebrated."

"We'll see," said Peter, and took the long plastic-covered menu with rather an air.

His wife was attentive to me. Parents of pupils always try to make me eat more than I care to, perhaps thinking that I would be less intractable if I were less thin. "Your daughter is not only a genius but will make a brilliant marriage," I am supposed to say over caramel cake. I let myself be coaxed by Peter's wife into having a speciality of the place – something monstrous, with boiled meat and dumplings that swam in broth. Having arranged this, she settled down to her tea and toast. As for Peter – well, what a performance! First he read the whole menu aloud and grimaced at everything; then he asked for a raw onion and a bunch of radishes and two pots of yoghurt, and cut up the onions and radishes in the yoghurt and ate the whole mess with a spoon. It was like the frantic exhibition of a child who has been made uneasy.

"He isn't well," said his wife, quite as though he weren't there. "He treats it like a joke, but you know, he was in jail after the Budapest uprising, and he was so badly treated that it ruined his stomach. He'll never be the same again."

He did not look up or kick me under the table or in any manner ask me not to betray him. It occurred to me he had forgotten I knew. I felt my face flushing, as if I had been boiled in the same water as the beef and dumplings. I thought I would choke. I looked, this time with real longing, at the mountain peaks. They seem so near in the clear weather that sometimes innocent foot travellers set off thinking they will be there in three-quarters of an hour. The pockets of snow looked as if they could have been scooped up with a coffee spoon. The cows on the lower slopes were the size of thimbles.

"Do you ski at this time of year?" said Peter's wife, without turning to see what I was staring at.

"One can, but I don't go up any more. There's an hour-and-a-half walk to the middle station, and the road isn't pleasant. It's all slush and mud." I thought they would ask what "the middle station" meant, but they didn't, which meant they weren't really listening.

When I refused a pudding, Peter said, with his old teasing, "I told you she was frugal. Her father was a German professor at Debrecen, the Protestant university."

"So was yours," said his wife sharply, as though reminding him of a truth he forgot from time to time.

"It never affected me," said Peter, smiling.

"That's where you met, then," said his wife, taking her eyes from me at last.

"No," said Peter. "We were only children then. We met when we were grown up, at the University of Lausanne. It was a coincidence, like meeting today. Erika and I will probably meet – I don't know where. On the moon."

It is difficult enough to listen to someone lying without looking shocked, but imagine what it might be to be part of the fantasy; his lies were a whirlwind, and I was at the core, trying to recognize something familiar. We met in Lausanne; that was true. We met on a bench in the public gardens. I told him I had lived in Hungary and could speak a few sentences of Hungarian still. He was four years younger than I. I told him about my father in Debrecen, and that we were Germans, and that my father had been shot by a Russian soldier. I said I was grateful for Switzerland. He told me he was a half Jew from Budapest and had been ill-used. His life had been saved in some remarkable way by a neutral embassy. He was grateful, too.

He was the first person to whom I had ever spoken spontaneously and without reserve. We met every day for ten days, and when he wanted to leave Switzerland because he thought it would be better somewhere else and would not go without me, I did not think twice. The evening lamps went on in the park where we were sitting, and I thought that if I did not go with him I would suffer every evening for the rest of my life, every time the lamps were lit. To avoid suffering, I went with him. Yet when I told my father's old friends, the people who had taken me in and welcomed me and kept me from starving, I said it was my duty. I said it was Peter who could not live without me. It is true I would never have gone out of Switzerland, out to the wilderness, but for him. My father had friends at the University of Lausanne, and although after the war some were afraid, because the wind had shifted, others took me in when I was seventeen and homeless and looked after me until I could work. I was afraid of telling about Peter. In the end, I had to. I quoted something my father had once said about duty, and no one could contradict that.

It lasted only a short time, the adventure, and can be briefly and accurately remembered. Quickly, then: He had heard there was a special university for refugees in a city on the Rhine, and thought they might admit him. We lived in a hotel over a café, and discovered we were living in a brothel. The university existed, but its quota was full. We were starving to death. We were so attractive a couple, so sympathetic-looking, that people dulled with eating looked at us fondly. We strolled along the Rhine and looked at excursion boats. "Your duty is always before you, plain as that," my father had said, pointing with his walking stick to some vista or tree or cloud. I do not know what he was pointing at – something in his mind.

Because of Peter I was on a sea without hope of landing anywhere. It grew on me that he had been jealous of my safety and had dragged me beyond my depth. There had been floods – I think in Holland – and money was being collected for the victims. Newspapers spoke of "Rhine solidarity," and I was envious, for I had solidarity with no one now. It took me time to think things out, for I had no illusions about my intelligence, and I wondered finally why I did not feel any solidarity with Peter. I loved him, but together we would starve or drown.

"You can't stay here," said the owner of the hotel one day. "It isn't safe for refugees. We have the police in too often."

"We can't move," said Peter. "My wife is ill." But that did not give me a feeling of solidarity, for I was not his wife, and he was a person who would keep moving from one place to another.

He never told the same story twice, except for some details. He said he was picked up and deported when he was ten or twelve. He was able to describe the Swiss or Swedish consulate where they tried to save him. In his memories, the person who hid him was always different. Sometimes he said it was a peasant, sometimes a fat woman who shut him in a cupboard. The forced march must have been true. Someone – he did not say who – was working on his behalf. He hinted he was illegitimate, and that a person of noble birth, who did not wish to be known, was his protector. It is true that sometimes in the marches from Budapest to the border one person in the column was saved, if the order came through in time. It was often at night. The column stopped by the side of the road, and the torches, hooded because of the air raids, moved from face to face. One night, the light picked out an old man who would have died soon in any case, and Peter. He could not see his deliverers – he saw the light moving from face to face. The light was lowered. He tried to hide, but they spoke his name. He thought the light meant an execution. He was taken away in a car, back to Budapest, and in the car was comforted with chocolates. These were the details he repeated: the light on his face, the voice saying his name, and the chocolates. Sometimes, being boastful, he said he was active in the Arrow Cross Party; but he was a victim, and a child. Once, he said he was poor and had sold papers in the street to pay for his shoes. But he was such a liar. He may have been poor, or he may have been from a solid family who lost him along the way; but it was not a Protestant family, and his father was not a professor at Debrecen. Also, he was not in Budapest during the uprising in 1956. He was in a city on the Rhine, starving, with me.

We stood at the foot of the cathedral in this city one day. We had nothing to eat and nothing to do. I could not understand why Peter had brought me here or what he wanted now. He urged me to write my father's old friends in Lausanne, or to my aunt in Paris, but I was proud, and ashamed that he would ask such a thing. I think he believed I was a magic solution just in myself. He lived in a fantasy of false names, false fortunes, false parents, and here was a reality of expired visas and dry bread he could not explain away.

"Goethe climbed to the top of this cathedral to cure himself of vertigo. You should try it," Peter said.

"Oh, Goethe would," I said, and that was the only thing that autumn that made Peter laugh. We climbed and climbed, and looked down at matchbox cars. I felt vertigo, and was surprised he did not. I held out my arms to receive him if he fainted – I was so sure he would not stand this – but he stood smiling down with no intention of toppling over. Below was the sweet nursery world, nursery-sized, with toy trams and toy people. It smiled back at him; he was its lord, at least from up here. My world was my size, and often bigger. I was afraid of the shrunken world as he saw it; he made me unsteady. I left him that day. He went alone to the post office to see if there were phantom letters from ghost friends, and I made myself as tidy as I could and went to my own consulate with a plausible story. And that was the last Peter saw of me, until Peter, or Poodlie, called my name at the station.

I don't know what he remembered. He had taken my family as his, and expected me to smile. Actually, I did. I made him a present of my family. But by now he must have believed that whatever came into his head was true, for he did not thank me – neither then nor later. I leaned over the table and said, "I see what is making the difference. It is the dark glasses." He immediately took them off, but I saw that I still did not recognize him.

An excursion party now trooped into the buffet. Their accents were, I think, industrial England over, I think, Viennese. One of the women smeared thick white cream on her sunburned arms. "Let's finish and pay and get out of here," said Peter's wife, sharply. I stared at him then, but his face showed nothing. He did not add or contribute. It might have had nothing to do with him. She slipped him folded money so that he could pay the bill. I tried to think, but they had stuffed me with food. I clung to one idea: no one would get me out of Switzerland again, as he once had to a city on the Rhine, as my old aunt had got me to Paris. Each time I returned I was wounded, or had failed. Outside the station, I stopped at the kiosk, but of course my newspapers were gone.

The next afternoon, I sat in the lobby of their hotel. His wife now looked through the windows to the station, as if afraid of missing the train out. She poured tea from a leaky pot, and passed chocolate biscuits, shell-shaped, in a thin coating of sugar. They were Poodlie's favorites; she was sorry he wasn't here. She poured with a tense, strong hand – I admired the long fingers, and the short nails, on which the red was thickly spread. Absently but politely, she asked about my work, as if she were a headmistress interviewing me for a post.

I described flowers next to snow, and plants so perfect and minute, rooted on stone, that they must be like the algae on Mars.

"Oh, yes, edelweiss," she said.

He was a parcel posted without an address, and he had come to her. Now I heard her inviting me to join them. I heard the words "The twins would adore you, and he is a different person when you're there. I've never seen him so gay and happy as he was yesterday at lunch." He had put her up to it, and now he was out, walking around in the village, waiting for the barter to be completed. "He has talked about you such a lot," she said.

"What did he tell you?"

"Why, that you were a wonderful person. He said you had been so kind to him."

That part of it ended there. She explained that Peter was walking, not in the village, as I had supposed, but somewhere up a mountain. He had gone up in a cable car. "I didn't bring the right clothes," she said. "We could drive somewhere, but we never do." It was the only sign of her discontent. The person she had gone to consult when she contemplated this marriage – a rapid psychotherapy, she explained – had warned her not to take over too many head-of-the-family functions from a young husband. That meant, among other things, that she was never to drive the car. But Poodlie was too wild to drive. She gave him cars, but could not trust him to drive them. I thought of him wandering along a steep, windy slope now, not knowing how to keep a foothold in his slippery shoes. He was up above the village in his dark suit and dark glasses and shoes. How could she let him go that way – as if he were lost or had strayed from the towns? He was alone, shivering (no one had told him how cold it would be), dreaming and inventing things to be remembered.

I did not meet her children, but I saw her with them in a tearoom: two plump girls of about fourteen, in clay-colored tights and long pullovers that covered their sturdy hips. They were not girls I had ever seen before. They looked sullen there in the dark shop, which was suffocating with the smell of chocolate. They were choosing éclairs, pointing, discontented and curt. Their school had not yet taught them manners, and their mother, with a stiff smile on her lips and her sunglasses hiding her opinion, could see only the distance between what they were and what they ought to be. She was not an educator. The girls' clumsiness was a twist of the spirit, a sprain. She watched them choose and eat, and I thought how much time she spent watching people choose and eat their food. She removed the glasses and rubbed the space between her eyes. She saw me, and her glance meeting mine almost begged something. Information? Advice? She had the psychotherapy for advice, and she had Peter to tell her stories. Perhaps she wanted me to change my mind about going with them. He must have asked for me, as he asked for cars she would not let him drive because he broke them.

It would have been easy for her to make me believe my choices were wrong, but it would have been another matter to make me change my mind. Once when she was busy with the twins, he came to me. He looked at the saucer full of moss and Alpine plants; and the shelf with tea and hard biscuits and cereal and powdered milk; and at my bed with its shabby cushions; and my walls decorated with photographs of snow and skiers – searching for something. He twitched a curtain as if it hid a view he liked and said, "It's all dirty green, like a customs inspector's uniform."

But I had travelled nearly as much as Peter, and over some of the same frontiers. He could not impress me. I think (like the remark about semiprecious stones and snow-capped mountains) it was a way of talking he had developed because it amused his wife. He knew it was no good talking about the past, because we were certain to remember it differently. He daren't be nostalgic about anything, because of his inventions. He would never be certain if the memory he was feeling tender about was true.

I watched him at the window – the town lad, hating the quiet. "What is that racket?" he said angrily. It was the stream running outside through the garden. There was also Coco, the donkey, braying in his enclosure. He would have preferred a deafening, continued, city noise. I remembered him on streets full of trams and traffic; I remembered the quick turn of his head. When I remembered the horror of the room over the café, I thought it had been the horror of living on a street.

The view here, after the long garden, was of the roof of the chalet farther down the slope. A crash: my bookshelf, containing *Wild Flowers of Germany*, fell from the wall. The house shook.

He looked at the perpendicular, windless rain that had begun to fall. He turned back to the room; he was still searching. "You used to read," he said, still in pursuit of something. I pointed to the floor. "Didn't you hear them fall?" He made a silly remark – I remember the sense of it, not the words. He could not trust me, because I had once run away, vanished, but as he had long ago fabricated something else, he could not remember why he could not trust me. The room grew dark. I served coffee in cups with *Liberté* and *Patrie* and a green-and-white shield of the Vaud on them. The parents of a pupil had bought them in Montreux for me once. He held his cup close to his eyes and read the words, and put it down without saying anything.

I said to myself that he was only a man about whom I had known a great deal and it was so long ago that much of it might have been told to me by someone else. Nostalgia is a weakness; he would be the one to indulge in it, if he dared. I had not gone to him out of duty and had not left him out of self-preservation. It was not that simple. I would have talked, for I knew he was waiting for me to scrape away the dreams and begin again with the truth, but I thought, I shall write him a letter. That will be easier. I shall write about everything, all of the truth.

They came up by train and they left by train – the little red train that has its start among the hotels and swimming pools along the lake. As neither of them could drive the other, they had to take the train. They were leaving the twins behind.

The twins were happy, and the fresh air was doing them good. They were enrolled for the autumn term.

The first-class carriages of those trains look as if they had been built for miniature royal tours. There are oval satin-wood panels and Art Nouveau iron roses. Some of the roses had iron worms eating their hearts. I imagine the artist meant something beautiful and did not know it was hideous. As you can imagine, the trains are beautifully polished. The panels gleam, and dust is not allowed to accumulate in the rose petals. The windows are clear for a view of cows and valleys, the ashtrays are emptied and polished, and the floors are swept. I like best the deep-rose velvet, with its pattern of brown leaves and ferns, that covers the seats. It wears slowly; in some very worn places the color is light apricot and the palest lemon, and the pattern can scarcely be seen. Somewhere in storage, preserved from dust and the weather, are bales of the same velvet, and when a seat becomes too worn they simply patch it up again.

He would have stayed if I had wanted. Yes, Poodlie would have left Poodlie. He knew *I* would never go with them. I might have been for sale, but not to her. At a word of truth he would have stayed, if only to hear the rest. He would have made furious plans, and left such an imprint on this place that after his departure I could not have lived here any more. Or perhaps this time one of us would have stayed forever. These are the indecisions that rot the fabric, if you let them. The shutter slams to in the wind and sways back; the rain begins to slant as the wind increases. This is the season for mountain storms. The wind rises, the season turns; no autumn is quite like another. The autumn children pour out of the train, and the clouds descend the mountain slopes, and there we are with walls and a ceiling to the village. Here is the pattern on the carpet where he walked, and the cup he drank from. I have learned to be provident. I do not waste a sheet of writing paper, or a postage stamp, or a tear. The stream outside the window, deep with rain, receives rolled in a pellet the letter to Peter. Actually, it is a blank sheet on which I intended to write a long letter about everything – about Véronique. I have wasted the sheet of paper. There has been such a waste of everything; such a waste.

1964

Saturday

I

AFTER THE girl across the aisle had glanced at Gérard a few times (though he was not talking to her, not even trying to), she went down to sit at the front of the bus, near the driver. She left behind a bunch of dark, wet, purple lilacs wrapped in wet newspaper. When Gérard followed to tell her, she did not even turn her head. Feeling foolish, he suddenly got down anywhere, in a part of Montreal he had never seen before, and in no time at all he was lost. He stood on the curb of a gloomy little street recently swept by a spring tempest of snow. A few people, bundled as Russians, scuffled by. A winter haze like a winter evening sifted down through a lattice of iron and steel. The sudden lowering of day, he saw, was caused by an overhead railway. This railway was smart and new, as if it had been unpacked out of sawdust quite recently and snapped into place.

What was it for? "Of all the unnecessary . . ." Gérard muttered, just as his father might. Talking aloud to oneself was a family habit. You could grumble away for minutes at home without anyone's taking the least notice. "Yes, they have to spend our money somehow," he went on, just as if he were old enough to vote and pay taxes. Luckily no one heard him. Everyone's attention had been fixed by a funeral procession of limousines grinding along in inches of slush. The Russian

91

bundles crossed themselves, but Gérard kept his hands in his pockets. "Clogging up the streets," he offered, as an opinion about dying and being taken somewhere for burial. At that moment the last cars broke away, climbed the curb, and continued along the sidewalk. Gérard pressed back to the wall behind him, as he saw the others doing. No one appeared astonished, and he supposed that down here, in the east end, where there was a funeral a minute, this was the custom. "Otherwise you'd never have any normal traffic," he said. "Only all these hearses."

He thought, all at once, Why is everybody looking at me?

He was smiling. That was why. He could not help smiling. It was like a cinématèque comedy – the black cars in the whitish fog, the solemn bystanders wiping their noses on their gloves and crossing themselves, and everyone in winter cocoon clothes, with a white bubble of breath. But it was not black and gray, like an old film: it was the color of winter and cities, brown and brick and sand. What was more, the friends and relations of the dead were now descending from their stopped cars, and he feared that his smile might have offended them, or made him seem gross and unfeeling; and so, in a propitiatory gesture he at once regretted, he touched his forehead, his chest, and a point on each shoulder.

He had never done this for himself. Until now, he had never craved approval. From the look of the mourners, they were all Protestants anyway. He wanted to tell them he had crossed himself by mistake; that he was an atheist, from a singular and perhaps a unique family of anti-clerics. But the mourners were too grieved to pay attention. Even the men were sobbing. They held their hands against their mouths, they blinked and choked, they all but doubled over with pain – they were laughing at something. Perhaps at Gérard? Well, they were terrible people. He had always known. He was relieved to see one well-behaved person among them. She had been carried from her car and placed, with gentle care, in a collapsible aluminum wheelchair. Loving friends attended her, one to hold her purse, another to tie her scarf, a third to tuck a fur robe around her knees. Gérard had often been ill, and he recognized on her face the look of someone who knows about separateness and nightmares and all the vile tricks that the body can play. Her hair was careless, soft, and long, but the face seemed thirty, which was, to him, rather old. She turned her dark head and he heard her say gravely, "Not since the liberation of Elizabeth Barrett . . ."

The coffin lay in the road. It had been let down from a truck, parked there as if workmen were about to jump out and begin shovelling snow or mending the pavement. The dead man must have left eccentric instructions, Gérard thought, for his coffin was nothing more than pieces of brown carton stapled together in a rough shape. The staples were slipping out: that was how carelessly and above all how cheaply the thing had been done. Gérard had a glimpse of a dark suit and a watch chain before he looked away. The hands, he saw, rested upon a long white envelope. He was to be buried with a packet of securities, as all Protestants probably were. The crippled woman touched Gérard on the arm and said, "Just reach over and get it, will you?" – that way, casually, used to service. No one stopped Gérard or asked him what he thought he was doing. As he slipped the envelope away he knew that this impertinence, this violation, would turn the dead man into a fury where he was concerned. By his desire to be agreeable, Gérard had deliberately and foolishly given himself some bad nights.

Jazz from an all-night program invaded the house until Gérard's mother, discovering its source in the kitchen, turned the radio off. She supposed Gérard had walked in his sleep. What else could she think when she found him kneeling, in the dark, with his head against the refrigerator door? Beside him was a smashed plate and the leftover ham that had been on it, and an overturned stool. She knelt too, and drew his head on her shoulder. His father stood in the doorway. The long underwear he wore at all times and in every season showed at his wrists and ankles, where the pajamas stopped. Without his teeth and without his glasses he seemed younger and clearer about the eyes, but frighteningly helpless and almost female. His head and his hands were splashed with large, soft-looking freckles.

"He looks so peaceful," the old man said. "This is how he always looks when we aren't around."

She did not answer, for once, "Oh, nobody cares," but her expression cried for her, "What useless, pointless remark will you think of next?" She clasped her son and tried to rock him. As Gérard resisted, she held still. Of all her children, he was the one with whom she blundered most. His uneven health, his moods, his temper, his choked breathing, were signs of starvation, she had been told, but not of the body. The mother was to blame. How to blame? How? Why not the father? They hadn't said. Her daughters were married; Léopold was still small; in between came this strange boy. One of Queen Victoria's children had been flogged for having asthma. Why should she think of this now? She had never punished her children. The very word had been banned.

Gérard heard his father open the refrigerator and then heard him pouring beer in a glass.

"He's been out with his girl," his father said. "She's no Cleopatra, but it's better than having him queer."

All Gérard felt then was how her grip slackened. She said softly, "Get rid of that girl. Just until you've passed your exams. Look at what she's doing to you. One day you'll meet her in the street and you'll wonder why you fought with your mother over her. Get rid of her and I'll believe everything you ever say. You've never walked in your sleep. You came in late. You were hungry . . ."

"What about the funeral?" the old man said. "Whose funeral?"

"Leave him," said his mother. "He's been dreaming."

Gérard, no longer refusing, let his mother rock him. If it had been a dream, then why in English? Dreaming in English made him feel powerless, as if his mind were dying, ill-fed from the soil. They spoke English at home, but he, Gérard, tried to dream in French. He read French; he went to French movies; he tried to speak it with his little brother; and yet his mind made fun of him and sent up to the surface "Elizabeth Barrett." The family had not deserted French for social betterment, or for business reasons, but on the matter of belief that set them apart. His mother wanted English to be freedom, at least from the Church. There were no public secular schools, but that was only part of it. Church and language were inextricably enmeshed, and you had to leave the language if you wanted your children brought up some other way. That was how it was. It was as simple, and as complex, as that. But (still pressed to his mother) he thought that here in the house there had never been freedom, only tension and conversation (oh, such a lot of conversation!) and a few corrupted qualities disguised as "speaking your mind," "taking a stand," and "drawing the line somewhere." Caressed by his mother, he seemed privileged. Being privileged, he weakened, and that meant even his rage was fouled. He had so much to hate that he seemed to carry in his brain a miniature Gérard, sneering and dark.

"If you would just do something about your children instead of all the time thinking about yourself," he heard his mother say. "Oh, anything. Do anything. Who cares what you do now? Nobody cares."

There had been a shortage of bedrooms until Gérard's five sisters married. His mother kept for her private use a sitting room with periwinkle paper on the walls. It could have done as a bedroom for the two boys, but her need for this extra space was never questioned. She had talks with her daughters there, and she kept the household accounts. Believing it her duty, she read her children's personal letters and their diaries as long as they lived under her roof. She carried the letters to the bright room and sat, leaning her head on her hand, reading. If someone came in she never tried to hide what she read, or slip it under a book, but let her hand fall, indifferently. In this room Gérard had lived the most hideous adventure of his life. Sometimes he thought it was a dream and he willed it to be a dream, even if it meant reversing sleeping and waking forever and accepting as friends and neighbors the strangers he saw in his sleep. He would remember it sometimes and say, "I must have dreamed it." His collection of pornography was heaped in plain sight on his mother's desk. There were the pictures, the books carefully dissimulated under fake covers, and the postcards from France and India turned face down. His mother sat with these at her elbow, and, of course, he could see them, and she said, "Gérard, I won't always be here. I'm not immortal. Your father is thirty years older than I am but he didn't have to bear his own children and he's as sound as this house. He might very well outlive me. I want you to see that he is always looked after and that he always uses saccharine to sweeten his tea. There is a little box I slip in his pajama pocket and another in the kitchen. Promise me. Now, the sweater you had on yesterday. I want to throw it out. It's past mending. I don't want you to sulk for a week, and that's why I'm asking you first." He wanted to say, "Those things aren't mine, I've got to give them back." He saw through her eyes and all at once understood that the cards from India were the worst of all, for they were all about people scarcely older than Léopold, and the reason they looked so funny was that they were starving to death. All Gérard had seen until now was what they were doing, not who they were, or could be. Meanwhile the room rocked around him, and his mother stood up to show that was all she had to say.

She did not sleep in the pretty room, but in a Spartan cell where there were closets full of linen and soap, and a shelf of preserves behind a curtain, and two painters' stepladders, and two large speckled mirrors in gilt frames. One wall was covered with photographs of a country house the children had never seen, and of her old convent school. The maid, when there was one, went freely in without knocking if she needed a jar of fruit or clean bedsheets. Even when her daughters married and liberated their rooms one by one, she stayed where she was. The bed was hard and narrow and the old man could not comfortably spend the night. For years Gérard had slept in a basement room that contained a Ping-Pong table, and from which he could hear, at odd hours, the furnace coming to life with a growl. A lighted tank of tropical fish separated two divans, one of which was used now by his father, now by his little brother. He had never understood why his father would suddenly appear in the middle of the night, and why the little brother, aged three and four and five, was led, stumbling and protesting, to finish the night in his mother's bed. Gérard was used to someone's presence at night, the warm light of the tank had comforted him. Now that he had a room of his own and slept alone in it, he discovered he was afraid of the dark.

His mother sat by his bed, holding his hand, until he pretended to be asleep. His door was open and a ray from the passage bent over the bed and along the wall. "I'm sure I must be pale," she said, though her cheeks and brow were rosy. She believed her children had taken her blood to make their own and that hers was diminished. Having had seven babies, she could not have left much over a pint. Bitterly anti-clerical, she sometimes hinted that nuns had the best of it after all. Gérard had been wrong to wake her, he had no business walking in his sleep. Tomorrow was what she called "a hell day." It was

Léopold's ninth birthday, she was without help, and twenty-two people were going to sit down to lunch. Directly after the meal, she was to take all the uneaten cake to an aged religious who had once been a teacher of hers and was now ending her life bedridden in a convent for the old. The home was seventy miles north of the city, but might have been seven hundred. One son-in-law had undertaken to drive her. Instead of coming back with him, she proposed to spend the night. This meant that another son-in-law would have to fetch her the next day. The interlocked planning this required surpassed tunnelling under the Alps. "Hell day," she said, but she said it so often that Gérard supposed most days were some kind of hell.

The first thing he did when he wakened was light a cigarette, the second turn on his radio. He felt oddly drunk, as if he might miss his footing stumbling down to breakfast. She was already prepared for the last errand of the day. She wore a tweed suit and her overnight case stood in the hall. She moved back and forth between the kitchen and the dining room. His father, still in underwear and pajamas, sat breakfasting at the counter in the kitchen. She paused and watched him stir too much sugar into his coffee, but did not, this time, remark on it. The old man, excited, tapped his spoon on his saucer.

"It was a movie," he said. "Your dream. I saw it, I think, in a movie about an old man. You've dreamed an old man's dream. I've looked through the paper," he said, pushing it toward his son. "There's nothing about that funeral. It couldn't have been a funeral. Anyway, not anyone important."

"Leave him," said the mother, patiently. "He dreamed it. There is something you can do today. Take over the dog. *Completely.* Léopold has him now." Gérard knew it was his father thus addressed. He held his cup in both hands. "As for you, Gérard, I want a word with you."

"Another thing I thought," continued the old man. "Maybe they were making a movie around there and you got mixed up with the crowd. What you took for a railway was some kind of scaffolding, cameras. Eh?"

"Gérard, I want you to . . ." She turned to her husband: "Back me up! He's your son, too! Gérard, I want you to tell that girl you're too young to be tied to one person." Her face was blazing, her eyes brilliant and clear. "What will you do when she starts a baby? Marry her? I want you to tell that girl there's no money to inherit in this family, and that after Léopold's education is finished there won't be a cent for anybody. Not even us."

"She's not really a dancer," said the old man, forestalling the next bit. "She gives dancing *lessons.* It's not the same thing."

"I don't care what she gives. What about your son?"

Gérard was about to say, "I did tell her," but he remembered, "I never got there. I only started out."

He stopped hearing them. He had set his cup down as his mother spoke his name, and pushed it to the back of the counter. As his father handed him the paper, he remembered, he had taken it with his left hand, and opened it wide instead of carefully folding it, as he usually did. This was so important that he did not hear what was said after a minute or two. He had always given importance to his gestures, noticing whether he put his watch or his glasses to the left or the right of a bedlamp. He always left his coffee cup about four inches from the edge of the counter. When he studied, he piled his books on the right, and whatever text he was immediately using was at his left hand. His radio had to be dead center. He saw, and had been noticing for some time, that his mind was not keeping quiet order for him anymore and that his gestures were not automatic. He felt that if he did not pay close attention to everything now, something literally fantastic could happen.

Gestures had kept things controlled, as they ought to be. Whatever could happen now was in the domain of magic.

II

The conviction that she was married against her will never leaves her. If she had been born royal it could not have been worse. She has led the life of a crown princess, sapped by boredom and pregnancies. She told each of her five daughters as they grew up that they were conceived in horror; that she could have left them in their hospital cots and not looked back, so sickened was she by their limp spines and the autumn smell of their hair, by their froglike movements and their animal wails. She liked them when they could reason, and talk, and answer back – when they became what she calls "people."

She makes the girls laugh. She is French-Canadian, whether she likes it or not. They see at the heart of her a sacrificial mother, her education has removed her in degree only from the ignorant, tiresome, moralizing mother, given to mysterious female surgery, subjugated by miracles, a source of infinite love. They have heard her saying, "Why did I get married? Why did I have all these large dull children?" They have heard, "If any of my children had been brilliant or unusual, it would have justified my decision. Yes, they might have been narrow and warped in French, but oh how commonplace they became in English!" "We are considered traitors and renegades," she says. "And I can't point to even one of my children and say, 'Yes, but it was worth it – look at Pauline – or Lucia – or Gérard.'" The girls ought to be wounded at this, but in fact they are impermeable. They laugh and call it "Mother putting on an act." Her passionate ambition for them is her own affair. They have chosen exactly the life she tried to renounce for them; they married young, they are frequently pregnant, and sometimes bored.

This Saturday she has reunited them, the entire family and one guest, for Léopold's ninth birthday. There are fourteen adults at the dining-room table and eight at the children's, which is in the living room, through the arch. Léopold, so small he seems two years younger than nine, so clever and quick that other children are slightly afraid of him, keeps an eye on his presents. He has inherited his brother's electric train. It is altogether old-fashioned; Gérard has had it nine years. Still, Léopold will not let anyone near it. It is his now, and therefore charmed. If any of these other children, these round-eyed brats with English names, lays a hand on the train, he disconnects it; if the outrage is repeated, he goes in the kitchen and stands on a stool and turns off the electricity for the whole house. No one reprimands him. He is not like other children. He is more intelligent, for one thing, and so much uglier. Unlike Gérard, who speaks French as if through a muslin curtain, or as if translating from another language, who wears himself out struggling for one complete dream, Léopold can, if he likes, say anything in a French more limpid and accurate than anything they are used to hearing. He goes to a private, secular school, the only French one in the province; he has had a summer in Montreux. Either his parents have more money than when the others were small, or they have chosen to invest in their last chance. French is Léopold's private language; he keeps it as he does his toys, to himself, polished, personal, a lump of crystalline rock he takes out, examines, looks through, and conceals for another day.

Léopold's five sisters think his intelligence is a disease, and one they hope their own children will not contract. Their mother is *bright*, their father is *thoughtful* (*deep* is another explanation for him), but Léopold's intelligence will always show him the limit of a situation and the last point of possibility where people are concerned; and so, of course, he is bound to be unhappy forever. How will he be able to love? To his elder brother, he seems like a small illegitimate creature raised in secret, in the wrong house. One day Léopold will show them extraordinary credentials. But this is a fancy, for Léopold is where he belongs, in the right family; he has simply been planted – little stunted, ugly thing – in the wrong generation. The children at his table are his nieces and nephews, and the old gentleman at the head of the adult table, the old man bowed over a dish of sieved, cooked fruit, is his father. Léopold is evidence of an old man's foolishness. His existence is an embarrassment. The girls wish he had never been born, and so they are especially kind, and they load him with presents. Even Gérard, who would have found the family quite complete, quite satisfactory, without any Léopold, ever, has given the train (which he was keeping for his own future children) and his camera.

When Léopold is given something, he walks round it and decides what the gift is worth in terms of the giver. If it seems cheap, he mutters without raising his eyes. If it seems important, he flashes a brief, shrewd look that any adult, but no child, mistakes for a glance of complicity. The camera, though second-hand, has been well received. It is round his neck; he puts down his fork and holds the camera and makes all the children uneasy by staring at each in turn and deciding none of them worth an inch of film.

"Poor little lad," says his mother, who flings out whatever she feels, no matter who is in the way. "He has never had a father – only a grandfather."

The old man may not have heard. He is playing his private game of trying to tell his five English-Canadian sons-in-law apart. The two Bobs, the Don, the Ian, and the Ken are interchangeable, like postage stamps of the Queen's profile. Two are Anglicans, two United Church, and the most lackluster is a Lutheran, but which is he? The old man lifts his head and smiles a great slow smile. His smile acquits his daughters; he forgives them for having ever thought him a shameless old person; but the five sons-in-law are made uneasy. They wonder if they are meant to smile back, or something *weird* like that. Well, they may not have much in common with each

other, but here they are five together, not isolated, not alone.
Their children, with round little noses, and round little blue
eyes, are at the next table, and two or three babies are sleeping
in portable cots upstairs.

It is a windy spring day, with a high clean sky, and black
branches hitting on the windows. The family's guest that day
is Father Zinkin, who is dressed just like anyone, without even
a clerical collar to make him seem holy. This, to the five men, is
another reason for discomposure; for they might be respectful
of a robe, but *what* is this man, with his polo-necked sweater
and his nose in the wine and his rough little jokes? Is he really
the Lord's eunuch? I mean, they silently ask each other, would
you trust him? You know what I mean . . . Father Zinkin has
just come back from Rome. He says that the trees are in leaf,
and he got his pale jaundiced sunburn sitting at a sidewalk
café. This is Montreal, it is still cold, and the daughters' five fur
coats are piled upstairs on their mother's bed. They accept the
news about Rome without grace. If he thinks it is so sunny in
Rome, why didn't he stay there? Who asked him to come back?
That is how every person at that table feels about news from
abroad, and it is the only sentiment that can ever unite them.
When you say it is sunny elsewhere, you are suggesting it is
never sunny here. When you describe the trees of Rome, what
you are *really* saying is there are no trees in Montreal.

Why is he at the table, then, since he brings them nothing
but unwelcome news? The passionately anti-clerical family
cannot keep away from priests. They will make an excuse: they
will say they admire his mind, or his gifts with language – he
speaks seven. He eats and drinks just like anyone, he has
travelled, and been psychoanalyzed, and is not frightened by
women. At least, he does not seem to be. Look at the way he
pours wine for Lucia, and then for Pauline, and how his tone is
just right, not a scrap superior. And then, he is not Canadian.
He does not remind them of anything. None of the children,
from Lucia, who is twenty-nine, to Léopold, nine today, has

been baptized. Father Zinkin sits down and eats with them as if they were. Until the girls grew up and married they never went to church. Now that they are Protestants they go because their husbands want to; so, their mother thinks, this is what all the fighting and the courage came to, finally; all the struggling and being condemned and cut off from one's own kind: the five girls simply joined another kind, just as stupid.

No, thinks the old father at the head of the table: more stupid. At any rate, less interesting. Less interesting because too abstract. You would have to be a genius to be a true Protestant, and those he has met . . . At night, when he is trying to get to sleep, he thinks of his sons-in-law. He remembers their names without trouble: the two Bobs, the Don, the Ian, and the last one – Keith, or Ken? Ken. Monique married Ken. Alone, in the dark, he tries to match names and faces. Are both Bobs thin? Pink in the face? Yes, and around the neck. They lose their hair young – something to do with English hairbrushes, he invents. The old man droops now, for the sight of his sons-in-law can send him off to sleep. His five daughters – he knows their names, and he knows his own sons. His grandchildren seem to belong to a new national type, with round heads, and quite large front teeth. You would think some Swede or other had been around Montreal on a bicycle so as to create this new national type. Sharon, and Marilyn and Cary and Gary and Gail. Cary and *Gary.*

"Nobody cares," his wife says, very sharply.

He has been mumbling, talking to himself, saying the names of children aloud. She minds because of Father Zinkin. When she and her husband are alone, and he talks too much, repeats the same thing over and over, she squeezes her eyes until only a pinpoint of amber glows between the lids, and she squeezes out through a tight throat, "All right, all *right,*" and even, "Shut UP" in a rising crescendo of three. Not even her children know she says "Shut up" to the old man; "nobody cares" is just a family phrase. When it is used on Don Carlos, the basset, now under the children's table, it makes him look as if he might cry real tears.

She speaks lightly, quickly now, in English. She sits, very straight, powdered and pretty, and says, in a musical English all her own, not the speech of the city at all, "They say Jews look after their own people, but it's not true. I was told about some people who had a very old sick father. They had to tie him to a chair sometimes, because he would go downtown and steal things or start to cry in the street. As they couldn't afford a home for him, and he wouldn't have gone anyway, they decided to leave him. They moved half the furniture away and the old man sat crying on a chair and saw his family go. He sat weeping, not protesting, and his children slouched out without saying goodbye. Yes, he sat weeping, a respectable old man. Now, this man's wife gave Russian lessons to earn her living, and one day, when she was giving a lesson to a woman I know, she said, 'Come to the window.' My friend looked out and saw an old-fashioned Jew going by. The woman said, 'That was my husband.' She seemed pleased with herself, as though she had done what was right for her children."

"Was he dead?" asks Gérard. He is always waiting for some simple, casual confirmation about the existence of ghosts.

"No, of course not. He was just an old man, and someone had taken him in. Some Russian. So," she concedes, "he was looked after." But, as she likes her stories cruel, so that her children will know more about life than she once did, unhappy endings are her habit. She feels obliged to add, "Someone took him in, but probably gave him a miserable time. He must be dead now. This was long ago, during the last war, when people were learning Russian. It was the thing to do then."

Her children are worried by this story, but perhaps the father has not heard it. He is still eating his fruit, taking a mouthful and then forgetting to swallow. Suddenly something he has been thinking silently must have excited him, for he taps his spoon on the edge of the glass dish.

"As you get old you lose everything," he says. "You lose your God, if you ever had one. When you know they want you to die, you want to live. You want to be loved. Even that."

His children are so embarrassed, so humiliated, they feel as if ashes and sand were being ground in their skins. The sons-in-law are revolted. They look at their plates. Honestly, they can never come to this house without something being said about religion or something personal.

"You lose your parents," the old man continues. "You have to outlive them. Everything is loss." Before they can say "nobody cares" he is off once more: "No need for priests," he mutters. "If there is no sin, then no need for redemption. Dead words. Tell me, Father whoever you are," (he asks the glass dish of fruit) "will you explain why these words should be used?" Muttering – he has been muttering all his life.

"Oh, shut *up*," they are thinking. A chorus of silent English: "Shut *up*!" If only the old man could hear the words, he would see a great black wall; he would hear a sigh, a rattle, like the black trees outside the windows, hitting the panes.

The old man shakes his head over his plate: No, no, he never wanted to marry. He wanted to become a priest. Either God is, or He is not. If He is, I shall live for Him. If He is not, I shall fight His ghost. At forty-nine he was married off by a Jesuit, who was an old school friend. He and the shy, soft, orphaned girl who had been placed in a convent at six, and had left it, now, at eighteen, exchanged letters about comparative religion. She seemed intelligent – he has forgotten now what he imagined their life could ever be like. Presently what they had in common was her physical horror of him and his knowledge of it, and then they had in common all their children.

III

When the old man had finished his long thoughts, everyone except Gérard and Father Zinkin had disappeared. The small children were made to kiss him – moist reluctant mouths on his cheek – "before Granpa takes his nap." Léopold, who never touched anyone, looked at him briefly through his new camera and said softly to him, and only to him, "*Il n'y a pas assez de lumière.*" Their dark identical eyes reflected each other. Then everyone vanished, the women to rattle plates in the kitchen, Léopold to his room, the five fathers to play some game with the children at the back of the house. He sat in his leather armchair, sometimes he slept, and he heard Gérard protesting, "I know the difference between seeing and dreaming."

"Well, it was a waking dream," said the priest. "There is no snow on the streets, but you say there had been a storm."

The old man looked. The white light in the room surely was the reflection of a snowy day? The room seemed filled with white furniture, white flowers. The priest, because he was dressed like Gérard, tried to sound like a young man and an old friend. Only when the priest turned his head, seeking an ashtray, did the old man see what Father Zinkin knew. His interest in Gérard was intellectual. His mind was occupied with its own power. The old man imagined him, narrow, suspicious, in a small parish, lording it over a flock of old maids. They were thin, their eyebrows met over their noses.

Gérard said, "All right, what if I was analyzed? What difference would it make?"

"You would be yourself. You would be yourself *without eVort.*"

The old man had been waiting for him to say, "it would break the mirror;" for what is the good of being yourself, if you are Gérard?

"What I mean is, you can't understand about this girl. So there's no use talking about her."

"I know about girls," said the other. "I went out. I even danced."

It struck the old man how often he had been told by priests they knew about life because they had, once, danced with girls. He was willing to let them keep that as a memory of life, but what about Gérard, as entangled with a woman as a man of thirty? But then Gérard lost interest and said, "I'd want to be analyzed in French," so it didn't matter.

"It wouldn't work. Your French isn't spontaneous enough. Now, begin again. You were on the street, it was daylight, then you were in the kitchen in the dark."

How the old man despised this self-indulgence! He felt it was not his business to put a stop to it. His wife stopped it simply by coming in and beginning to talk about herself. When she talked about her children she seemed to be talking about herself, and when the priest said, to console some complaint she was making, "The little one will be brilliant," meaning Léopold, he seemed to be prophesying a future in which she would shine. Outside, the others were breaking up into groups, carrying cots, ushering children into cars. It would take a good ten minutes, and so she sat perched on the arm of a sofa with her hat on her head and her coat on her arm, and said, "Léopold will be brilliant, but I never wanted him. I'd had six children, five close together. French Canadians of our background, for I daren't say class, it sounds so . . . Well, we, people like ourselves, do *not* usually have these monstrous families, regardless of what you may have been told, Father. My mother had no one but me, and when she tried having a second child, it killed her. When I knew I was having Léopold I took ergot. I lay here, on this very sofa, in the middle of the afternoon. Nothing happened, and nothing showed. He was born without even a strawberry mark to condemn me."

She likes to shock, the old man remembered. How much you can take is measure of your intelligence. So she thinks. Oddly enough, she can be shocked.

She stopped speaking and sighed and smoothed the collar of her coat. When she thought, "My son Gérard is sleeping with a common girl," it shocked her. She thought, now, seeing him slouch past the doorway, scarcely able to wait for the house to empty so that he could go off and find that girl and spend a disgusting Saturday night with her, "Gérard knows. He looks at his father, and me, and now he knows. Before, he only thought he knew. He knows now why the old man follows me up the stairs."

She said very lightly, "My son has sex on the brain. It's all he thinks about now. I suppose all boys are the same. You must have been that way once, Father." Really, that was farther than she had ever gone. The priest looked like a statue resembling the person he had been a moment before.

Once she had departed the house seemed to relax, like an animal that feels safe and can sleep. The old man was to walk the dog and do something about his children. Those had been his instructions for the day. Oh, yes, and he was to stop thinking about himself. He put on his hat and coat and walked down the street with Don Carlos. Don Carlos dug the wet spring lawns with tortoiseshell nails. Let off the leash, he at once rolled in something horrible. The old man wanted to scold, but the wind made all conversation between himself and the dog impossible. The wind suddenly dropped; it was to the old man like a sudden absence of fear. He could dream as well as Gérard. He invented: he and Don Carlos went through the gap of a fence and were in a large sloping pasture. He trod on wildflowers. From the spongy spring soil grew crab apple trees and choke cherries, and a hedge of something he no longer remembered, that was sweet and white. Presently they – he and the dog – looked down on a village and the two silvery spires of a church. He saw the date over the door: 1885. The hills on the other side of the water were green and black with shadows. He had never seen such a blue and green day. But he was still here, on the street, and had not forgotten it for a second. Imagination was as good as sleepwalking any day.

Léopold stood on the porch, watching him through his camera. He seemed to be walking straight into Léopold's camera, magically reduced in size.

"Why, Léo," he said. "You're not supposed to be here," not caring to show how happy it made him that Léopold was here. They were bound so soon to lose each other – why start?

"Wouldn't."

"Wouldn't what?"

"Wouldn't go to Pauline's. She's coming back to get us for supper."

"I don't want anything more to eat today."

"Neither do I. And I'm not going."

Who would dare argue with Léopold? He put his camera down. One day he would have the assurance of a real street, a real father, a real afternoon.

"Well, well," his father said. "So they're all gone." He felt shy. He would never have enough of Léo – he would never know what became of him. He edged past and held the door open for the dog.

"All gone. *Il n'y a que moi.*" Léopold, who never touched anyone, pressed his lips to his father's hand.

1968

The Latehomecomer

WHEN I came back to Berlin out of captivity in the spring of 1950, I discovered I had a stepfather. My mother had never mentioned him. I had been writing from Brittany to "Grete Bestermann," but the "Toeppler" engraved on a brass plate next to the bellpull at her new address turned out to be her name, too. As she slipped the key in the lock, she said quietly, "Listen, Thomas. I'm Frau Toeppler now. I married a kind man with a pension. This is his key, his name, and his apartment. He wants to make you welcome." From the moment she met me at the railway station that day, she must have been wondering how to break it.

I put my hand over the name, leaving a perfect palm print. I said, "I suppose there are no razor blades and no civilian shirts in Berlin. But some ass is already engraving nameplates."

Martin Toeppler was an old man who had been a tram conductor. He was lame in one arm as the result of a working accident and carried that shoulder higher than the other. His eyes had the milky look of the elderly, lighter round the rim than at the center of the iris, and he had an old woman's habit of sighing, "Ah, yes, yes." The sigh seemed to be his way of pleading, "It can't be helped." He must have been forty-nine, at the most, but aged was what he seemed to me, and more than aged – useless, lost. His mouth hung open much of the time, as

111

though he had trouble breathing through his nose, but it was only because he was a chronic talker, always ready to bite down on a word. He came from Franconia, near the Czech border, close to where my grandparents had once lived.

"Grete and I can understand each other's dialects," he said – but we were not a dialect-speaking family. My brother and I had been made to say "bread" and "friend" and "tree" correctly. I turned my eyes to my mother, but she looked away.

Martin's one dream was to return to Franconia; it was almost the first thing he said to me. He had inherited two furnished apartments in a town close to an American military base. One of the two had been empty for years. The occupants had moved away, no one knew where – perhaps to Sweden. After their departure, which had taken place at five o'clock on a winter morning in 1943, the front door had been sealed with a government stamp depicting a swastika and an eagle. The vanished tenants must have died, perhaps in Sweden, and now no local person would live in the place, because a whole family of ghosts rattled about, opening and shutting drawers, banging on pipes, moving chairs and ladders. The ghosts were looking for a hoard of gold that had been left behind, Martin thought. The second apartment had been rented to a family who had disappeared during the confused migrations of the end of the war and were probably dead, too; at least they were dead officially, which was all that mattered. Martin intended to modernize the two flats, raise them up to American standards – he meant by this putting venetian blinds at the windows and gas-heated water tanks in the bathrooms – and let them to a good class of American officer, too foreign to care about a small-town story, too educated to be afraid of ghosts. But he would have to move quickly; otherwise his inheritance, his sole postwar capital, his only means of getting started again, might be snatched away from him for the sake of shiftless and illiterate refugees from the Soviet zone, or bombed-out families still huddled in barracks, or for latehomecomers.

This last was a new category of persons, all one word. It was out of his mouth before he remembered that I was one, too. He stopped talking, and then he sighed and said, "Ah, yes, yes."

He could not keep still for long: he drew out his wallet and showed me a picture of himself on horseback. He may have wanted to substitute this country image for any idea I had of him on the deck of a tram. He held the snapshot at arm's length and squinted at it. "That was Martin Toeppler once," he said. "It will be Martin Toeppler again." His youth, and a new right shoulder and arm, and the hot, leafy summers everyone his age said had existed before the war were waiting for him in Franconia. He sounded like a born winner instead of a physically broken tram conductor on the losing side. He put the picture away in a cracked celluloid case, pocketed his wallet, and called to my mother, "The boy will want a bath."

My mother, who had been preparing a bath for minutes now, had been receiving orders all her life. As a girl she had worked like a slave in her mother's village guesthouse, and after my father died she became a servant again, this time in Berlin, to my powerful Uncle Gerhard and his fat wife. My brother and I spent our winters with her, all three sleeping in one bed sometimes, in a cold attic room, sharing bread and apples smuggled from Uncle Gerhard's larder. In the summer we were sent to help our grandmother. We washed the chairs and tables, cleaned the toilets of vomit, and carried glasses stinking with beer back to the kitchen. We were still so small we had to stand on stools to reach the taps.

"It was lucky you had two sons," Uncle Gerhard said to my mother once. "There will never be a shortage of strong backs in the family."

"No one will exploit my children," she is supposed to have replied, though how she expected to prevent it only God knows, for we had no roof of our own and no money and we ate such food as we were given. Our uniforms saved us. Once we had joined the Hitler Jugend, even Uncle Gerhard never dared ask, "Where are you going?" or "Where have you been?" My brother was quicker than I. By the time he was twelve he knew he had been trapped; I was sixteen and a prisoner before I understood. But from our mother's point of view we were free, delivered; we would not repeat her life. That was all she wanted.

In captivity I had longed for her and for the lost paradise of our poverty, where she had belonged entirely to my brother and to me and we had slept with her, one on each side. I had written letters to her full of remorse for past neglect and containing promises of future goodness: I would work hard and look after her forever. These letters, sent to blond, young, soft-voiced Grete Bestermann, had been read by Grete Toeppler, whose greying hair was pinned up in a sort of oval balloon, and who was anxious and thin, as afraid of things to come as she was of the past. I had not recognized her at the station, and when she said timidly, "Excuse me? Thomas?" I thought she was her own mother. I did not know then, or for another few minutes, that my grandmother had died or that my rich Uncle Gerhard, now officially de-Nazified by a court of law, was camped in two rooms carved out of a ruin, raising rabbits for a living and hoping that no one would notice him. She had last seen me when I was fifteen. We had been moving toward each other since early this morning, but I was exhausted and taciturn, and we were both shy, and we had not rushed into each other's arms, because we had each been afraid of embracing a stranger. I had one horrible memory of her, but it may have been only a dream. I was small, but I could speak and walk. I came into a room where she was nursing a baby. Two other women were with her. When they saw me they started to laugh, and one said to her, "Give some to Thomas." My mother leaned over and put her breast in my mouth. The taste was disgustingly sweet, and because of the two women I felt humiliated: I spat and backed off and began to cry. She said something to the women and they laughed harder than ever.

It must have been a dream, for who could the baby have been? My brother was eleven months older than I.

She was cautious as an animal with me now, partly because of my reaction to the nameplate. She must have feared there was more to come. She had been raised to respect men, never to interrupt their conversation, to see that their plates were filled before hers – even, as a girl, to stand when they were sitting down. I was twenty-one, I had been twenty-one for three days, I had crossed over to the camp of the bullies and strangers. All the while Martin was talking and boasting and showing me himself on horseback, she crept in and out of the parlor, fetching wood and the briquettes they kept by the tile stove, carrying them down the passage to build a fire for me in the bathroom. She looked at me sidelong sometimes and smiled with her hand before her mouth – a new habit of hers – but she kept silent until it was time to say that the bath was ready.

My mother spread a towel for me to stand on and showed me a chair where, she said, Martin always sat to dry his feet. There was a shelf with a mirror and comb but no washbasin. I supposed that he shaved and they cleaned their teeth in the kitchen. My mother said the soap was of poor quality and would not lather, but she asked me, again from behind the screen of her hand, not to leave it underwater where it might melt and be wasted. A stone underwater might have melted as easily. "There is a hook for your clothes," she said, though of course I had seen it. She hesitated still, but when I began to unbutton my shirt she slipped out.

The bath, into which a family could have fitted, was as rough as lava rock. The water was boiling hot. I sat with my knees drawn up as if I were in the tin tub I had been lent sometimes in France. The starfish scar of a grenade wound was livid on one knee, and that leg was misshapen, as though it had been pressed the wrong way while the bones were soft. Long underwear I took to be my stepfather's hung over a line. I sat looking at it, and at a stiff thin towel hanging next to it, and at the water condensing on the cement walls, until the skin of my hands and feet became as ridged and soft as corduroy.

There is a term for people caught on a street crossing after the light has changed: "pedestrian-traffic residue." I had been in a prisoner-of-war camp at Rennes when an order arrived to repatriate everyone who was under eighteen. For some reason, my name was never called. Five years after that, when I was in Saint-Malo, where I had been assigned to a druggist and his wife as a "free worker" – which did not mean free but simply not in a camp – the police sent for me and asked what I was doing in France with a large "PG," for "*prisonnier de guerre*," on my back. Was I a deserter from the Foreign Legion? A spy? Nearly every other prisoner in France had been released at least ten months before, but the file concerning me had been lost or mislaid in Rennes, and I could not leave until it was found – I had no existence. By that time the French were sick of me, because they were sick of the war and its reminders, and the scheme of using the prisoners the Americans had taken to rebuild the roads and bridges of France had not worked out. The idea had never been followed by a plan, and so some of the prisoners became farm help, some became domestic servants, some went into the Foreign Legion because the food was better, some sat and did nothing for three or four years, because no one could discover anything for them to do. The police hinted to me that if I were to run away no one would mind. It would have cleared up the matter of the missing file. But I was afraid of putting myself in the wrong, in which case they might have an excuse to keep me forever. Besides, how far could I have run with a large "PG" painted on my jacket and trousers? Here, where it would not be necessary to wear a label, because "latehomecomer" was written all over me, I sensed that I was an embarrassment, too; my appearance, my survival, my bleeding gums and loose teeth, my chronic dysentery and anemia, my craving for sweets, my reticence with strangers, the cast-off rags I had worn on arrival, all said "war" when everyone wanted peace, "captivity" when the word was "freedom," and "dry bread" when everyone was thinking "jam and butter." I guessed that now, after five years of peace, most of the population must have elbowed onto the right step of the right staircase and that there was not much room left for pedestrian-traffic residue.

My mother came in to clean the tub after I was partly dressed. She used fine ash from the stove and a cloth so full of holes it had to be rolled into a ball. She said, "I called out to you but you didn't hear. I thought you had fallen asleep and drowned."

I was hard of hearing because of the anti-aircraft duty to which I'd been posted in Berlin while I was still in high school. After the boys were sent to the front, girls took our places. It was those girls, still in their adolescence, who defended the grown men in uniform down in the bunkers. I wondered if they had been deafened, too, and if we were a generation who would never hear anything under a shout. My mother knelt by the tub, and I sat on Martin's chair, like Martin, pulling on clean socks she had brought me. In a low voice, which I heard perfectly, she said that I had known Martin in my childhood. I said I had not. She said then that my father had known him. I stood up and waited until she rose from her knees, and I looked down at her face. I was afraid of touching her, in case we should both cry. She muttered that her family must surely have known him, for the Toepplers had a burial plot not far from the graveyard where my grandmother lay buried, and some thirty miles from where my father's father had a bakery once. She was looking for any kind of a link.

"I wanted you and Chris to have a place to stay when you came back," she said, but I believed she had not expected to see either of us again and that she had been afraid of being homeless and alone. My brother had vanished in Czechoslovakia

with the Schörner army. All of that army had been given up for
dead. My Uncle Gerhard, her only close relative, could not
have helped her even if it had occurred to him; it had taken
him four years to become officially and legally de-Nazified,
and now, "as white as a white lilac," according to my mother,
he had no opinions about anything and lived only for his
rabbits.

"It is nice to have a companion at my age," my mother said.
"Someone to talk to." Did the old need more than conversation? My mother must have been about forty-two then. I had
heard the old men in prison camp comparing their wives and
saying that no hen was ever too tough for boiling.

"Did you marry him before or after he had this apartment?"

"After." But she had hesitated, as if wondering what I
wanted to hear.

The apartment was on the second floor of a large dark
block – all that was left of a workers' housing project of the
nineteen-twenties. Martin had once lived somewhere between the bathroom window and the street. Looking out, I
could easily replace the back walls of the vanished houses, and
the small balconies festooned with brooms and mops, and the
moist oily courtyard. Winter twilight must have been the prevailing climate here until an air raid let the seasons in. Cinders
and gravel had been raked evenly over the crushed masonry
now; the broad concourse between the surviving house – ours
– and the road beyond it that was edged with ruins looked
solid and flat.

But no, it was all shaky and loose, my mother said. Someone ought to cause a cement walk to be laid down; the women
were always twisting their ankles, and when it rained you
walked in black mud, and there was a smell of burning. She
had not lost her belief in an invisible but well-intentioned
"someone." She then said, in a hushed and whispery voice,
that Martin's first wife, Elke, was down there under the rubble

and cinders. It had been impossible to get all the bodies out, and one day a bulldozer covered them over for all time. Martin had inherited those two apartments in a town in Franconia from Elke. The Toepplers were probably just as poor as the Bestermanns, but Martin had made a good marriage.

"She had a dog, too," said my mother. "When Martin married her she had a white spitz. She gave it a bath in the bathtub every Sunday." I thought of Martin Toeppler crossing this new wide treacherous front court and saying, "Elke's grave. Ah, yes, yes." I said it, and my mother suddenly laughed loudly and dropped her hand, and I saw that some of her front teeth were missing.

"The house looks like an old tooth when you see it from the street," she said, as though deliberately calling attention to the very misfortune she wanted to hide. She knew nothing about the people who had lived in this apartment, except that they had left in a hurry, forgetting to pack a large store of black-market food, some pretty ornaments in a china cabinet, and five bottles of wine. "They left without paying the rent," she said, which didn't sound like her.

It turned out to be a joke of Martin Toeppler's. He repeated it when I came back to the parlor wearing a shirt that I supposed must be his, and with my hair dark and wet and combed flat. He pointed to a bright rectangle on the brown wallpaper. "That is where they took Adolf's picture down," he said. "When they left in a hurry without paying the rent."

My father had been stabbed to death one night when he was caught tearing an election poster off the schoolhouse wall. He left my mother with no money, two children under the age of five, and a political reputation. After that she swam with the current. I had worn a uniform of one kind or another most of my life until now. I remembered wearing civilian clothes once, when I was fourteen, for my confirmation. I had felt disguised, and wondered what to do with my hands; from the age of seven I had stuck my thumbs in a leather belt. I had impressions, not memories, of my father. Pictures were frozen things; they told me nothing. But I knew that when my hair was wet I looked something like him. A quick flash would come back out of a mirror, like a secret message, and I would think, There, that is how he was. I sat with Martin at the table, where my mother had spread a lace cloth (the vanished tenants') and over which the April sun through lace curtains laid still another design. I placed my hands flat under lace shadows and wondered if they were like my father's, too.

She had put out everything she could find to eat and drink – a few sweet biscuits, cheese cut almost as thin as paper, dark bread, small whole tomatoes, radishes, slices of salami arranged in a floral design on a dish to make them seem more. We had a bottle of fizzy wine that Martin called champagne. It had a brown tint, like watered iodine, and a taste of molasses. Through this murk bubbles climbed. We raised our glasses without saying what we drank to, other than my return. Perhaps Martin drank to his destiny in Franconia with the two apartments. I had a plan, but it was my own secret. By a common accord, there was no mutual past. Then my mother spoke from behind the cupped hand and said she would like us to drink to her missing elder son. She looked at Martin as she said this, in case the survival of Chris might be a burden, too.

Toward the end of that afternoon, a neighbor came in with a bottle of brandy – a stout man with three locks of slick grey hair across his skull. All the fat men of comic stories and of literature were to be Willy Wehler to me, in the future. But he could not have been all that plump in Berlin in 1950; his chin probably showed the beginnings of softness, and his hair must have been dark still, and there must have been plenty of it. I can see the start of his baldness, the two deep peninsulas of polished skin running from the corners of his forehead to just above his ears. Willy Wehler was another Franconian. He and Martin began speaking in dialect almost at once. Willy was at a remove, however – he mispronounced words as though to be funny, and he would grin and look at me. This was to say that he knew better, and he knew that I knew. Martin and Willy hated Berlin. They sounded as if they had been dragged to Berlin against their will, like displaced persons. In their eyes the deepest failure of a certain political authority was that it had enticed peace-loving persons with false promises of work, homes, pensions, lives afloat like little boats at anchor; now these innocent provincials saw they had been tricked, and they were going back where they had started from. It was as simple to them as that – the equivalent of an insurance company's no longer meeting its obligations. Willy even described the life he would lead now in a quiet town, where, in sight of a cobbled square with a fountain and an equestrian statue, he planned to open a perfume-and-cosmetics shop; people wanted beauty now. He would live above the shop – he was not too proud for that – and every morning he would look down on his blue store awnings, over window boxes stuffed with frilled petunias. My stepfather heard this with tears in his eyes, but perhaps he was thinking of his two apartments and of Elke and the spitz. Willy's future seemed so real, so close at hand, that it was almost as though he had dropped in to say goodbye. He sat with his daughter on his knees, a baby not yet three. This little girl, whose name was Gisela, became a part of my life from that afternoon, and so did fat Willy, though none of us knew it then. The secret to which I had drunk my silent toast was a girl in France, who would be a middle-aged woman, beyond my imagining now, if she had lived. She died by jumping or accidentally falling out of a fifth-floor window in Paris. Her parents had locked her in a room when they found out she was corresponding with me.

This was still an afternoon in April in Berlin, the first of my freedom. It was one day after old Adolf's birthday, but that was not mentioned, not even in dialect or in the form of a Berlin joke. I don't think they were avoiding it; they had simply forgotten. They would always be astonished when other people turned out to have more specific memories of time and events.

This was the afternoon about which I would always say to myself, "I should have known," and even "I knew" – knew that I would marry the baby whose movements were already so willful and quick that her father complained, "We can't take her anywhere," and sat holding both her small hands in his; otherwise she would have clutched at every glass within reach. Her winged brows reminded me of the girl I wanted to see again. Gisela's eyes were amber in color, and luminous, with the whites so pure they seemed blue. The girl in France had eyes that resembled dark petals, opaque and velvety, and slightly tilted. She had black hair from a Corsican grandmother, and long fine lashes. Gisela's lashes were stubby and thick. I found that I was staring at the child's small ears and her small perfect teeth, thinking all the while of the other girl, whose smile had been spoiled by the malnutrition and the poor dentistry of the Occupation. I should have realized then, as I looked at Willy and his daughter, that some people never go without milk and eggs and apples, whatever the landscape, and that the sparse feast on our table had more to do with my mother's long habit of poverty – a kind of fatalistic incompetence that came from never having had enough money – than with a real shortage of food. Willy had on a white nylon shirt, which was a luxury then. Later, Martin would say to me, "That Willy! Out of a black uniform and into the black market before you could say 'democracy,'" but I never knew whether it was a common Berlin joke or something Martin had made up or the truth about Willy.

Gisela, who was either slow to speak for her age or only lazy, looked at me and said, "Man" – all she had to declare. Her hair was so silky and fine that it reflected the day as a curve of mauve light. She was all light and sheen, and she was the first person – I can even say the first *thing* – I had ever seen that was

unflawed, without shadow. She was as whole and as innocent
as a drop of water, and she was without guilt.

Her hands, released when her father drank from his wineglass, patted the tablecloth, seized a radish, tried to stuff it in
his mouth.

My mother sat with her chair pushed back a few respectful
inches. "Do you like children, Thomas?" she said. She knew
nothing about me now except that I was not a child.

The French girl was sixteen when she came to Brittany on
a holiday with her father and mother. The next winter she
sent me books so that I would not drop too far behind in my
schooling, and the second summer she came to my room.
The door to the room was in a bend of the staircase, halfway
between the pharmacy on the ground floor and the flat where
my employers lived. They were supposed to keep me locked
in this room when I wasn't working, but the second summer
they forgot or could not be bothered, and in any case I had
made a key with a piece of wire by then. It was the first room
I'd had to myself. I whitewashed the walls and boxed in the
store of potatoes they kept on the floor in a corner. Bunches
of wild plants and herbs the druggist used in prescriptions
hung from hooks in the ceiling. One whole wall was taken up
with shelves of drying leaves and roots – walnut leaves for
treating anemia, camomile for fainting spells, thyme and
rosemary for muscular cramps, and nettles and mint, sage
and dandelions. The fragrance in the room and the view of
the port from the window could have given me almost
enough happiness for a lifetime, except that I was too young
to find any happiness in that.

How she escaped from her parents the first afternoon I
never knew, but she was a brave, careless girl and had already
escaped from them often. They must have known what could
happen when they locked that wild spirit into a place where
the only way out was a window. Perhaps they were trying to
see how far they could go with a margin of safety. She left a

message for them: "To teach you a lesson." She must have thought she would be there and not there, lost to them and yet able to see the result. There was no message for me, except that it is a terrible thing to be alone; but I had already learned it. She must have knelt on the windowsill. The autumn rain must have caught her lashes and hair. She was already alien on the windowsill, beyond recognition.

I had made my room as neat for her as though I were expecting a military inspection. I wondered if she knew how serious it would be for both of us if we were caught. She glanced at the view, but only to see if anyone could look in on us, and she laughed, starting to take off her pullover, arms crossed; then stopped and said, "What is it – are you made of ice?" How could she know that I was retarded? I had known nothing except imagination and solitude, and the preying of old soldiers; and I was too old for one and repelled by the other. I thought she was about to commit the sacrifice of her person – her physical self and her immortal soul. I had heard the old men talking about women as if women were dirt, but needed for "that." One man said he would cut off an ear for "that." Another said he would swim the Atlantic. I thought she would lie in some way convenient to me and that she would feel nothing but a kind of sorrow, which would have made it a pure gift. But there was nothing to ask; it was not a gift. It was her decision and not a gift but an adventure. She hadn't come here to look at the harbor, she told me, when I hesitated. I may even have said, "No," and it might have been then that she smiled at me over crossed arms, pulling off her sweater, and said, "Are you made of ice?" For all her jauntiness, she thought she was deciding her life, though she continued to use the word "adventure." I think it was the only other word she knew for "love." But all we were settling was her death, and my life was decided in Berlin when Willy Wehler came in with a bottle of brandy and Gisela, who refused to say more than "Man." I can still see the lace curtains, the mark on the wallpaper, the china ornaments left by the people who had gone in such a hurry – the chimney sweep with his matchstick broom, the girl with bobbed orange hair sitting on a crescent moon, the dog with the ruff around his neck – and when I remember this I say to myself, "I must have known."

We finished two bottles of Martin's champagne, and then my mother jumped to her feet to remove the glasses and bring others so that we could taste Willy Wehler's brandy.

"The dirty Belgian is still hanging around," he said to Martin, gently rocking the child, who now had her thumb in her mouth.

"What does he want?" said my stepfather. He repeated the question; he was slow and he thought that other people, unless they reacted at once and with a show of feeling, could not hear him.

"He was in the Waffen-S.S. – he says. He complains that the girls here won't go out with him, though only five or six years ago they were like flies."

"They are afraid of him," came my mother's timid voice. "He stands in the court and stares . . ."

"I don't like men who look at pure young girls," said Willy Wehler. "He said to me, 'Help me; you owe me help.' He says he fought for us and nobody thanked him."

"He did? No wonder we lost," said Martin. I had already seen that the survivors of the war were divided into those who said they had always known how it would all turn out and those who said they had been indifferent. There are also those who like wars and those who do not. Martin had never been committed to winning or to losing or to anything – that explained his jokes. He had gained two apartments and one requisitioned flat in Berlin. He had lost a wife, but he often said to me later that people were better off out of this world.

"In Belgium he was in jail," said Willy. "He says he fought for us and then he was in jail and now we won't help him and the girls won't speak to him."

"Why is he here?" my stepfather suddenly shouted. "Who let him in? All this is his own affair, not ours." He rocked in his chair in a peculiar way, perhaps only imitating the gentle motion Willy made to keep Gisela asleep and quiet. "Nobody owes him anything," cried my stepfather, striking the table so that the little girl started and shuddered. My mother touched his arm and made a sort of humming sound, with her lips pressed together, that I took to be a signal between them, for he at once switched to another topic. It was a theme of conversation I was to hear about for many years after that afternoon. It was what the old men had to say when they were not boasting about women or their own past, and it was this: What should the Schörner army have done in Czechoslovakia to avoid capture by the Russians, and why did General Eisenhower (the villain of the story) refuse to help?

Eisenhower was my stepfather's left hand, General Schörner was his right, and the Russians were a plate of radishes. I turned very slightly to look at my mother. She had that sad cast of feature women have when their eyes are fixed nowhere. Her hand still lay lightly on Martin Toeppler's sleeve. I supposed then that he really was her husband and that they slept in the same bed. I had seen one or two closed doors in the passage on my way to the bath. Of my first prison camp, where everyone had been under eighteen or over forty, I remembered the smell of the old men – how they stopped being clean when there were no women to make them wash – and I remembered their long boasting. And yet, that April afternoon, as the sunlight of my first hours of freedom moved over the table and up along the brown wall, I did my boasting, too. I told about a prisoner I had captured. It seemed to be the thing I had to say to two men I had never seen before.

"He landed in a field just outside my grandmother's village," I told them. "I was fourteen. Three of us saw him – three boys. We had French rifles captured in the 1870 war. He'd had time to fold his parachute and he was sitting on it. I knew only one thing in English; it was 'Hands up.'"

My stepfather's mouth was open, as it had been when I first walked into the flat that day. My mother stood just out of sight.

"We advanced, pointing our 1870 rifles," I went on, droning, just like the old prisoners of war. "We all now said, 'Hands up.' The prisoner just –" I made the gesture the American had made, of chasing a fly away, and I realized I was drunk. "He didn't stand up. He had put everything he had on the ground – a revolver, a wad of German money, a handkerchief with a map of Germany, and some smaller things we couldn't identify at once. He had on civilian shoes with thick soles. He very slowly undid his watch and handed it over, but we had no ruling about that, so we said no. He put the watch on the ground next to the revolver and the map. Then he slowly got up and strolled into the village, with his hands in his pockets. He was chewing gum. I saw he had kept his cigarettes, but I didn't know the rule about that, either. We kept our guns trained on him. The schoolmaster ran out of my grandmother's guesthouse – everyone ran to stare. He was excited and kept saying in English, 'How do you do? How do you do?' but then an officer came running, too, and he was screaming, 'Why are you interfering? You may ask only one thing: Is he English or American.' The teacher was glad to show off his English, and he asked, 'Are you English or American?' and the American seemed to move his tongue all round his mouth before he answered. He was the first foreigner any of us had ever seen, and they took him away from us. We never saw him again."

That seemed all there was to it, but Martin's mouth was still open. I tried to remember more. "There was hell because we had left the gun and the other things on the ground. By the time they got out to the field, someone had stolen the parachute – probably for the cloth. We were in trouble over that, and we never got credit for having taken a prisoner. I went back to the field alone later on. I wanted to cry, for some reason – because it was over. He was from an adventure story to me. The whole war was a Karl May adventure, when I was fourteen and running around in school holidays with a gun. I found some small things in the field that had been overlooked – pills for keeping awake, pills in transparent envelopes. I had never seen that before. One envelope was called 'motion sickness.' It was a crime to keep anything, but I kept it anyway. I still had it when the Americans captured me, and they took it away. I had kept it because it was from another world. I would look at it and wonder. I kept it because of *The Last of the Mohicans*, because, because."

This was the longest story I had ever told in my life. I added, "My grandmother is dead now." My stepfather had finally shut his mouth. He looked at my mother as if to say that she had brought him a rival in the only domain that mattered – the right to talk everyone's ear off. My mother edged close to Willy Wehler and urged him to eat bread and cheese. She was still in the habit of wondering what the other person thought and how important he might be and how safe it was to speak. But Willy had not heard more than a sentence or two. That was plain from the way the expression on his face came slowly awake. He opened his eyes wide, as if to get sleep out of them, and – evidently imagining I had been talking about my life in France – said, "What were you paid as a prisoner?"

I had often wondered what the first question would be once I was home. Now I had it.

"Ha!" said my stepfather, giving the impression that he expected me to be caught out in a monstrous lie.

"One franc forty centimes a month for working here and there on a farm," I said. "But when I became a free worker with a druggist the official pay was three thousand francs a month, and that was what he gave me." I paused. "And of course I was fed and housed and had no laundry bills."

"Did you have bedsheets?" said my mother.

"With the druggist's family, always. I had one sheet folded in half. It was just right for a small cot."

"Was it the same sheet as the kind the family had?" she said, in the hesitant way that was part of her person now.

"They didn't buy sheets especially for me," I said. "I was treated fairly by the druggist, but not by the administration."

"Ah ha," said the two older men, almost together.

"The administration refused to pay my fare home," I said, looking down into my glass the way I had seen the men in prison camp stare at a fixed point when they were recounting a grievance.

"A prisoner of war has the right to be repatriated at administration expense. The administration would not pay my fare because I had stayed too long in France – but that was their mistake. I bought a ticket as far as Paris on the pay I had saved. The druggist sold me some old shoes and trousers and a jacket of his. My own things were in rags. In Paris I went to the Y.M.C.A. The Y.M.C.A. was supposed to be in charge of prisoners' rights. The man wouldn't listen to me. If I had been left behind, then I was not a prisoner, he said; I was a tourist. It was his duty to help me. Instead of that, he informed the police." For the first time my voice took on the coloration of resentment. I knew that this complaint about a niggling matter of train fare made my whole adventure seem small, but I had become an old soldier. I remembered the police commissioner, with his thin lips and dirty nails, who said, "You should have been repatriated years ago, when you were sixteen."

"It was a mistake," I told him.

"Your papers are full of strange mistakes," he said, bending over them. "There, one capital error. An omission, a grave omission. What is your mother's maiden name?"

"Wickler," I said.

I watched him writing "W-i-e-c-k-l-a-i-r," slowly, with the tip of his tongue sticking out of the corner of his mouth as he wrote. "You have been here for something like five years with an incomplete dossier. And what about this? Who crossed it out?"

"I did. My father was not a pastry cook."

"You could be fined or even jailed for this," he said.

"My father was not a pastry cook," I said. "He had tuberculosis. He was not allowed to handle food."

Willy Wehler did not say what he thought of my story. Perhaps not having any opinion about injustice, even the least important, had become a habit of his, like my mother's of speaking through her fingers. He was on the right step of that staircase I've spoken of. Even the name he had given his daughter was a sign of his sensitivity to the times. Nobody wanted to hear the pagan, Old Germanic names anymore – Sigrun and Brunhilde and Sieglinde. Willy had felt the change. He would have called any daughter something neutral and pretty – Gisela, Marianne, Elisabeth – any time after the battle of Stalingrad. All Willy ever had to do was sniff the air.

He pushed back his chair (in later years he would be able to push a table away with his stomach) and got to his feet. He had to tip his head to look up into my eyes. He said he wanted to give me advice that would be useful to me as a latehomecomer. His advice was to forget. "Forget everything," he said. "Forget, forget. That was what I said to my good neighbor Herr Silber when I bought his wife's topaz brooch and earrings before he emigrated to Palestine. I said, 'Dear Herr Silber, look forward, never back, and forget, forget, forget.'"

The child in Willy's arms was in the deepest of sleeps. Martin Toeppler followed his friend to the door, they whispered together; then the door closed behind both men.

"They have gone to have a glass of something at Herr Wehler's," said my mother. I saw now that she was crying quietly. She dried her eyes on her apron and began clearing the table of the homecoming feast. "Willy Wehler has been kind to us," she said. "Don't repeat that thing."

"About forgetting?"

"No, about the topaz brooch. It was a crime to buy anything from Jews."

"It doesn't matter now."

She lowered the tray she held and looked pensively out at the wrecked houses across the street. "If only people knew beforehand what was allowed," she said.

"My father is probably a hero now," I said.

"Oh, Thomas, don't travel too fast. We haven't seen the last of the changes. Yes, a hero. But too late for me. I've suffered too much."

"What does Martin think that he died of?"

"A working accident. He can understand that."

"You could have said consumption. He did have it." She shook her head. Probably she had not wanted Martin to imagine he could ever be saddled with two sickly stepsons. "Where do you and Martin sleep?"

"In the room next to the bathroom. Didn't you see it? You'll be comfortable here in the parlor. The couch pulls out. You can stay as long as you like. This is your home. A home for you and Chris." She said this so stubbornly that I knew some argument must have taken place between her and Martin.

I intended this room to be my home. There was no question about it in my mind. I had not yet finished high school; I had been taken out for anti-aircraft duty, then sent to the front. The role of adolescents in uniform had been to try to prevent the civilian population from surrendering. We were expected to die in the ruins together. When the women ran pillowcases up flagpoles, we shinnied up to drag them down. We were prepared to hold the line with our 1870 rifles until we saw the American tanks. There had not been tanks in our Karl May adventure stories, and the Americans, finally, were not out of *The Last of the Mohicans*. I told my mother that I had to go back to high school and then I would apply for a scholarship and take a degree in French. I would become a schoolmaster. French was all I had from my captivity; I might as well use it. I would earn money doing translations.

That cheered her up. She would not have to ask the ex-tram conductor too many favors. "Translations" and "scholarship" were an exalted form of language, to her. As a schoolmaster, I would have the most respectable job in the family, now that Uncle Gerhard was raising rabbits. "As long as it doesn't cost *him* too much," she said, as if she had to say it and yet was hoping I wouldn't hear.

It was not strictly true that all I had got out of my captivity was the ability to speak French. I had also learned to cook, iron, make beds, wait on table, wash floors, polish furniture, plant a vegetable garden, paint shutters. I wanted to help my mother in the kitchen now, but that shocked her. "Rest," she said, but I did not know what "rest" meant. "I've never seen a man drying a glass," she said, in apology. I wanted to tell her that while the roads and bridges of France were still waiting for someone to rebuild them I had been taught how to make a tomato salad by the druggist's wife; but I could not guess what the word "France" conveyed to her imagination. I began walking about the apartment. I looked in on a store cupboard, a water closet smelling of carbolic, the bathroom again, then a room containing a high bed, a brown wardrobe, and a table covered with newspapers bearing half a dozen of the flowerless spiky dull green plants my mother had always tended with so much devotion. I shut the door as if on a dark past, and I said to myself, "I am free. This is the beginning of life. It is also the start of the good half of a rotten century. Everything ugly and corrupt and vicious is behind us." My thoughts were not exactly in those words, but something like them. I said to myself, "This apartment has a musty smell, an old and dirty smell that sinks into clothes. After a time I shall probably smell like the dark parlor. The smell must be in the cushions, in the bed that pulls out, in the lace curtains. It is a smell that creeps into nightclothes. The blankets will be permeated." I thought, I shall get used to the smell, and the smell of burning in the stone outside. The view of ruins will be my view. Every day on my way home from school I shall walk over Elke. I shall get used to the wood staircase, the bellpull, the polished name-plate, the white enamel fuses in the hall – my mother had said, "When you want light in the parlor you give the center fuse in the lower row a half turn." I looked at a framed drawing of car-toon people with puffy hair. A strong wind had blown their umbrella inside out. They would be part of my view, like the ruins. I took in the ancient gas bracket in the kitchen and the stone sink. My mother, washing glasses without soap, smiled at me, forgetting to hide her teeth. I reëxamined the tiled stove in the parlor, the wood and the black briquettes that would be next to my head at night, and the glass-fronted cabinet full of the china ornaments God had selected to survive the Berlin air raids. These would be removed to make way for my books. For Martin Toeppler need not imagine he could count on my pride, or that I would prefer to starve rather than take his cha-rity, or that I was too arrogant to sleep on his dusty sofa. I would wear out his soap, borrow his shirts, spread his butter on my bread. I would hang on Martin like an octopus. He had a dependent now – a ravenous, egocentric, latehomecoming high-school adolescent of twenty-one. The old men owed this much to me – the old men in my prison camp who would have sold mother and father for an extra ounce of soup, who had already sold their children for it; the old men who had fouled my idea of women; the old men in the bunkers who had let the girls defend them in Berlin; the old men who had dared to survive.

The bed that pulled out was sure to be all lumps. I had slept on worse. Would it be wide enough for Chris, too?

People in the habit of asking themselves silent useless

questions look for answers in mirrors. My hair was blond again now that it had dried. I looked less like my idea of my father. I tried to see the reflection of the man who had gone out in the middle of the night and who never came back. You don't go out alone to tear down election posters in a village where nobody thinks as you do – not unless you *want* to be stabbed in the back. So the family had said.

"You were well out of it," I said to the shadow that floated on the glass panel of the china cabinet, though it would not be my father's again unless I could catch it unaware.

I said to myself, "It is quieter than France. They keep their radios low."

In captivity I had never suffered a pain except for the cramps of hunger the first years, which had been replaced by a scratching, morbid anxiety, and the pain of homesickness, which takes you in the stomach and the throat. Now I felt the first of the real pains that were to follow me like little dogs for the rest of my life, perhaps: the first compressed my knee, the second tangled the nerves at the back of my neck. I discovered that my eyes were sensitive and that it hurt to blink.

This was the hour when, in Brittany, I would begin peeling the potatoes for dinner. I had seen food my mother had never heard of – oysters, and artichokes. My mother had never seen a harbor or a sea.

My American prisoner had left his immediate life spread on an alien meadow – his parachute, his revolver, his German money. He had strolled into captivity with his hands in his pockets.

"I know what you are thinking," said my mother, who was standing behind me. "I know that you are judging me. If you could guess what my life has been – the whole story, not only the last few years – you wouldn't be hard on me."

I turned too slowly to meet her eyes. It was not what I had been thinking. I had forgotten about her, in that sense.

"No, no, nothing like that," I said. I still did not touch her.

What I had been moving along to in my mind was: Why am I in this place? Who sent me here? Is it a form of justice or injustice? How long does it last?

"Now we can wait together for Chris," she said. She seemed young and happy all at once. "Look, Thomas. A new moon. Bow to it three times. Wait – you must have something silver in your hand." I saw that she was hurrying to finish with this piece of nonsense before Martin came back. She rummaged in the china cabinet and brought out a silver napkin ring – left behind by the vanished tenants, probably. The name on it was "Meta" – no one we knew. "Bow to the moon and hold it and make your wish," she said. "Quickly."

"You first."

She wished, I am sure, for my brother. As for me, I wished that I was a few hours younger, in the corridor of a packed train, clutching the top of the open window, my heart hammering as I strained to find the one beloved face.

1974

In Youth Is Pleasure

M Y FATHER died, then my grandmother; my mother was left, but we did not get on. I was probably disagreeable with anyone who felt entitled to give me instructions and advice. We seldom lived under the same roof, which was just as well. She had found me civil and amusing until I was ten, at which time I was said to have become pert and obstinate. She was impulsive, generous, in some ways better than most other people, but without any feeling for cause and effect; this made her at the least unpredictable and at the most a serious element of danger. I was fascinated by her, though she worried me; then all at once I lost interest. I was fifteen when this happened. I would forget to answer her letters and even to open them. It was not rejection or anything so violent as dislike but a simple indifference I cannot account for. It was much the way I would be later with men I fell out of love with, but I was too young to know that then. As for my mother, whatever I thought, felt, said, wrote, and wore had always been a positive source of exasperation. From time to time she attempted to alter the form, the outward shape at least, of the creature she thought she was modelling, but at last she came to the conclusion there must be something wrong with the clay. Her final unexpected upsurge of attention coincided with my abrupt unconcern: one may well have been the reason for the other.

It took the form of digging into my diaries and notebooks and it yielded, among other documents, a two-year-old poem, Kiplingesque in its rhythms, entitled "Why I Am a Socialist." The first words of the first line were "You ask . . . ," then came a long answer. But it was not an answer to anything she'd wondered. Like all mothers – at least, all I have known – she was obsessed with the entirely private and possibly trivial matter of a daughter's virginity. Why I was a Socialist I rightly conceded to be none of her business. Still, she must have felt she had to say something, and that something was "You had better be clever, because you will never be pretty." My response was to take – take, not grab – the poem from her and tear it up. No voices were raised. I never mentioned the incident to anyone. That is how it was. We became, presently, mutually unconcerned. My detachment was put down to the coldness of my nature, hers to the exhaustion of trying to bring me up. It must have been a relief to her when, in the first half of Hitler's war, I slipped quietly and finally out of her life. I was now eighteen, and completely on my own. By "on my own" I don't mean a show of independence with Papa-Mama footing the bills: I mean that I was solely responsible for my economic survival and that no living person felt any duty toward me.

On a bright morning in June I arrived in Montreal, where I'd been born, from New York, where I had been living and going to school. My luggage was a small suitcase and an Edwardian picnic hamper – a preposterous piece of baggage my father had brought from England some twenty years before; it had been with me since childhood, when his death turned my life into a helpless migration. In my purse was a birth certificate and five American dollars, my total fortune, the parting gift of a Canadian actress in New York, who had taken me to see *Mayerling* before I got on the train. She was kind and good and terribly hard up, and she had no idea that apart from some loose change I had nothing more. The birth certificate, which testified I was Linnet Muir, daughter of Angus and of Charlotte, was my right of passage. I did not own a passport and possibly never had seen one. In those days there was almost no such thing as a "Canadian." You were Canadian-born, and a British subject, too, and you had a third label with no consular reality, like the racial tag that on Soviet passports will make a German of someone who has never been to Germany. In Canada you were also whatever your father happened to be, which in my case was English. He was half Scot, but English by birth, by mother, by instinct. I did not feel a scrap British or English, but I was not an American either. In American schools I had refused to salute the flag. My denial of that curiously Fascist-looking celebration, with the right arm stuck straight out, and my silence when the others intoned the trusting ". . . and justice for all" had never been thought offensive, only stubborn. Americans then were accustomed to gratitude from foreigners but did not demand it; they quite innocently could not imagine any country fit to live in except their own. If I could not recognize it, too bad for me. Besides, I was not a refugee – just someone from the backwoods. "You got schools in Canada?" I had been asked. "You got radios?" And once, from a teacher, "What do they major in up there? Basket-weaving?"

My travel costume was a white piqué jacket and skirt that must have been crumpled and soot-flecked, for I had sat up all night. I was reading, I think, a novel by Sylvia Townsend Warner. My hair was thick and long. I wore my grandmother's wedding ring, which was too large, and which I would lose before long. I desperately wanted to look more than my age, which I had already started to give out as twenty-one. I was travelling light; my picnic hamper contained the poems and journals I had judged fit to accompany me into my new, unfettered existence, and some books I feared I might not find again in clerical Quebec – Zinoviev and Lenin's *Against the Stream*, and a few beige pamphlets from the Little Lenin

Library, purchased second hand in New York. I had a picture of Mayakovsky torn out of *Cloud in Trousers* and one of Paddy Finucane, the Irish R.A.F. fighter pilot, who was killed the following summer. I had not met either of these men, but I approved of them both very much. I had abandoned my beloved but cumbersome anthologies of American and English verse, confident that I had whatever I needed by heart. I knew every word of Stephen Vincent Benét's "Litany for Dictatorships" and "Notes to be Left in a Cornerstone," and the other one that begins:

> They shot the Socialists at half-past five
> In the name of victorious Austria. . . .

I could begin anywhere and rush on in my mind to the end. "Notes . . ." was the New York I knew I would never have again, for there could be no journeying backward; the words "but I walked it young" were already a gate shut on a part of my life. The suitcase held only the fewest possible summer clothes. Everything else had been deposited at the various war-relief agencies of New York. In those days I made symbols out of everything, and I must have thought that by leaving a tartan skirt somewhere I was shedding past time. I remember one of those wartime agencies well because it was full of Canadian matrons. They wore pearl earrings like the Duchess of Kent's and seemed to be practicing her tiny smile. Brooches pinned to their cashmere cardigans carried some daft message about the Empire. I heard one of them exclaiming, "You don't expect me, a Britisher, to drink tea made with tea bags!" Good plain girls from the little German towns of Ontario, christened probably Wilma, Jean, and Irma, they had flowing eighteenth-century names like Georgiana and Arabella now. And the Americans, who came in with their arms full of every stitch they could spare, would urge them, the Canadian matrons, to stand fast on the cliffs, to fight the fight, to slug the enemy on the landing fields, to belt him one on the beaches, to keep going with whatever iron rations they could scrape up in Bronxville and Scarsdale; and the Canadians half-shut their eyes and tipped their heads back like Gertrude Lawrence and said in thrilling Benita Hume accents that they would do that – indeed they would. I recorded "They're all trained nurses, actually. The Canadian ones have a good reputation. They managed to marry those American doctors."

Canada had been in Hitler's war from the very beginning, but America was still uneasily at peace. Recruiting had already begun; I had seen a departure from New York for Camp Stewart in Georgia, and some of the recruits' mothers crying and even screaming and trying to run alongside the train. The recruits were going off to drill with broomsticks because there weren't enough guns; they still wore old-fashioned headgear and were paid twenty-one dollars a month. There was a song about it: "For twenty-one dollars a day, once a month." As my own train crossed the border to Canada I expected to sense at once an air of calm and grit and dedication, but the only changes were from prosperous to shabby, from painted to unpainted, from smiling to dour. I was entering a poorer and a curiously empty country, where the faces of the people gave nothing away. The crossing was my sea change. I silently recited the vow I had been preparing for weeks: that I would never be helpless again and that I would not let anyone make a decision on my behalf.

When I got down from the train at Windsor Station, a man sidled over to me. He had a cap on his head and a bitter Celtic face, with deep indentations along his cheeks, as if his back teeth were pulled. I thought he was asking a direction. He repeated his question, which was obscene. My arms were pinned by the weight of my hamper and suitcase. He brushed the back of his hand over my breasts, called me a name, and edged away. The murderous rage I felt and the revulsion that followed were old friends. They had for years been my reaction to what my diaries called "their hypocrisy." "They" was a world of sly and mumbling people, all of them older than myself. I must have substituted "hypocrisy" for every sort of aggression, because fright was a luxury I could not afford. What distressed me was my helplessness – I who had sworn only a few hours earlier that I'd not be vulnerable again. The man's gaunt face, his drunken breath, the flat voice which I assigned to the graduate of some Christian Brothers teaching establishment haunted me for a long time after that. "The man at Windsor Station" would lurk in the windowless corridors of my nightmares; he would be the passenger, the only passenger, on a dark train. The first sight of a city must be the measure for all second looks.

But it was not my first sight. I'd had ten years of it here – the first ten. After that, and before New York (in one sense, my deliverance), there had been a long spell of grief and shadow in an Ontario city, a place full of mean judgments and grudging minds, of paranoid Protestants and slovenly Catholics. To this day I cannot bear the sight of brick houses, or of a certain kind of empty treeless street on a Sunday afternoon. My memory of Montreal took shape while I was there. It was not a random jumble of rooms and summers and my mother singing "We've Come to See Miss Jenny Jones," but the faithful record of the true survivor. I retained, I rebuilt a superior civilization. In that drowned world, Sherbrooke Street seemed to be glittering and white; the vision of a house upon that street was so painful that I was obliged to banish it from the memorial. The small hot rooms of a summer cottage became enormous and cool. If I say that Cleopatra floated down the Chateauguay River, that the Winter Palace was stormed on Sherbrooke Street, that Trafalgar was fought on Lake St. Louis, I mean it naturally; they were the natural backgrounds of my exile and fidelity. I saw now at the far end of Windsor Station – more foreign, echoing, and mysterious than any American station could be – a statue of Lord Mount Stephen, the founder of the Canadian Pacific, which everyone took to be a memorial to

Edward VII. Angus, Charlotte, and the smaller Linnet had truly been: this was my proof; once upon a time my instructions had been to make my way to Windsor Station should I ever be lost and to stand at the foot of Edward VII and wait for someone to find me.

I have forgotten to say that no one in Canada knew I was there. I looked up the number of the woman who had once been my nurse, but she had no telephone. I found her in a city directory, and with complete faith that "O. Carette" was indeed Olivia and that she would recall and welcome me I took a taxi to the east end of the city – the French end, the poor end. I was so sure of her that I did not ask the driver to wait (to take me where?) but dismissed him and climbed two flights of dark-brown stairs inside a house that must have been built soon after Waterloo. That it was Olivia who came to the door, that the small gray-haired creature I recalled as dark and towering had to look up at me, that she unhesitatingly offered me shelter all seem as simple now as when I broke my fiver to settle the taxi. Believing that I was dead, having paid for years of Masses for the repose of my heretic soul, almost the first thing she said to me was "*Tu vis?*" I understood "*Tu es ici?*" We straightened it out later. She held both my hands and cried and called me *belle et grande. Grande* was good, for among American girls I'd seemed a shrimp. I did not see what there was to cry for; I was here. I was as naturally selfish with Olivia as if her sole reason for being was me. I stayed with her for a while and left when her affection for me made her possessive, and I think I neglected her. On her deathbed she told one of her daughters, the reliable one, to keep an eye on me forever. Olivia was the only person in the world who did not believe I could look after myself. Where she and I were concerned I remained under six.

Now, at no moment of this remarkable day did I feel anxious or worried or forlorn. The man at Windsor Station could not really affect my view of the future. I had seen some of the worst of life, but I had no way of judging it or of knowing what the worst could be. I had a sensation of loud, ruthless power, like an enormous waterfall. The past, the part I would rather not have lived, became small and remote, a dark pinpoint. My only weapons until now had been secrecy and insolence. I had stopped running away from schools and situations when I finally understood that by becoming a name in a file, by attracting attention, I would merely prolong my stay in prison – I mean, the prison of childhood itself. My rebellions then consisted only in causing people who were physically larger and legally sovereign to lose their self-control, to become bleached with anger, to shake with such temper that they broke cups and glasses and bumped into chairs. From the malleable, sunny child Olivia said she remembered, I had become, according to later chroniclers, cold, snobbish, and presumptuous. "You need an iron hand, Linnet." I can still hear that melancholy voice, which belonged to a friend of my mother's. "If anybody ever marries you he'd better have an iron hand." After today I would never need to hear this, or anything approaching it, for the rest of my life.

And so that June morning and the drive through empty, sun-lit, wartime streets are even now like a roll of drums in the mind. My life was my own revolution – the tyrants deposed, the constitution wrenched from unwilling hands; I was, all by myself, the liberated crowd setting the palace on fire; I was the flags, the trees, the bannered windows, the flower-decked trains. The singing and the skyrockets of the 1848 I so trustingly believed would emerge out of the war were me, no one but me; and, as in the lyrical first days of any revolution, as in the first days of any love affair, there wasn't the whisper of a voice to tell me, "You might compromise."

If making virtue of necessity has ever had a meaning it must be here: for I was independent *inevitably*. There were good-hearted Americans who knew a bit of my story – as much as I wanted anyone to know – and who hoped I would swim and not drown, but from the moment I embarked on my journey I went on the dark side of the moon. "You seemed so sure of yourself," they would tell me, still troubled, long after this. In the cool journals I kept I noted that my survival meant nothing in the capitalist system; I was one of those not considered to be worth helping, saving, or even investigating. Thinking with care, I see this was true. What could I have turned into in another place? Why, a librarian at Omsk or a file clerk at Tomsk. Well, it hadn't happened that way; I had my private revolution and I settled in with Olivia in Montreal. Sink or swim? Of course I swam. Jobs were for the having; you could pick them up off the ground. Working for a living meant just what it says – a brisk necessity. It would be the least important fragment of my life until I had what I wanted. The cheek of it, I think now: penniless, sleeping in a shed room behind the kitchen of Olivia's cold-water flat, still I pointed across the wooden balustrade in a long open office where I was being considered for employment and said, "But I won't sit there." Girls were *there*, penned in like sheep. I did not think men better than women – only that they did more interesting work and got more money for it. In my journals I called other girls "coolies." I did not know if life made them bearers or if they had been born with a natural gift for giving in. "Coolie" must have been the secret expression of one of my deepest fears. I see now that I had an immense conceit: I thought I occupied a world other people could scarcely envision, let alone attain. It involved giddy risks and changes, stepping off the edge blindfolded, one's hand on nothing more than a birth certificate and a five-dollar bill. At this time of sitting in judgment I was earning nine dollars a week (until I was told by someone that the local minimum wage was twelve, on which I left for greener fields) and washing my white piqué skirt at night and ironing at dawn, and coming home at all hours so I could pretend to Olivia I had dined. Part of this impermeable sureness that I needn't waver or doubt came out of my having lived in New York. The first time I ever heard people laughing in a cinema was there. I can still remember the wonder and excitement and amazement I felt. I was just under fourteen and I had never heard people expressing their feelings in a public place in my life. The easy reactions, the way a poignant moment caught them, held them still – all that was new. I had come there straight from Ontario, where the reaction to a love scene was a kind of unhappy giggling, while the image of a kitten or a baby induced a long flat "Aaaah," followed by shamed silence. You could imagine them blushing in the dark for having said that – just that "Aaaah." When I heard that open American laughter I thought I could be like these people too, but had been told not to be by everyone, beginning with Olivia: "*Pas si fort*" was something she repeated to me so often when I was small that my father had made a tease out of it, called "passy four." From a tease it became oppressive too: "For the love of God, Linnet, passy four." What were these new people? Were they soft, too easily got at? I wondered that even then. Would a dictator have a field day here? Were they, as Canadian opinion had it, vulgar? Perhaps the notion of vulgarity came out of some incapacity on the part of the refined. Whatever they were, they couldn't all be daft; if they weren't I probably wasn't either. I supposed I stood as good a chance of being miserable here as anywhere, but at least I would not have to pretend to be someone else.

Now, of course there is much to be said on the other side: people who do not display what they feel have practical advantages. They can go away to be killed as if they didn't mind; they can see their sons off to war without a blink. Their upbringing is intended for a crisis. When it comes, they behave themselves. But it is murder in everyday life – truly murder. The dead of heart and spirit litter the landscape. Still, keeping a straight face makes life tolerable under stress. It makes *public* life tolerable – that is all I am saying; because in private people still got drunk, went after each other with bottles and knives, rang the police to complain that neighbors were sending poison gas over the transom, abandoned infant children and aged parents, wrote letters to newspapers in favor of corporal punishment, with inventive suggestions. When I came back to Canada that June, at least one thing had been settled: I knew that it was all right for people to laugh and cry and even to make asses of themselves. I had actually known people like that, had lived with them, and they were fine, mostly – not crazy at all. That was where a lot of my confidence came from when I began my journey into a new life and a dream past.

My father's death had been kept from me. I did not know its exact circumstances or even the date. He died when I was ten. At thirteen I was still expected to believe a fable about his being in England. I kept waiting for him to send for me, for my life was deeply wretched and I took it for granted he knew. Finally I began to suspect that death and silence can be one. How to be sure? Head-on questions got me nowhere. I had to create a situation in which some adult (not my mother, who was far too sharp) would lose all restraint and hurl the truth at me. It was easy: I was an artist at this. What I had not foreseen was the verbal violence of the scene or the effect it might have. The storm that seemed to break in my head, my need to maintain the pose of indifference ("What are you telling me that for? What makes you think I care?") were such a strain that I had physical reactions, like stigmata, which doctors would hopelessly treat on and off for years and which vanished when I became independent. The other change was that if anyone asked about my father I said, "Oh, he died." Now, in Montreal, I could confront the free adult world of falsehood and evasion on an equal footing; they would be forced to talk to me as they did to each other. Making appointments to meet my father's friends – Mr. Archie McEwen, Mr. Stephen Ross-Colby, Mr. Quentin Keller – I left my adult name, "Miss Muir." These were the men who eight, nine, ten years ago had asked, "Do you like your school?" – not knowing what else to say to children. I had curtsied to them and said, "Good night." I think what I wanted was special information about despair, but I should have known that would be taboo in a place where "like" and "don't like" were heavy emotional statements.

Archie McEwen, my father's best friend, or the man I mistook for that, kept me standing in his office on St. James Street West, he standing too, with his hands behind his back, and he said the following – not reconstructed or approximate but recalled, like "The religions of ancient Greece and Rome are extinct" or "O come, let us sing unto the Lord":

"Of course, Angus was a very sick man. I saw him walking along Sherbrooke Street. He must have just come out of hospital. He couldn't walk upright. He was using a stick. Inching along. His hair had turned gray. Nobody knew where Charlotte had got to, and we'd heard you were dead. He obviously wasn't long for this world either. He had too many troubles for any one man. I crossed the street because I didn't have the heart to shake hands with him. I felt terrible."

Savage? Reasonable? You can't tell, with those minds. Some recent threat had scared them. The Depression was too close, just at their heels. Archie McEwen did not ask where I was staying or where I had been for the last eight years; in fact, he asked only two questions. In response to the first I said, "She is married."

There came a gleam of interest – distant, amused: "So she decided to marry him, did she?"

My mother was highly visible; she had no secrets except unexpected ones. My father had nothing but. When he asked,

"Would you like to spend a year in England with your Aunt Dorothy?" I had no idea what he meant and I still don't. His only brother, Thomas, who was killed in 1918, had not been married; he'd had no sisters, that anyone knew. Those English mysteries used to be common. People came out to Canada because they did not want to think about the Thomases and Dorothys anymore. Angus was a solemn man, not much of a smiler. My mother, on the other hand – I won't begin to describe her, it would never end – smiled, talked, charmed anyone she didn't happen to be related to, swam in scandal like a partisan among the people. She made herself the central figure in loud, spectacular dramas which she played with the houselights on; you could see the audience too. That was her mistake; they kept their reactions, like their lovemaking, in the dark. You can imagine what she must have been in this world where everything was hushed, muffled, disguised: she must have seemed all they had by way of excitement, give or take a few elections and wars. It sounds like a story about the old and stale, but she and my father had been quite young eight and ten years before. The dying man creeping along Sherbrooke Street was thirty-two. First it was light chatter, then darker gossip, and then it went too far (*he* was ill and he couldn't hide it; *she* had a lover and didn't try); then suddenly it became tragic, and open tragedy was disallowed. And so Mr. Archie McEwen could stand in his office and without a trace of feeling on his narrow Lowland face – not unlike my father's in shape – he could say, "I crossed the street."

Stephen Ross-Colby, a bachelor, my father's painter chum: the smell of his studio on St. Mark Street was the smell of a personal myth. I said timidly, "Do you happen to have anything of his – a drawing or anything?" I was humble because I was on a private, personal terrain of vocation that made me shy even of the dead.

He said, "No, nothing. You could ask around. She junked a

lot of his stuff and he junked the rest when he thought he wouldn't survive. You might try . . ." He gave me a name or two. "It was all small stuff," said Ross-Colby. "He didn't do anything big." He hurried me out of the studio for a cup of coffee in a crowded place – the Honey Dew on St. Catherine Street, it must have been. Perhaps in the privacy of his studio I might have heard him thinking. Years after that he would try to call me "Lynn," which I never was, and himself "Steve." He'd come into his own as an artist by then, selling wash drawings of Canadian war graves, sun-splashed, wisteria-mauve, lime-green, with drifts of blossom across the name of the regiment; gained a reputation among the heartbroken women who bought these impersonations, had them framed – the only picture in the house. He painted the war memorial at Caen. ("Their name liveth forever.") His stones weren't stones but mauve bubbles – that is all I have against them. They floated off the page. My objection wasn't to "He didn't do anything big" but to Ross-Colby's way of turning the dead into thistledown. He said, much later, of that meeting, "I felt like a bastard, but I was broke, and I was afraid you'd put the bite on me."

Let me distribute demerits equally and tell about my father's literary Jewish friend, Mr. Quentin Keller. He was older than the others, perhaps by some twelve years. He had a whispery voice and a long pale face and a daughter older than I. "Bossy Wendy" I used to call her when, forced by her parents as I was by mine, Bossy Wendy had to take a whole afternoon of me. She had a room full of extraordinary toys, a miniature kitchen in which everything worked, of which all I recall her saying is "Don't touch." Wendy Keller had left Smith after her freshman year to marry the elder son of a Danish baron. Her father said to me, "There is only one thing you need to know and that is that your father was a gentleman."

Jackass was what I thought. Yes, Mr. Quentin Keller was a

jackass. But he was a literary one, for he had once written a play called *Forbearance,* in which I'd had a role. I had bounded across the stage like a tennis ball, into the arms of a young woman dressed up like an old one, and cried my one line: "Here I am, Granny!" Of course, he did not make his living fiddling about with amateur theatricals; thanks to our meeting I had a good look at the inside of a conservative architect's private office – that was about all it brought me.

What were they so afraid of, I wondered. I had not yet seen that I was in a false position where they were concerned; being "Miss Muir" had not made equals of us but lent distance. I thought they had read my true passport, the invisible one we all carry, but I had neither the wealth nor the influence a provincial society requires to make a passport valid. My credentials were lopsided: the important half of the scales was still in the air. I needed enormous collateral security – fame, an alliance with a powerful family, the power of money itself. I remember how Archie McEwen, trying to place me in some sensible context, to give me a voucher so he could take me home and show me to his wife, perhaps, asked his second question: "Who inherited the – ?"

"The what, Mr. McEwen?"

He had not, of course, read "Why I Am a Socialist." I did not believe in inherited property. "Who inherited the – ?" would not cross my mind again for another ten years, and then it would be a drawer quickly opened and shut before demons could escape. To all three men the last eight years were like minutes; to me they had been several lives. Some of my confidence left me then. It came down to "Next time I'll know better," but would that be enough? I had been buffeted until now by other people's moods, principles, whims, tantrums; I had survived, but perhaps I had failed to grow some outer skin it was now too late to acquire. Olivia thought that; she was the only one. Olivia knew more about the limits of nerve than I did. Her knowledge came out of the clean, swept, orderly poverty that used to be tucked away in the corners of cities. It didn't spill out then, or give anyone a bad conscience. Nobody took its picture. Anyway, Olivia would not have sat for such a portrait. The fringed green rug she put over her treadle sewing machine was part of a personal fortune. On her mantelpiece stood a copper statuette of Voltaire in an armchair. It must have come down to her from some robustly anticlerical ancestor. "Who is he?" she said to me. "You've been to school in a foreign country." "A governor of New France," I replied. She knew Voltaire was the name of a bad man and she'd have thrown the figurine out, and it would have made one treasure less in the house. Olivia's maiden name was Ouvrardville, which was good in Quebec, but only really good if you were one of the rich ones. Because of her maiden name she did not want anyone ever to know she had worked for a family; she impressed this on me delicately – it was like trying to understand what a dragonfly wanted to tell. In the old days she had gone home every weekend, taking me with her if my parents felt my company was going to make Sunday a very long day. Now I understood what the weekends were about: her daughters, Berthe and Marguerite, for whose sake she worked, were home from their convent schools Saturday and Sunday and had to be chaperoned. Her relatives pretended not to notice that Olivia was poor or even that she was widowed, for which she seemed grateful. The result of all this elegant sham was that Olivia did not say, "I was afraid you'd put the bite on me," or keep me standing. She dried her tears and asked if there was a trunk to follow. No? She made a pot of tea and spread a starched cloth on the kitchen table and we sat down to a breakfast of toast and honey. The honey tin was a ten-pounder decorated with bees the size of hornets. Lifting it for her, I remarked, "*C'est collant,*" a word out of a frozen language that started to thaw when Olivia said, "*Tu vis?*"

On the advice of her confessor, who was to be my rival from now on, Olivia refused to tell me whatever she guessed or knew, and she was far too dignified to hint. Putting together the three men's woolly stories, I arrived at something about tuberculosis of the spine and a butchery of an operation. He started back to England to die there but either changed his mind or was too ill to begin the journey; at Quebec City, where he was to have taken ship, he shot himself in a public park at five o'clock in the morning. That was one version; another was that he died at sea and the gun was found in his luggage. The revolver figured in all three accounts. It was an officer's weapon from the Kaiser's war, that had belonged to his brother. Angus kept it at the back of a small drawer in the tall chest used for men's clothes and known in Canada as a high-boy. In front of the revolver was a pigskin stud box and a pile of ironed handkerchiefs. Just describing that drawer dates it. How I happen to know the revolver was loaded and how I learned never to point a gun even in play is another story. I can tell you that I never again in my life looked inside a drawer that did not belong to me.

I know a woman whose father died, she thinks, in a concentration camp. Or was he shot in a schoolyard? Or hanged and thrown in a ditch? Were the ashes that arrived from some eastern plain his or another prisoner's? She invents different deaths. Her inventions have become her conversation at dinner parties. She takes on a child's voice and says, "My father died at Buchenwald." She chooses and rejects elements of the last act; one avoids mentioning death, shooting, capital punishment, cremation, deportation, even fathers. Her inventions are not thought neurotic or exhibitionist but something sanctioned by history. Peacetime casualties are not like that. They are lightning bolts out of a sunny sky that strike only one house. All around the ashy ruin lilacs blossom, leaves gleam. Speculation in public about the disaster would be indecent.

Nothing remains but a silent, recurring puzzlement to the survivors: Why here and not there? Why this and not that? Before July was out I had settled his fate in my mind and I never varied: I thought he had died of homesickness; sickness for England was the consumption, the gun, the everything. "Everything" had to take it all in, for people in Canada then did not speak of irrational endings to life, and newspapers did not print that kind of news: this was because of the spiritual tragedy for Catholic families, and because the act had long been considered a criminal one in British law. If Catholic feelings were spared it gave the impression no one but Protestants ever went over the edge, which was unfair; and so the possibility was eliminated, and people came to a natural end in a running car in a closed garage, hanging from a rafter in the barn, in an icy lake with a canoe left to drift empty. Once I had made up my mind, the whole story somehow became none of my business: I had looked in a drawer that did not belong to me. More, if I was to live my own life I had to let go. I wrote in my journal that "they" had got him but would not get me, and after that there was scarcely ever a mention.

My dream past evaporated. Montreal, in memory, was a leafy citadel where I knew every tree. In reality I recognized nearly nothing and had to start from scratch. Sherbrooke Street had been the dream street, pure white. It was the avenue poor Angus descended leaning on a walking stick. It was a moat I was not allowed to cross alone; it was lined with gigantic spreading trees through which light fell like a rain of coins. One day, standing at a corner, waiting for the light to change, I understood that the Sherbrooke Street of my exile – my Mecca, my Jerusalem – was this. It had to be: there could not be two. It was *only* this. The limitless green where in a perpetual spring I had been taken to play was the campus of McGill University. A house, whose beauty had brought tears to my sleep, to which in sleep I'd returned to find it inhabited by ugly strangers, gypsies, was a narrow stone thing with a shop on the ground floor and offices above – if that was it, for there were several like it. Through the bare panes of what might have been the sitting room, with its deep private window seats, I saw neon striplighting along a ceiling. Reality, as always, was narrow and dull. And yet what dramatic things had taken place on this very corner: Once Satan had approached me – furry dark skin, claws, red eyes, the lot. He urged me to cross the street and I did, in front of a car that braked in time. I explained, "The Devil told me to." I had no idea until then that my parents did not believe what I was taught in my convent school. (Satan is not bilingual, by the way; he speaks Quebec French.) My parents had no God and therefore no Fallen Angel. I was scolded for lying, which was a thing my father detested, and which my mother regularly did but never forgave in others.

Why these two nonbelievers wanted a strong religious education for me is one of the mysteries. (Even in loss of faith they were unalike, for he was ex-Anglican and she was ex-Lutheran and that is not your same atheist – no, not at all.) "To make you tolerant" was a lame excuse, as was "French," for I spoke fluent French with Olivia, and I could read in two languages before I was four. Discipline might have been one reason – God knows, the nuns provided plenty of that – but according to Olivia I did not need any. It cannot have been for the quality of the teaching, which was lamentable. I suspect that it was something like sending a dog to a trainer (they were passionate in their concern for animals, especially dogs), but I am not certain it ever brought me to heel. The first of my schools, the worst, the darkest, was on Sherbrooke Street too. When I heard, years later, it had been demolished, it was like the burial of a witch. I had remembered it penitentiary size, but what I found myself looking at one day was simply a very large stone house. A crocodile of little girls emerged from the front gate and proceeded along the street – white-faced, black-clad, eyes cast down. I knew they were bored, fidgety, anxious, and probably hungry. I should have felt pity, but at eighteen all that came to me was thankfulness that I had been correct about one thing throughout my youth, which I now considered ended: time had been on my side, faithfully, and unless you died you were always bound to escape.

1975

The Moslem Wife

IN THE SOUTH of France, in the business room of a hotel quite near to the house where Katherine Mansfield (whom no one in this hotel had ever heard of) was writing "The Daughters of the Late Colonel," Netta Asher's father announced that there would never be a man-made catastrophe in Europe again. The dead of that recent war, the doomed nonsense of the Russian Bolsheviks had finally knocked sense into European heads. What people wanted now was to get on with life. When he said "life," he meant its commercial business.

Who would have contradicted Mr. Asher? Certainly not Netta. She did not understand what he meant quite so well as his French solicitor seemed to, but she did listen with interest and respect, and then watched him signing papers that, she knew, concerned her for life. He was renewing the long lease her family held on the Hotel Prince Albert and Albion. Netta was then eleven. One hundred years should at least see her through the prime of life, said Mr. Asher, only half jokingly, for of course he thought his seed was immortal.

Netta supposed she might easily live to be more than a hundred – at any rate, for years and years. She knew that her father did not want her to marry until she was twenty-six and that she was then supposed to have a pair of children, the elder a boy. Netta and her father and the French lawyer shook hands on the lease, and she was given her first glass of champagne. The date on the bottle was 1909, for the year of her birth. Netta bravely pronounced the wine delicious, but her father said she would know much better vintages before she was through.

Netta remembered the handshake but perhaps not the terms. When the lease had eighty-eight years to run, she married her first cousin, Jack Ross, which was not at all what her father had had in mind. Nor would there be the useful pair of children – Jack couldn't abide them. Like Netta he came from a hotelkeeping family where the young were like blight. Netta had up to now never shown a scrap of maternal feeling over anything, but Mr. Asher thought Jack might have made an amiable parent – a kind one, at least. She consoled Mr. Asher on one count, by taking the hotel over in his lifetime. The hotel was, to Netta, a natural life; and so when Mr. Asher, dying, said, "She behaves as I wanted her to," he was right as far as the drift of Netta's behavior was concerned but wrong about its course.

The Ashers' hotel was not down on the seafront, though boats and sea could be had from the south-facing rooms. Across a road nearly empty of traffic were handsome villas, and behind and to either side stood healthy olive trees and a large lemon grove. The hotel was painted a deep ochre with white trim. It had white awnings and green shutters and black iron balconies as lacquered and shiny as Chinese boxes. It possessed two tennis courts, a lily pond, a sheltered winter garden, a formal rose garden, and trees full of nightingales. In the summer dark, *belles-de-nuit* glowed pink, lemon, white, and after their evening watering they gave off a perfume that varied from plant to plant and seemed to match the petals' coloration. In May the nights were dense with stars and fireflies. From the rose garden one might have seen the twin pulse of cigarettes on a balcony, where Jack and Netta sat drinking a last brandy-and-soda before turning in. Most of the rooms were shuttered by then, for no traveller would have dreamed of being south except in winter. Jack and Netta and a few servants had the whole place to themselves. Netta would hire workmen and have the rooms that needed it repainted – the blue cardroom, and the red-walled bar, and the white dining room, where Victorian mirrors gave back glossy walls and blown curtains and nineteenth-century views of the Ligurian coast, the work of an Asher great-uncle. Everything upstairs and down was soaked and wiped and polished, and even the pictures were relentlessly washed with soft cloths and ordinary laundry soap. Netta also had the boiler overhauled and the linen mended and new monograms embroidered and the looking glasses resilvered and the shutters taken off their hinges and scraped and made spruce green again for next year's sun to fade, while Jack talked about decorators and expert gardeners and even wrote to some, and banged tennis balls against the large new garage. He also read books and translated poetry for its own sake and practiced playing the clarinet. He had studied music once, and still thought that an important life, a musical life, was there in the middle distance. One summer, just to see if he could, he translated pages of St. John Perse, which were as blank as the garage wall to Netta, in any tongue.

Netta adored every minute of her life, and she thought Jack had a good life too, with nearly half the year for the pleasures that suited him. As soon as the grounds and rooms and cellar and roof had been put to rights, she and Jack packed and went travelling somewhere. Jack made the plans. He was never so cheerful as when buying Baedekers and dragging out their stickered trunks. But Netta was nothing of a traveller. She would have been glad to see the same sun rising out of the same sea from the window every day until she died. She loved Jack, and what she liked best after him was the hotel. It was a place where, once, people had come to die of tuberculosis, yet it held no trace or feeling of danger. When Netta walked with her workmen through sheeted summer rooms, hearing the cicadas and hearing Jack start, stop, start some deeply alien music (alien even when her memory automatically gave her a composer's name), she was reminded that here the dead had never been allowed to corrupt the living; the dead had been dressed for an outing and removed as soon as their first muscular stiffness relaxed. Some were wheeled out in chairs, sitting, and some reclined on portable cots, as if merely resting.

That is why there is no bad atmosphere here, she would say to herself. Death has been swept away, discarded. When the shutters are closed on a room, it is for sleep or for love. Netta could think this easily because neither she nor Jack was ever sick. They knew nothing about insomnia, and they made love every day of their lives – they had married in order to be able to.

Spring had been the season for dying in the old days. Invalids who had struggled through the dark comfort of winter took fright as the night receded. They felt without protection. Netta knew about this, and about the difference between darkness and brightness, but neither affected her. She was not afraid of death or of the dead – they were nothing but cold, heavy furniture. She could have tied jaws shut and weighted eyelids with native instinctiveness, as other women were born knowing the temperature for an infant's milk.

"There are no ghosts," she could say, entering the room where her mother, then her father had died. "If there were, I would know."

Netta took it for granted, now she was married, that Jack felt as she did about light, dark, death, and love. They were as alike in some ways (none of them physical) as a couple of twins, spoke much the same language in the same accents, had the same jokes – mostly about other people – and had been together as much as their families would let them for most of their lives. Other men seemed dull to Netta – slower, perhaps, lacking the spoken shorthand she had with Jack. She never mentioned this. For one thing, both of them had the idea that, being English, one must not say too much. Born abroad, they worked hard at an Englishness that was innocently inaccurate, rooted mostly in attitudes. Their families had been innkeepers along this coast for a century, even before Dr. James Henry Bennet had discovered "the Genoese Rivieras." In one of his guides to the region, a "Mr. Ross" is mentioned as a hotel owner who will accept English bank checks, and there is a "Mr. Asher," reliable purveyor of English groceries. The most trustworthy shipping agents in 1860 are the Montale brothers, converts to the Anglican Church, possessors of a British *laissez-passer* to Malta and Egypt. These families, by now plaited like hair, were connections of Netta's and Jack's and still in business from beyond Marseilles to Genoa. No wonder that other men bored her, and that each thought the other both familiar and unique. But of course they were unalike too. When once someone asked them, "Are you related to Montale, the poet?" Netta answered, "What poet?" and Jack said, "I wish we were."

There were no poets in the family. Apart from the great-uncle who had painted landscapes, the only person to try anything peculiar had been Jack, with his music. He had been allowed to study, up to a point; his father had been no good with hotels – had been a failure, in fact, bailed out four times by his cousins, and it had been thought, for a time, that Jack Ross might be a dunderhead too. Music might do him; he might not be fit for anything else.

Information of this kind about the meaning of failure had been gleaned by Netta years before, when she first became aware of her little cousin. Jack's father and mother – the commercial blunderers – had come to the Prince Albert and Albion to ride out a crisis. They were somewhere between undischarged bankruptcy and annihilation, but one was polite: Netta curtsied to her aunt and uncle. Her eyes were on Jack. She could not read yet, though she could sift and classify attitudes. She drew near him, sucking her lower lip, her hands behind her back. For the first time she was conscious of the beauty of another child. He was younger than Netta, imprisoned in a portable-fence arrangement in which he moved tirelessly, crabwise, hanging on a barrier he could easily have climbed. He was as fair as his Irish mother and sunburned a deep brown. His blue gaze was not a baby's – it was too challenging. He was naked except for shorts that were large and seemed about to fall down. The sunburn, the undress were because his mother was reckless and rather odd. Netta – whose mother was perfect – wore boots, stockings, a longsleeved frock, and a white sun hat. She heard the adults laugh and say that Jack looked like a prizefighter. She walked around his prison, staring, and the blue-eyed fighter stared back.

The Rosses stayed for a long time, while the family sent telegrams and tried to raise money for them. No one looked after Jack much. He would lie on a marble step of the staircase watching the hotel guests going into the cardroom or the dining room. One night, for a reason that remorse was to wipe out in a minute, Netta gave him such a savage kick (though he was not really in her way) that one of his legs remained paralyzed for a long time.

"*Why* did you do it?" her father asked her – this in the room where she was shut up on bread and water. Netta didn't know. She loved Jack, but who would believe it now? Jack learned to walk, then to run, and in time to ski and play tennis; but her lifelong gift to him was a loss of balance, a sudden lopsided bend of a knee. Jack's parents had meantime been given a small hotel to run at Bandol. Mr. Asher, responsible for a bank loan, kept an eye on the place. He went often, in a hotel car with a chauffeur, Netta perched beside him. When, years later, the families found out that the devoted young cousins had become lovers, they separated them without saying much. Netta was too independent to be dealt with. Besides, her father did not want a rift; his wife had died, and he needed Netta. Jack, whose claim on music had been the subject of teasing until now, was suddenly sent to study in England. Netta saw that he was secretly dismayed. He wanted to be almost anything as long as it was impossible, and then only as an act of grace. Netta's father did think it was his duty to tell her that marriage was, at its best, a parched arrangement, intolerable without a flow of golden guineas and fresh blood. As cousins, Jack and Netta could not bring each other anything except stale money. Nothing stopped them: they were married four months after Jack became twenty-one. Netta heard someone remark at her wedding, "She doesn't need a husband," meaning perhaps the practical, matter-of-fact person she now seemed to be. She did have the dry, burned-out look of someone turned inward. Her dark eyes glowed out of a thin face. She had the shape of a girl of fourteen. Jack, who was large, and fair, and who might be stout at forty if he wasn't careful, looked exactly his age, and seemed quite ready to be married.

Netta could not understand why, loving Jack as she did, she did not look more like him. It had troubled her in the past when they did not think exactly the same thing at almost the same time. During the secret meetings of their long engagement she had noticed how even before a parting they were nearly apart – they had begun to "unmesh," as she called it. Drinking a last drink, usually in the buffet of a railway station, she would see that Jack was somewhere else, thinking about the next-best thing to Netta. The next-best thing might only be a book he wanted to finish reading, but it was enough to make her feel exiled. He often told Netta, "I'm not holding on to you. You're free," because he thought it needed saying, and of course he wanted freedom for himself. But to Netta "freedom" had a cold sound. Is that what I do want, she would wonder. Is that what I think he should offer? Their partings were often on the edge of parting forever, not just because Jack had said or done or thought the wrong thing but because between them they generated the high sexual tension that leads to quarrels. Barely ten minutes after agreeing that no one in the world could possibly know what they knew, one of them, either one, could curse the other out over something trivial. Yet they were, and remained, much in love, and when they were apart Netta sent him letters that were almost despairing with enchantment.

Jack answered, of course, but his letters were cautious. Her exploration of feeling was part of an unlimited capacity she seemed to have for passionate behavior, so at odds with her appearance, which had been dry and sardonic even in childhood. Save for an erotic sentence or two near the end (which Netta read first) Jack's messages might have been meant for any girl cousin he particularly liked. Love was memory, and he was no good at the memory game; he needed Netta there. The instant he saw her he knew all he had missed. But Netta, by then, felt forgotten, and she came to each new meeting aggressive and hurt, afflicted with the physical signs of her doubts and injuries – cold sores, rashes, erratic periods, mysterious temperatures. If she tried to discuss it he would say, "We aren't going over all that again, are we?" Where Netta was concerned he had settled for the established faith, but Netta, who had a wilder, more secret God, wanted a prayer a minute, not to speak of unending miracles and revelations.

When they finally married, both were relieved that the strain of partings and of tense disputes in railway stations would come to a stop. Each privately blamed the other for past violence, and both believed that once they could live openly, without interference, they would never have a disagreement again. Netta did not want Jack to regret the cold freedom he had vainly tried to offer her. He must have his liberty, and his music, and other people, and, oh, anything he wanted – whatever would stop him from saying he was ready to let her go free. The first thing Netta did was to make certain they had the best room in the hotel. She had never actually owned a room until now. The private apartments of her family had always been surrendered in a crisis: everyone had packed up and moved as beds were required. She and Jack were hopelessly untidy, because both had spent their early years moving down hotel corridors, trailing belts and raincoats, with tennis shoes hanging from knotted strings over their shoulders, their arms around books and sweaters and gray flannel bundles. Both had done lessons in the corners of lounges, with cups and glasses rattling, and other children running, and English voices louder than anything. Jack, who had been vaguely educated, remembered his boarding schools as places where one had a permanent bed. Netta chose for her marriage a south-facing room with a large balcony and an awning of dazzling white. It was furnished with lemonwood that had been brought to the Riviera by Russians for their own villas long before. To the lemonwood Netta's mother had added English chintzes; the result, in Netta's eyes, was not bizarre but charming. The room was deeply mirrored; when the shutters were closed on hot afternoons a play of light became as green as a forest on the walls, and as blue as seawater in the glass. A quality of suspension, of disbelief in gravity, now belonged to Netta. She became tidy, silent, less introspective, as watchful and as reflective as her bedroom mirrors. Jack stayed as he was, luckily; any alteration would have worried her, just as a change in an often-read story will trouble a small child. She was intensely, almost unnaturally happy.

One day she overheard an English doctor, whose wife played bridge every afternoon at the hotel, refer to her, to Netta, as "the little Moslem wife." It was said affectionately, for the doctor liked her. She wondered if he had seen through walls and had watched her picking up the clothing and the wet towels Jack left strewn like clues to his presence. The phrase was collected and passed from mouth to mouth in the idle English colony. Netta, the last person in the world deliberately to eavesdrop (she lacked that sort of interest in other people), was sharp of hearing where her marriage was concerned. She had a special antenna for Jack, for his shades of meaning, secret intentions, for his innocent contradictions. Perhaps "Moslem wife" meant several things, and possibly it was plain to anyone with eyes that Jack, without meaning a bit of harm by it, had a way with women. Those he attracted were a puzzling lot, to Netta. She had already catalogued them – elegant elderly parties with tongues like carving knives; gentle, clever girls who flourished on the unattainable; untouchable-daughter types, canny about their virginity, wondering if Jack would be father enough to justify the sacrifice. There was still another kind – tough, sunburned, clad in dark colors – who made Netta think in the vocabulary of horoscopes: Her gem – diamonds. Her color – black. Her language – worse than Netta's. She noticed that even when Jack had no real use for a woman he never made it apparent; he adopted anyone who took a liking to him. He assumed – Netta thought – a tribal, paternal air that was curious in so young a man. The plot of attraction interested him, no matter how it turned out. He was like someone reading several novels at once, or like someone playing simultaneous chess.

Netta did not want her marriage to become a world of stone. She said nothing except, "Listen, Jack, I've been at this hotel business longer than you have. It's wiser not to be too pally with the guests." At Christmas the older women gave him boxes of expensive soap. "They must think someone around here wants a good wash," Netta remarked. Outside their fenced area of private jokes and private love was a landscape too open, too light-drenched, for serious talk. And then, when? Jack woke up quickly and early in the morning and smiled as naturally as children do. He knew where he was and the day of the week and the hour. The best moment of the day was the first cigarette. When something bloody happened, it was never before six in the evening. At night he had a dark look that went with a dark mood, sometimes. Netta would tell him that she could see a cruise ship floating on the black horizon like a piece of the Milky Way, and she would get that look for an answer. But it never lasted. His memory was too short to let him sulk, no matter what fragment of night had crossed his mind. She knew, having heard other couples all her life, that at least she and Jack never made the conjugal sounds that passed for conversation and that might as well have been bow-wow and quack quack.

If, by chance, Jack found himself drawn to another woman, if the tide of attraction suddenly ran the other way, then he would discover in himself a great need to talk to his wife. They sat out on their balcony for much of one long night and he told her about his Irish mother. His mother's eccentricity – "Vera's dottiness," where the family was concerned – had kept Jack from taking anything seriously. He had been afraid of pulling her mad attention in his direction. Countless times she had faked tuberculosis and cancer and announced her own imminent death. A telephone call from a hospital had once declared her lost in a car crash. "It's a new life, a new life," her husband had babbled, coming away from the phone. Jack saw his father then as beautiful. Women are beautiful when they fall in love, said Jack; sometimes the glow will last a few hours, sometimes even a day or two.

"You know," said Jack, as if Netta knew, "the look of amazement on a girl's face . . ."

Well, that same incandescence had suffused Jack's father when he thought his wife had died, and it continued to shine until a taxi deposited dotty Vera with her cheerful announcement that she had certainly brought off a successful April Fool. After Jack's father died she became violent. "Getting away from her was a form of violence in me," Jack said. "But I did it." That was why he was secretive; that was why he was independent. He had never wanted any woman to get her hands on his life.

Netta heard this out calmly. Where his own feelings were

concerned she thought he was making them up as he went along. The garden smelled coolly of jasmine and mimosa. She wondered who his new girl was, and if he was likely to blurt out a name. But all he had been working up to was that his mother – mad, spoiled, devilish, whatever she was – would need to live with Jack and Netta, unless Netta agreed to giving her an income. An income would let her remain where she was – at the moment, in a Rudolf Steiner community in Switzerland, devoted to medieval gardening and to getting the best out of Goethe. Netta's father's training prevented even the thought of spending the money in such a manner.

"You won't regret all you've told me, will you?" she asked. She saw that the new situation would be her burden, her chain, her mean little joke sometimes. Jack scarcely hesitated before saying that where Netta mattered he could never regret anything. But what really interested him now was his mother.

"Lifts give her claustrophobia," he said. "She mustn't be higher than the second floor." He sounded like a man bringing a legal concubine into his household, scrupulously anxious to give all his women equal rights. "And I hope she will make friends," he said. "It won't be easy, at her age. One can't live without them." He probably meant that he had none. Netta had been raised not to expect to have friends: you could not run a hotel and have scores of personal ties. She expected people to be polite and punctual and to mean what they said, and that was the end of it. Jack gave his friendship easily, but he expected considerable diversion in return.

Netta said dryly, "If she plays bridge, she can play with Mrs. Blackley." This was the wife of the doctor who had first said "Moslem wife." He had come down here to the Riviera for his wife's health; the two belonged to a subcolony of flat-dwelling expatriates. His medical practice was limited to hypochondriacs and rheumatic patients. He had time on his hands: Netta often saw him in the hotel reading room, standing, leafing – he took pleasure in handling books. Netta, no reader, did not like touching a book unless it was new. The doctor had a trick of speech Jack loved to imitate: he would break up his words with an extra syllable, some words only, and at that not every time. "It is all a matter of stu-hyle," he said, for "style," or, Jack's favorite, "Oh, well, in the end it all comes down to su-hex." "Uh-hebb and flo-ho of hormones" was the way he once described the behavior of saints – Netta had looked twice at him over that. He was a firm agnostic and the first person from whom Netta heard there existed a magical Dr. Freud. When Netta's father had died of pneumonia, the doctor's "I'm su-horry, Netta" had been so heartfelt she could not have wished it said another way.

His wife, Georgina, could lower her blood pressure or stop her heartbeat nearly at will. Netta sometimes wondered why Dr. Blackley had brought her to a soft climate rather than to the man at Vienna he so admired. Georgina was well enough to play fierce bridge, with Jack and anyone good enough. Her husband usually came to fetch her at the end of the afternoon when the players stopped for tea. Once, because he was obliged to return at once to a patient who needed him, she said, "Can't you be competent about anything?" Netta thought she understood, then, his resigned repetition of "It's all su-hex." "Oh, don't explain. You bore me," said his wife, turning her back.

Netta followed him out to his car. She wore an India shawl that had been her mother's. The wind blew her hair; she had to hold it back. She said, "Why don't you kill her?"

"I am not a desperate person," he said. He looked at Netta, she looking up at him because she had to look up to nearly everyone except children, and he said, "I've wondered why we haven't been to bed."

"Who?" said Netta. "You and your wife? Oh. You mean me." She was not offended, she just gave the shawl a brusque tug and said, "Not a hope. Never with a guest," though of course that was not the reason.

"You might have to, if the guest were a maharaja," he said, to make it all harmless. "I am told it is pu-hart of the courtesy they expect."

"We don't get their trade," said Netta. This had not stopped her liking the doctor. She pitied him, rather, because of his wife, and because he wasn't Jack and could not have Netta.

"I do love you," said the doctor, deciding finally to sit down in his car. "Ee-nee-ormously." She watched him drive away as if she loved him too, and might never see him again. It never crossed her mind to mention any of this conversation to Jack.

That very spring, perhaps because of the doctor's words, the hotel did get some maharaja trade – three little sisters with ebony curls, men's eyebrows, large heads, and delicate hands and feet. They had four rooms, one for their governess. A chauffeur on permanent call lodged elsewhere. The governess, who was Dutch, had a perfect triangle of a nose and said "whom" for "who," pronouncing it "whum." The girls were to learn French, tennis, and swimming. The chauffeur arrived with a hairdresser, who cut their long hair; it lay on the governess's carpet, enough to fill a large pillow. Their toe- and fingernails were filed to points and looked like a kitten's teeth. They came smiling down the marble staircase, carrying new tennis racquets, wearing blue linen skirts and navy blazers. Mrs. Blackley glanced up from the bridge game as they went by the cardroom. She had been one of those opposed to their having lessons at the English Lawn Tennis Club, for reasons that were, to her, perfectly evident.

She said, loudly, "They'll have to be in white."

"End whay, pray?" cried the governess, pointing her triangle nose.

"They can't go on the courts except in white. It is a private club. Entirely white."

"Whum do they all think they are?" the governess asked, prepared to stalk on. But the girls, with their newly cropped heads, and their vulnerable necks showing, caught the drift and refused to go.

"Whom indeed," said Georgina Blackley, fiddling with her bridge hand and looking happy.

"My wife's seamstress could run up white frocks for them in a minute," said Jack. Perhaps he did not dislike children all that much.

"Whom could," muttered Georgina.

But it turned out that the governess was not allowed to choose their clothes, and so Jack gave the children lessons at the hotel. For six weeks they trotted around the courts looking angelic in blue, or hopelessly foreign, depending upon who saw them. Of course they fell in love with Jack, offering him a passionate loyalty they had nowhere else to place. Netta watched the transfer of this gentle, anxious gift. After they departed, Jack was bad-tempered for several evenings and then never spoke of them again; they, needless to say, had been dragged from him weeping.

When this happened the Rosses had been married nearly five years. Being childless but still very loving, they had trouble deciding which of the two would be the child. Netta overheard "He's a darling, but she's a sergeant major and no mistake. And so *mean*." She also heard "He's a lazy bastard. He bullies her. She's a fool." She searched her heart again about children. Was it Jack or had it been Netta who had first said no? The only child she had ever admired was Jack, and not as a child but as a fighter, defying her. She and Jack were not the sort to have animal children, and Jack's dotty mother would probably soon be child enough for any couple to handle. Jack still seemed to adopt, in a tribal sense of his, half the women who fell in love with him. The only woman who resisted adoption was Netta – still burned-out, still ardent, in a manner of speaking still fourteen. His mother had turned up meanwhile, getting down from a train wearing a sly air of enjoying her own jokes, just as she must have looked on the day of the April

Fool. At first she was no great trouble, though she did complain about an ulcerated leg. After years of pretending, she at last had something real. Netta's policy of silence made Jack's mother confident. She began to make a mockery of his music: "All that money gone for nothing!" Or else, "The amount we wasted on schools! The hours he's thrown away with his nose in a book. All that reading – if at least it had got him somewhere." Netta noticed that he spent more time playing bridge and chatting to cronies in the bar now. She thought hard, and decided not to make it her business. His mother had once been pretty; perhaps he still saw her that way. She came of a ramshackle family with a usable past; she spoke of the Ashers and the Rosses as if she had known them when they were tinkers. English residents who had a low but solid barrier with Jack and Netta were fences-down with his mad mother: they seemed to take her at her own word when it was about herself. She began then to behave like a superior sort of guest, inviting large parties to her table for meals, ordering special wines and dishes at inconvenient hours, standing endless rounds of drinks in the bar.

Netta told herself, Jack wants it this way. It is his home too. She began to live a life apart, leaving Jack to his mother. She sat wearing her own mother's shawl, hunched over a new, modern adding machine, punching out accounts. "Funny couple," she heard now. She frowned, smiling in her mind; none of these people knew what bound them, or how tied they were. She had the habit of dodging out of her mother-in-law's parties by saying, "I've got such an awful lot to do." It made them laugh, because they thought this was Netta's term for slave-driving the servants. They thought the staff did the work, and that Netta counted the profits and was too busy with bookkeeping to keep an eye on Jack – who now, at twenty-six, was as attractive as he ever would be.

A woman named Iris Cordier was one of Jack's mother's new friends. Tall, loud, in winter dully pale, she reminded

Netta of a blond penguin. Her voice moved between a squeak and a moo, and was a mark of the distinguished literary family to which her father belonged. Her mother, a Frenchwoman, had been in and out of nursing homes for years. The Cordiers haunted the Riviera, with Iris looking after her parents and watching their diets. Now she lived in a flat somewhere in Roquebrune with the survivor of the pair – the mother, Netta believed. Iris paused and glanced in the business room where Mr. Asher had signed the hundred-year lease. She was on her way to lunch – Jack's mother's guest, of course.

"I say, aren't you Miss Asher?"

"I was." Iris, like Dr. Blackley, was probably younger than she looked. Out of her own childhood Netta recalled a desperate adolescent Iris with middle-aged parents clamped like handcuffs on her life. "How is your mother?" Netta had been about to say "How is Mrs. Cordier?" but it sounded servile.

"I didn't know you knew her."

"I remember her well. Your father too. He was a nice person."

"And still is," said Iris, sharply. "He lives with me, and he always will. French daughters don't abandon their parents." No one had ever sounded more English to Netta. "And your father and mother?"

"Both dead now. I'm married to Jack Ross."

"Nobody told me," said Iris, in a way that made Netta think, Good Lord, Iris too? Jack could not possibly seem like a patriarchal figure where she was concerned; perhaps this time the game was reversed and Iris played at being tribal and maternal. The idea of Jack, or of any man, flinging himself on that iron bosom made Netta smile. As if startled, Iris covered her mouth. She seemed to be frightened of smiling back.

Oh, well, and what of it, Iris too, said Netta to herself, suddenly turning back to her accounts. As it happened, Netta was mistaken (as she never would have been with a bill). That day Jack was meeting Iris for the first time.

The upshot of these errors and encounters was an invitation to Roquebrune to visit Iris's father. Jack's mother was ruthlessly excluded, even though Iris probably owed her a return engagement because of the lunch. Netta supposed that Iris had decided one had to get past Netta to reach Jack – an inexactness if ever there was one. Or perhaps it was Netta Iris wanted. In that case the error became a farce. Netta had almost no knowledge of private houses. She looked around at something that did not much interest her, for she hated to leave her own home, and saw Iris's father, apparently too old and shaky to get out of his armchair. He smiled and he nodded, meanwhile stroking an aged cat. He said to Netta, "You resemble your mother. A sweet woman. Obliging and quiet. I used to tell her that I longed to live in her hotel and be looked after."

Not by me, thought Netta.

Iris's amber bracelets rattled as she pushed and pulled everyone through introductions. Jack and Netta had been asked to meet a young American Netta had often seen in her own bar, and a couple named Sandy and Sandra Braunsweg, who turned out to be Anglo-Swiss and twins. Iris's long arms were around them as she cried to Netta, "Don't you know these babies?" They were, like the Rosses, somewhere in their twenties. Jack looked on, blue-eyed, interested, smiling at everything new. Netta supposed that she was now seeing some of the rather hard-up snobbish – snobbish what? "Intelligum-hen-sia," she imagined Dr. Blackley supplying. Having arrived at a word, Netta was ready to go home; but they had only just arrived. The American turned to Netta. He looked bored, and astonished by it. He needs the word for "bored," she decided. Then he can go home, too. The Riviera was no place for Americans. They could not sit all day waiting for mail and the daily papers and for the clock to show a respectable drinking time. They made the best of things when they were caught with a house they'd been rash enough to rent unseen. Netta often had them then *en pension* for meals: a hotel dining room was one way of meeting people. They paid a fee to use the tennis courts, and they liked the bar. Netta would notice then how Jack picked up any accent within hearing.

Jack was now being attentive to the old man, Iris's father. Though this was none of Mr. Cordier's business, Jack said, "My wife and I are first cousins, as well as second cousins twice over."

"You don't look it."

Everyone began to speak at once, and it was a minute or two before Netta heard Jack again. This time he said, "We are from a family of great . . ." It was lost. What now? Great innkeepers? Worriers? Skinflints? Whatever it was, old Mr. Cordier kept nodding to show he approved.

"We don't see nearly enough of young men like you," he said.

"True!" said Iris loudly. "We live in a dreary world of ill women down here." Netta thought this hard on the American, on Mr. Cordier, and on the male Braunsweg twin, but none of them looked offended. "I've got no time for women," said Iris. She slapped down a glass of whiskey so that it splashed, and rapped on a table with her knuckles. "Shall I tell you why? Because women don't tick over. They just simply don't tick over." No one disputed this. Iris went on: Women were underinformed. One could have virile conversations only with men. Women were attached to the past through fear, whereas men had a fearless sense of history. "Men tick," she said, glaring at Jack.

"I am not attached to a past," said Netta, slowly. "The past holds no attractions." She was not used to general conversation. She thought that every word called for consideration and for an answer. "Nothing could be worse than the way we children were dressed. And our mothers – the hard waves of their hair, the white lips. I think of those pale profiles and I wonder if those women were ever young."

Poor Netta, who saw herself as profoundly English, spread consternation by being suddenly foreign and gassy. She talked the English of expatriate children, as if reading aloud. The twins looked shocked. But she had appealed to the American. He sat beside her on a scuffed velvet sofa. He was so large that she slid an inch or so in his direction when he sat down. He was Sandra Braunsweg's special friend: they had been in London together. He was trying to write.

"What do you mean?" said Netta. "Write what?"

"Well – a novel, to start," he said. His father had staked him to one year, then another. He mentioned all that Sandra had borne with, how she had actually kicked and punched him to keep him from being too American. He had embarrassed her to death in London by asking a waitress, "Miss, where's the toilet?"

Netta said, "Didn't you mind being corrected?"

"Oh, no. It was just friendly."

Jack meanwhile was listening to Sandra telling about her English forebears and her English education. "I had many years of undeniably excellent schooling," she said. "Mitten Todd."

"What's that?" said Jack.

"It's near Bristol. I met excellent girls from Italy, Spain. I took *him* there to visit," she said, generously including the American. "I said, 'Get a yellow necktie.' He went straight out and bought one. I wore a little Schiaparelli. Bought in Geneva but still a real . . . A yellow jacket over a gray . . . Well, we arrived at my excellent old school, and even though the day was drizzly I said, 'Put the top of the car back.' He did so at once, and then he understood. The interior of the car harmonized perfectly with the yellow and gray." The twins were orphaned. Iris was like a mother.

"When Mummy died we didn't know where to put all the Chippendale," said Sandra, "Iris took a lot of it."

Netta thought, She is so silly. How can he respond? The

girl's dimples and freckles and soft little hands were nothing Netta could have ever described: she had never in her life thought a word like "pretty." People were beautiful or they were not. Her happiness had always been great enough to allow for despair. She knew that some people thought Jack was happy and she was not.

"And what made you marry your young cousin?" the old man boomed at Netta. Perhaps his background allowed him to ask impertinent questions; he must have been doing so nearly forever. He stroked his cat; he was confident. He was spokesman for a roomful of wondering people.

"Jack was a moody child and I promised his mother I would look after him," said Netta. In her hopelessly un-English way she believed she had said something funny.

At eleven o'clock the hotel car expected to fetch the Rosses was nowhere. They trudged home by moonlight. For the last hour of the evening Jack had been skewered on virile conversations, first with Iris, then with Sandra, to whom Netta had already given "Chippendale" as a private name. It proved that Iris was right about concentrating on men and their ticking – Jack even thought Sandra rather pretty.

"Prettier than me?" said Netta, without the faintest idea what she meant, but aware she had said something stupid.

"Not so attractive," said Jack. His slight limp returned straight out of childhood. *She* had caused his accident.

"But she's not always clear," said Netta. "Mitten Todd, for example."

"Who're you talking about?"

"Who are *you*?"

"Iris, of course."

As if they had suddenly quarrelled they fell silent. In silence they entered their room and prepared for bed. Jack poured a whiskey, walked on the clothes he had dropped, carried his drink to the bathroom. Through the half-shut door he called suddenly, "Why did you say that asinine thing about promising to look after me?"

"It seemed so unlikely, I thought they'd laugh." She had a glimpse of herself in the mirrors picking up his shed clothes.

He said, "Well, is it true?"

She was quiet for such a long time that he came to see if she was still in the room. She said, "No, your mother never said that or anything like it."

"We shouldn't have gone to Roquebrune," said Jack. "I think those bloody people are going to be a nuisance. Iris wants her father to stay here, with the cat, while she goes to England for a month. How do we get out of that?"

"By saying no."

"I'm rotten at no."

"I told you not to be too pally with women," she said, as a joke again, but jokes were her way of having floods of tears.

Before this had a chance to heal, Iris's father moved in, bringing his cat in a basket. He looked at his room and said, "Medium large." He looked at his bed and said, "Reasonably long." He was, in short, daft about measurements. When he took books out of the reading room, he was apt to return them with "This volume contains about 70,000 words" written inside the back cover.

Netta had not wanted Iris's father, but Jack had said yes to it. She had not wanted the sick cat, but Jack had said yes to that too. The old man, who was lost without Iris, lived for his meals. He would appear at the shut doors of the dining room an hour too early, waiting for the menu to be typed and posted. In a voice that matched Iris's for carrying power, he read aloud, alone: "Consommé. Good Lord, again? Is there a choice between the fish and the cutlet? I can't possibly eat all of that. A bit of salad and a boiled egg. That's all I could possibly want." That was rubbish, because Mr. Cordier ate the menu and more, and if there were two puddings, or a pudding and ice cream, he ate both and asked for pastry, fruit, and cheese to

follow. One day, after Dr. Blackley had attended him for faint-
ness, Netta passed a message on to Iris, who had been back
from England for a fortnight now but seemed in no hurry to
take her father away.

"Keith Blackley thinks your father should go on a diet."

"He can't," said Iris. "Our other doctor says dieting causes
cancer."

"You can't have heard that properly," Netta said.

"It is like those silly people who smoke to keep their figures," said Iris. "Dieting."

"Blackley hasn't said he should smoke, just that he should
eat less of everything."

"My father has never smoked in his life," Iris cried. "As for
his diet, I weighed his food out for years. He's not here forever.
I'll take him back as soon as he's had enough of hotels."

He stayed for a long time, and the cat did too, and a nuisance they both were to the servants. When the cat was too ail-
ing to walk, the old man carried it to a path behind the tennis
courts and put it down on the gravel to die. Netta came out
with the old man's tea on a tray (not done for everyone, but
having him out of the way was a relief) and she saw the cat
lying on its side, eyes wide, as if profoundly thinking. She saw
unlicked dirt on its coat and ants exploring its paws. The old
man sat in a garden chair, wearing a panama hat, his hands
clasped on a stick. He called, "Oh, Netta, take her away. I am
too old to watch anything die. I know what she'll do," he said,
indifferently, his voice failing as she came near. "Oh, I know
that. Turn on her back and give a shriek. I've heard it often."

Netta disburdened her tray onto a garden table and pulled
the tray cloth under the cat. She was angered at the haste and
indecency of the ants. "It would be polite to leave her," she
said. "She doesn't want to be watched."

"I always sit here," said the old man.

Jack, making for the courts with Chippendale, looked as if

the sight of the two conversing amused him. Then he understood and scooped up the cat and tray cloth and went away with the cat over his shoulder. He laid it in the shade of a Judas tree, and within an hour it was dead. Iris's father said, "I've got no one to talk to here. That's my trouble. That shroud was too small for my poor Polly. Ask my daughter to fetch me."

Jack's mother said that night, "I'm sure you wish that I had a devoted daughter to take me away too." Because of the attention given the cat she seemed to feel she had not been nuisance enough. She had taken to saying, "My leg is dying before I am," and imploring Jack to preserve her leg, should it be amputated, and make certain it was buried with her. She wanted Jack to be close by at nearly any hour now, so that she could lean on him. After sitting for hours at bridge she had trouble climbing two flights of stairs; nothing would induce her to use the lift.

"Nothing ever came of your music," she would say, leaning on him. "Of course, you have a wife to distract you now. I needed a daughter. Every woman does." Netta managed to trap her alone, and forced her to sit while she stood over her. Netta said, "Look, Aunt Vera, I forbid you, I absolutely forbid you, do you hear, to make a nurse of Jack, and I shall strangle you with my own hands if you go on saying nothing came of his music. You are not to say it in my hearing or out of it. Is that plain?"

Jack's mother got up to her room without assistance. About an hour later the gardener found her on a soft bed of wallflowers. "An inch to the left and she'd have landed on a rake," he said to Netta. She was still alive when Netta knelt down. In her fall she had crushed the plants, the yellow minted *giroflées de Nice*. Netta thought that she was now, at last, for the first time, inhaling one of the smells of death. Her aunt's arms and legs were turned and twisted; her skirt was pulled so that her swollen leg showed. It seemed that she had jumped carrying her walking stick – it lay across the path. She often slept in an armchair, afternoons, with one eye slightly open. She opened that eye now and, seeing she had Netta, said, "My son." Netta was thinking, I have never known her. And if I knew her, then it was Jack or myself I could not understand. Netta was afraid of giving orders, and of telling people not to touch her aunt before Dr. Blackley could be summoned, because she knew that she had always been mistaken. Now Jack was there, propping his mother up, brushing leaves and earth out of her hair. Her head dropped on his shoulder. Netta thought from the sudden heaviness that her aunt had died, but she sighed and opened that one eye again, saying this time, "Doctor?" Netta left everyone doing the wrong things to her dying – no, her murdered – aunt. She said quite calmly into a telephone, "I am afraid that my aunt must have jumped or fallen from the second floor."

Jack found a letter on his mother's night table that began, "Why blame Netta? I forgive." At dawn he and Netta sat at a card table with yesterday's cigarettes still not cleaned out of the ashtray, and he did not ask what Netta had said or done that called for forgiveness. They kept pushing the letter back and forth. He would read it and then Netta would. It seemed natural for them to be silent. Jack had sat beside his mother for much of the night. Each of them then went to sleep for an hour, apart, in one of the empty rooms, just as they had done in the old days when their parents were juggling beds and guests and double and single quarters. By the time the doctor returned for his second visit Jack was neatly dressed and seemed wide awake. He sat in the bar drinking black coffee and reading a travel book of Evelyn Waugh's called *Labels*. Netta, who looked far more untidy and underslept, wondered if Jack wished he might leave now, and sail from Monte Carlo on the Stella Polaris.

Dr. Blackley said, "Well, you are a dim pair. She is not in

pu-hain, you know." Netta supposed this was the roundabout way doctors have of announcing death, very like "Her sufferings have ended." But Jack, looking hard at the doctor, had heard another meaning. "Jumped or fell," said Dr. Blackley. "She neither fell nor jumped. She is up there enjoying a damned good thu-hing."

Netta went out and through the lounge and up the marble steps. She sat down in the shaded room on the chair where Jack had spent most of the night. Her aunt did not look like anyone Netta knew, not even like Jack. She stared at the alien face and said, "Aunt Vera, Keith Blackley says there is nothing really the matter. You must have made a mistake. Perhaps you fainted on the path, overcome by the scent of wallflowers. What would you like me to tell Jack?"

Jack's mother turned on her side and slowly, tenderly, raised herself on an elbow. "Well, Netta," she said, "I daresay the fool is right. But as I've been given quite a lot of sleeping stuff, I'd as soon stay here for now."

Netta said, "Are you hungry?"

"I should very much like a ham sandwich on English bread, and about that much gin with a lump of ice."

She began coming down for meals a few days later. They knew she had crept down the stairs and flung her walking stick over the path and let herself fall hard on a bed of wallflowers – had even plucked her skirt up for a bit of accuracy; but she was also someone returned from beyond the limits, from the other side of the wall. Once she said, "It was like diving and suddenly realizing there was no water in the sea." Again, "It is not true that your life rushes before your eyes. You can see the flowers floating up to you. Even a short fall takes a long time."

Everyone was deeply changed by this incident. The effect on the victim herself was that she got religion hard.

"We are all hopeless nonbelievers!" shouted Iris, drinking

in the bar one afternoon. "At least, I hope we are. But when I see you, Vera, I feel there might be something in religion. You look positively temperate."

"I am allowed to love God, I hope," said Jack's mother.

Jack never saw or heard his mother anymore. He leaned against the bar, reading. It was his favorite place. Even on the sunniest of afternoons he read by the red-shaded light. Netta was present only because she had supplies to check. Knowing she ought to keep out of this, she still said, "Religion is more than love. It is supposed to tell you why you exist and what you are expected to do about it."

"You have no religious feelings at all?" This was the only serious and almost the only friendly question Iris was ever to ask Netta.

"None," said Netta. "I'm running a business."

"I love God as Jack used to love music," said his mother. "At least he said he did when we were paying for lessons."

"Adam and Eve had God," said Netta. "They had nobody *but* God. A fat lot of good that did them." This was as far as their dialectic went. Jack had not moved once except to turn pages. He read steadily but cautiously now, as if every author had a design on him. That was one effect of his mother's incident. The other was that he gave up bridge and went back to playing the clarinet. Iris hammered out an accompaniment on the upright piano in the old music room, mostly used for listening to radio broadcasts. She was the only person Netta had ever heard who could make Mozart sound like an Irish jig. Presently Iris began to say that it was time Jack gave a concert. Before this could turn into a crisis Iris changed her mind and said what he wanted was a holiday. Netta thought he needed something: he seemed to be exhausted by love, friendship, by being a husband, someone's son, by trying to make a world out of reading and sense out of life. A visit to England to meet some stimulating people, said Iris. To help Iris with her tiresome father during the journey. To visit art galleries and bookshops and go to concerts. To meet people. To talk.

This was a hot, troubled season, and many persons were planning journeys – not to meet other people but for fear of a war. The hotel had emptied out by the end of March. Netta, whose father had known there would never be another cata-strophe, had her workmen come in, as usual. She could hear the radiators being drained and got ready for painting as she packed Jack's clothes. They had never been separated before. They kept telling each other that it was only for a short holiday – for three or four weeks. She was surprised at how neat marriage was, at how many years and feelings could be folded and put under a lid. Once, she went to the window so that he would not see her tears and think she was trying to blackmail him. Looking out, she noticed the American, Chippendale's lover, idly knocking a tennis ball against the garage, as Jack had done in the early summers of their life; he had come round to the hotel looking for a partner, but that season there were none. She suddenly knew to a certainty that if Jack were to die she would search the crowd of mourners for a man she could live with. She would not return from the funeral alone.

Grief and memory, yes, she said to herself, but what about three o'clock in the morning?

By June nearly everyone Netta knew had vanished, or, like the Blackleys, had started to pack. Netta had new tablecloths made, and ordered new white awnings, and two dozen rose-bushes from the nursery at Cap Ferrat. The American came over every day and followed her from room to room, talking. He had nothing better to do. The Swiss twins were in England. His father, who had been backing his writing career until now, had suddenly changed his mind about it – now, when he needed money to get out of Europe. He had projects for living on his own, but they required a dose of funds. He wanted to open a restaurant on the Riviera where nothing but chicken pie would be served. Or else a vast and expensive café where people would pay to make their own sandwiches. He said that he was seeing the food of the future, but all that Netta could see was customers asking for their money back. He trapped her behind the bar and said he loved her; Netta made other women look like stuffed dolls. He could still remember the shock of meeting her, the attraction, the brilliant answer she had made to Iris about attachments to the past.

Netta let him rave until he asked for a loan. She laughed and wondered if it was for the chicken-pie restaurant. No – he wanted to get on a boat sailing from Cannes. She said, quite cheerfully, "I can't be Venus and Barclays Bank. You have to choose."

He said, "Can't Venus ever turn up with a letter of credit?"

She shook her head. "Not a hope."

But when it was July and Jack hadn't come back, he cornered her again. Money wasn't in it now: his father had not only relented but had virtually ordered him home. He was about twenty-two, she guessed. He could still plead successfully for parental help and for indulgence from women. She said, no more than affectionately, "I'm going to show you a very pretty room."

A few days later Dr. Blackley came alone to say goodbye.

"Are you really staying?" he asked.

"I am responsible for the last eighty-one years of this lease," said Netta. "I'm going to be thirty. It's a long tenure. Besides, I've got Jack's mother and she won't leave. Jack has a chance now to visit America. It doesn't sound sensible to me, but she writes encouraging him. She imagines him suddenly very rich and sending for her. I've discovered the limit of what you can feel about people. I've discovered something else," she said abruptly. "It is that sex and love have nothing in common. Only a coincidence, sometimes. You think the coincidence will go on and so you get married. I suppose that is what men are born knowing and women learn by accident."

"I'm su-horry."

"For God's sake, don't be. It's a relief."

She had no feeling of guilt, only of amazement. Jack, as a memory, was in a restricted area – the tennis courts, the card-room, the bar. She saw him at bridge with Mrs. Blackley and pouring drinks for temporary friends. He crossed the lounge jauntily with a cluster of little dark-haired girls wearing blue. In the mirrored bedroom there was only Netta. Her dreams were cleansed of him. The looking glasses still held their blue-and-silver-water shadows, but they lost the habit of giving back the moods and gestures of a Moslem wife.

About five years after this, Netta wrote to Jack. The war had caught him in America, during the voyage his mother had so wanted him to have. His limp had kept him out of the Army. As his mother (now dead) might have put it, all that reading had finally got him somewhere: he had spent the last years putting out a two-pager on aspects of European culture – part of a scrupulous effort Britain was making for the West. That was nearly all Netta knew. A Belgian Red Cross official had arrived, apparently in Jack's name, to see if she was still alive. She sat in her father's business room, wearing a coat and a shawl because there was no way of heating any part of the hotel now, and she tried to get on with the letter she had been writing in her head, on and off, for many years.

"In June, 1940, we were evacuated," she started, for the tenth or eleventh time. "I was back by October. Italians had taken over the hotel. They used the mirror behind the bar for target practice. Oddly enough it was not smashed. It is covered with spiderwebs, and the bullet hole is the spider. I had great trouble over Aunt Vera, who disappeared and was found finally in one of the attic rooms.

"The Italians made a pet of her. Took her picture. She enjoyed that. Everyone who became thin had a desire to be photographed, as if knowing they would use this intimidating evidence against those loved ones who had missed being starved. Guilt for life. After an initial period of hardship, during which she often had her picture taken at her request, the Italians brought food and looked after her, more than anyone. She was their mama. We were annexed territory and in time we had the same food as the Italians. The thin pictures of your mother are here on my desk.

"She buried her British passport and would never say where. Perhaps under the Judas tree with Mr. Cordier's cat, Polly. She remained just as mad and just as spoiled, and that became dangerous when life stopped being ordinary. She complained about me to the Italians. At that time a complaint was a matter of prison and of death if it was made to the wrong person. Luckily for me, there was also the right person to take the message.

"A couple of years after that, the Germans and certain French took over and the Italians were shut up in another hotel without food or water, and some people risked their well-being to take water to them (for not everyone preferred the new situation, you can believe me). When she was dying I asked her if she had a message for one Italian officer who had made such a pet of her and she said, 'No, why?' She died without a word for anybody. She was buried as 'Rossini,' because the Italians had changed people's names. She had said she was French, a Frenchwoman named Ross, and so some peculiar civil status was created for us – the two Mrs. Rossinis.

"The records were topsy-turvy; it would have meant going to the Germans and explaining my dead aunt was British, and of course I thought I would not. The death certificate and permission to bury are for a Vera Rossini. I have them here on my desk for you with her pictures.

"You are probably wondering where I have found all this

writing paper. The Germans left it behind. When we were being shelled I took what few books were left in the reading room down to what used to be the wine cellar and read by candlelight. You are probably wondering where the candles came from. A long story. I even have paint for the radiators, large buckets that have never been opened.

"I live in one room, my mother's old sitting room. The business room can be used but the files have gone. When the Italians were here your mother was their mother, but I was not their Moslem wife, although I still had respect for men. One yelled '*Luce, luce,*' because your mother was showing a light. She said, 'Bugger you, you little toad.' He said, 'Granny, I said "*luce,*" not "*Duce.*"'

"Not long ago we crept out of our shelled homes, looking like cave dwellers. When you see the hotel again, it will be functioning. I shall have painted the radiators. Long shoots of bramble come in through the cardroom windows. There are drifts of leaves in the old music room and I saw scorpions and heard their rustling like the rustle of death. Everything that could have been looted has gone. Sheets, bedding, mattresses. The neighbors did quite a lot of that. At the risk of their lives. When the Italians were here we had rice and oil. Your mother, who was crazy, used to put out grains to feed the mice.

"When the Germans came we had to live under Vichy law, which meant each region lived on what it could produce. As ours produces nothing, we got quite thin again. Aunt Vera died plump. Do you know what it means when I say she used to complain about me?

"Send me some books. As long as they are in English. I am quite sick of the three other languages in which I've heard so many threats, such boasting, such a lot of lying.

"For a time I thought people would like to know how the Italians left and the Germans came in. It was like this: They came in with the first car moving slowly, flying the French flag. The highest-ranking French official in the region. Not a

German. No, just a chap getting his job back. The Belgian Red Cross people were completely uninterested and warned me that no one would ever want to hear.

"I suppose that you already have the fiction of all this. The fiction must be different, oh very different, from Italians sobbing with homesickness in the night. The Germans were not real, they were specially got up for the events of the time. Sat in the white dining room, eating with whatever plates and spoons were not broken or looted, ate soups that were mostly water, were forbidden to complain. Only in retreat did they develop faces and I noticed then that some were terrified and many were old. A radio broadcast from some untouched area advised the local population not to attack them as they retreated, it would make wild animals of them. But they were attacked by some young boys shooting out of a window and eight hostages were taken, including the son of the man who cut the maharaja's daughters' black hair, and they were shot and left along the wall of a café on the more or less Italian side of the border. And the man who owned the café was killed too, but later, by civilians – he had given names to the Gestapo once, or perhaps it was something else. He got on the wrong side of the right side at the wrong time, and he was thrown down the deep gorge between the two frontiers.

"Up in one of the hill villages Germans stayed till no one was alive. I was at that time in the former wine cellar, reading books by candlelight.

"The Belgian Red Cross team found the skeleton of a German deserter in a cave and took back the helmet and skull to Knokke-le-Zoute as souvenirs.

"My war has ended. Our family held together almost from the Napoleonic adventures. It is shattered now. Sentiment does not keep families whole – only mutual pride and mutual money."

This true story sounded so implausible that she decided never to send it. She wrote a sensible letter asking for sugar and rice and for new books; nothing must be older than 1940.

Jack answered at once: there were no new authors (he had been asking people). Sugar was unobtainable, and there were queues for rice. Shoes had been rationed. There were no women's stockings but lisle, and the famous American legs looked terrible. You could not find butter or meat or tinned pineapple. In restaurants, instead of butter you were given miniature golf balls of cream cheese. He supposed that all this must sound like small beer to Netta.

A notice arrived that a CARE package awaited her at the post office. It meant that Jack had added his name and his money to a mailing list. She refused to sign for it; then she changed her mind and discovered it was not from Jack but from the American she had once taken to such a pretty room. Jack did send rice and sugar and delicious coffee but he forgot about books. His letters followed; sometimes three arrived in a morning. She left them sealed for days. When she sat down to answer, all she could remember were implausible things.

Iris came back. She was the first. She had grown puffy in England – the result of drinking whatever alcohol she could get her hands on and grimly eating her sweets allowance: there would be that much less gin and chocolate for the Germans if ever they landed. She put her now wide bottom on a comfortable armchair – one of the few chairs the first wave of Italians had not burned with cigarettes or idly hacked at with daggers – and said Jack had been living with a woman in America and to spare the gossip had let her be known as his wife. Another Mrs. Ross? When Netta discovered it was dimpled Chippendale, she laughed aloud.

"I've seen them," said Iris. "I mean I saw them together. King Charles and a spaniel. Jack wiped his feet on her."

Netta's feelings were of lightness, relief. She would not have to tell Jack about the partisans hanging by the neck in the arches of the Place Masséna at Nice. When Iris had finished talking, Netta said, "What about his music?"

"I don't know."

"How can you not know something so important?"

"Jack had a good chance at things, but he made a mess of everything," said Iris. "My father is still living. Life really is too incredible for some of us."

A dark girl of about twenty turned up soon after. Her costume, a gray dress buttoned to the neck, gave her the appearance of being in uniform. She unzipped a military-looking bag and cried, in an unplaceable accent, "*Ha*llo, *ha*llo, Mrs. Ross? A few small gifts for you," and unpacked a bottle of Haig, four tins of corned beef, a jar of honey, and six pairs of American nylon stockings, which Netta had never seen before, and were as good to have under a mattress as gold. Netta looked up at the tall girl.

"Remember? I was the middle sister. With," she said gravely, "the typical middle-sister problems." She scarcely recalled Jack, her beloved. The memory of Netta had grown up with her. "I remember you laughing," she said, without loving that memory. She was a severe, tragic girl. "You were the first adult I ever heard laughing. At night in bed I could hear it from your balcony. You sat smoking with, I suppose, your handsome husband. I used to laugh just to hear you."

She had married an Iranian journalist. He had discovered that political prisoners in the United States were working under lamentable conditions in tin mines. President Truman had sent them there. People from all over the world planned to unite to get them out. The girl said she had been to Germany and to Austria, she had visited camps, they were all alike, and that was already the past, and the future was the prisoners in the tin mines.

Netta said, "In what part of the country are these mines?"

The middle sister looked at her sadly and said, "Is there more than one part?"

For the first time in years, Netta could see Jack clearly. They were silently sharing a joke; he had caught it too. She and the girl lunched in a corner of the battered dining room. The tables were scarred with initials. There were no tablecloths. One of the great-uncle's paintings still hung on a wall. It showed the Quai Laurenti, a country road alongside the sea. Netta, who had no use for the past, was discovering a past she could regret. Out of a dark, gentle silence – silence imposed by the impossibility of telling anything real – she counted the cracks in the walls. When silence failed she heard power saws ripping into olive trees and a lemon grove. With a sense of deliverance she understood that soon there would be nothing left to spoil. Her great-uncle's picture, which ought to have changed out of sympathetic magic, remained faithful. She regretted everything now, even the three anxious little girls in blue linen. Every calamitous season between then and now seemed to descend directly from Georgina Blackley's having said "white" just to keep three children in their place. Clad in buttoned-up gray, the middle sister now picked at corned beef and said she had hated her father, her mother, her sisters, and most of all the Dutch governess.

"Where is she now?" said Netta.

"Dead, I hope." This was from someone who had visited camps. Netta sat listening, her cheek on her hand. Death made death casual: she had always known. Neither the vanquished in their flight nor the victors returning to pick over rubble seemed half so vindictive as a tragic girl who had disliked her governess.

Dr. Blackley came back looking positively cheerful. In those days men still liked soldiering. It made them feel young, if they needed to feel it, and it got them away from home. War made the break few men could make on their own. The doctor looked years younger, too, and very fit. His wife was not with him. She had survived everything, and the hardships she had undergone had completely restored her to health – which had made it easy for her husband to leave her. Actually, he had never gone back, except to wind up the matter.

"There are things about Georgina I respect and admire," he said, as husbands will say from a distance. His war had been in Malta. He had come here, as soon as he could, to the shelled, gnawed, tarnished coast (as if he had not seen enough at Malta) to ask Netta to divorce Jack and to marry him, or live with him – anything she wanted, on any terms.

But she wanted nothing – at least, not from him.

"Well, one can't defeat a memory," he said. "I always thought it was mostly su-hex between the two of you."

"So it was," said Netta. "So far as I remember."

"Everyone noticed. You would vanish at odd hours. Dis-huppear."

"Yes, we did."

"You can't live on memories," he objected. "Though I respect you for being faithful, of course."

"What you are talking about is something of which one has no specific memory," said Netta. "Only of seasons. Places. Rooms. It is as abstract to remember as to read about. That is why it is boring in talk except as a joke, and boring in books except for poetry."

"You never read poetry."

"I do now."

"I guessed that," he said.

"That lack of memory is why people are unfaithful, as it is so curiously called. When I see closed shutters I know there are lovers behind them. That is how the memory works. The rest is just convention and small talk."

"Why lovers? Why not someone sleeping off the wine he had for lunch?"

"No. Lovers."

"A middle-aged man cutting his toenails in the bathtub,"

he said with unexpected feeling. "Wearing bifocal lenses so that he can see his own feet."

"No, lovers. Always."

He said, "Have you missed him?"

"Missed who?"

"Who the bloody hell are we talking about?"

"The Italian commander billeted here. He was not a guest. He was here by force. I was not breaking a rule. Without him I'd have perished in every way. He may be home with his wife now. Or in that fortress near Turin where he sent other men. Or dead." She looked at the doctor and said, "Well, what would you like me to do? Sit here and cry?"

"I can't imagine you with a brute."

"I never said that."

"Do you miss him still?"

"The absence of Jack was like a cancer which I am sure has taken root, and of which I am bound to die," said Netta.

"You'll bu-hury us all," he said, as doctors tell the condemned.

"I haven't said I won't." She rose suddenly and straightened her skirt, as she used to do when hotel guests became pally. "Conversation over," it meant.

"Don't be too hard on Jack," he said.

"I am hard on myself," she replied.

After he had gone he sent her a parcel of books, printed on grayish paper, in warped wartime covers. All of the titles were, to Netta, unknown. There was *Fireman Flower* and *The Horse's Mouth* and *Four Quartets* and *The Stuff to Give the Troops* and *Better Than a Kick in the Pants* and *Put Out More Flags*. A note added that the next package would contain Henry Green and Dylan Thomas. She guessed he would not want to be thanked, but she did so anyway. At the end of her letter was "Please remember, if you mind too much, that I said no to you once before." Leaning on the bar, exactly as Jack used to, with a glass of the middle sister's drink at hand, she opened *Better Than a Kick in the Pants* and read, ". . . two Fascists came in, one of them tall and thin and tough looking; the other smaller, with only one arm and an empty sleeve pinned up to his shoulder. Both of them were quite young and wore black shirts."

Oh, thought Netta, I am the only one who knows all this. No one will ever realize how much I know of the truth, the truth, the truth, and she put her head on her hands, her elbows on the scarred bar, and let the first tears of her after-war run down her wrists.

The last to return was the one who should have been first. Jack wrote that he was coming down from the north as far as Nice by bus. It was a common way of travelling and much cheaper than by train. Netta guessed that he was mildly hard up and that he had saved nothing from his war job. The bus came in at six, at the foot of the Place Masséna. There was a deep-blue late-afternoon sky and pale sunlight. She could hear birds from the public gardens nearby. The Place was as she had always seen it, like an elegant drawing room with a blue ceiling. It was nearly empty. Jack looked out on this sunlighted, handsome space and said, "Well, I'll just leave my stuff at the bus office, for the moment" – perhaps noticing that Netta had not invited him anywhere. He placed his ticket on the counter, and she saw that he had not come from far away: he must have been moving south by stages. He carried an aura of London pub life; he had been in London for weeks.

A frowning man hurrying to wind things up so he could have his first drink of the evening said, "The office is closing and we don't keep baggage here."

"People used to be nice," Jack said.

"Bus people?"

"Just people."

She was hit by the sharp change in his accent. As for the

way of speaking, which is something else again, he was like the heir to great estates back home after a Grand Tour. Perhaps the estates had run down in his absence. She slipped the frowning man a thousand francs, a new pastel-tinted bill, on which the face of a calm girl glowed like an opal. She said, "We shan't be long."

She set off over the Place, walking diagonally – Jack beside her, of course. He did not ask where they were headed, though he did make her smile by saying, "Did you bring a car?," expecting one of the hotel cars to be parked nearby, perhaps with a driver to open the door; perhaps with cold chicken and wine in a hamper, too. He said, "I'd forgotten about having to tip for every little thing." He did not question his destination, which was no farther than a café at the far end of the square. What she felt at that instant was intense revulsion. She thought, I don't want him, and pushed away some invisible flying thing – a bat or a blown paper. He looked at her with surprise. He must have been wondering if hardship had taught Netta to talk in her mind.

This is it, the freedom he was always offering me, she said to herself, smiling up at the beautiful sky.

They moved slowly along the nearly empty square, pausing only when some worn-out Peugeot or an old bicycle, finding no other target, made a swing in their direction. Safely on the pavement, they walked under the arches where partisans had been hanged. It seemed to Netta the bodies had been taken down only a day or so before. Jack, who knew about this way of dying from hearsay, chose a café table nearly under a poor lad's bound, dangling feet.

"I had a woman next to me on the bus who kept a hedgehog all winter in a basketful of shavings," he said. "He can drink milk out of a wineglass." He hesitated. "I'm sorry about the books you asked for. I was sick of books by then. I was sick of rhetoric and culture and patriotic crap."

"I suppose it is all very different over there," said Netta.

"God, yes."

He seemed to expect her to ask questions, so she said, "What kind of clothes do they wear?"

"They wear quite a lot of plaids and tartans. They eat at peculiar hours. You'll see them eating strawberries and cream just when you're thinking of having a drink."

She said, "Did you visit the tin mines, where Truman sends his political prisoners?"

"*Tin* mines?" said Jack. "No."

"Remember the three little girls from the maharaja trade?"

Neither could quite hear what the other had to say. They were partially deaf to each other.

Netta continued softly, "Now, as I understand it, she first brought an American to London, and then she took an Englishman to America."

He had too much the habit of women, he was playing too close a game, to waste points saying, "Who? What?"

"It was over as fast as it started," he said. "But then the war came and we were stuck. She became a friend," he said. "I'm quite fond of her" — which Netta translated as, "It is a subterranean river that may yet come to light." "You wouldn't know her," he said. "She's very different now. I talked so much about the south, down here, she finally found some land going dirt cheap at Bandol. The mayor arranged for her to have an orchard next to her property, so she won't have neighbors. It hardly cost her anything. He said to her, 'You're very pretty.'"

"No one ever had a bargain in property because of a pretty face," said Netta.

"Wasn't it lucky," said Jack. He could no longer hear himself, let alone Netta. "The war was unsettling, being in America. She minded not being active. Actually she was using the Swiss passport, which made it worse. Her brother was killed over Bremen. She needs security now. In a way it was sorcerer and apprentice between us, and she suddenly grew up. She'll be better off with a roof over her head. She writes a little now.

Her poetry isn't bad," he said, as if Netta had challenged its quality.

"Is she at Bandol now, writing poetry?"

"Well, no." He laughed suddenly. "There isn't a roof yet. And, you know, people don't sit writing that way. They just think they're going to."

"Who has replaced you?" said Netta. "Another sorcerer?"

"Oh, *he* . . . he looks like George II in a strong light. Or like Queen Anne. Queen Anne and Lady Mary, somebody called them." Iris, that must have been. Queen Anne and Lady Mary wasn't bad – better than King Charles and his spaniel. She was beginning to enjoy his story. He saw it, and said lightly, "I was too preoccupied with you to manage another life. I couldn't see myself going on and on away from you. I didn't want to grow middle-aged at odds with myself."

But he had lost her; she was enjoying a reverie about Jack now, wearing one of those purple sunburns people acquire at golf. She saw him driving an open car, with large soft freckles on his purple skull. She saw his mistress's dog on the front seat and the dog's ears flying like pennants. The revulsion she felt did not lend distance but brought a dreamy reality closer still. He must be thirty-four now, she said to herself. A terrible age for a man who has never imagined thirty-four.

"Well, perhaps you have made a mess of it," she said, quoting Iris.

"What mess? I'm here. *He* –"

"Queen Anne?"

"Yes, well, actually Gerald is his name; he wears nothing but brown. Brown suit, brown tie, brown shoes. I said, '*He* can't go to Mitten Todd. He won't match.'"

"Harmonize," she said.

"That's it. Harmonize with the –"

"What about Gerald's wife? I'm sure he has one."

"Lucretia."

"No, really?"

"On my honor. When I last saw them they were all together, talking."

Netta was remembering what the middle sister had said about laughter on the balcony. She couldn't look at him. The merest crossing of glances made her start laughing rather wildly into her hands. The hysterical quality of her own laughter caught her in midair. What were they talking about? He hitched his chair nearer and dared to take her wrist.

"Tell me, now," he said, as if they were to be two old confidence men getting their stories straight. "What about you? Was there ever . . ." The glaze of laughter had not left his face and voice. She saw that he would make her his business, if she let him. Pulling back, she felt another clasp, through a wall of fog. She groped for this other, invisible hand, but it dissolved. It was a lost, indifferent hand; it no longer recognized her warmth. She understood: He is dead . . . Jack, closed to ghosts, deaf to their voices, was spared this. He would be spared everything, she saw. She envied him his imperviousness, his true unhysterical laughter.

Perhaps that's why I kicked him, she said. I was always jealous. Not of women. Of his short memory, his comfortable imagination. And I am going to be thirty-seven and I have a dark, an accurate, a deadly memory.

He still held her wrist and turned it another way, saying, "Look, there's paint on it."

"Oh, God, where is the waiter?" she cried, as if that were the one important thing. Jack looked his age, exactly. She looked like a burned-out child who had been told a ghost story. Desperately seeking the waiter, she turned to the café behind them and saw the last light of the long afternoon strike the mirror above the bar – a flash in a tunnel; hands juggling with fire. That unexpected play, at a remove, borne indoors, displayed to anyone who could stare without blinking, was a complete story. It was the brightness on the looking glass, the only part of a life, or a love, or a promise, that could never be concealed, changed, or corrupted.

Not a hope, she was trying to tell him. He could read her face now. She reminded herself, If I say it, I am free. I can finish painting the radiators in peace. I can read every book in the world. If I had relied on my memory for guidance, I would never have crept out of the wine cellar. Memory is what ought to prevent you from buying a dog after the first dog dies, but it never does. It should at least keep you from saying yes twice to the same person.

"I've always loved you," he chose to announce – it really was an announcement, in a new voice that stated nothing except facts.

The dark, the ghosts, the candlelight, her tears on the scarred bar – *they* were real. And still, whether she wanted to see it or not, the light of imagination danced all over the square. She did not dare to turn again to the mirror, lest she confuse the two and forget which light was real. A pure white awning on a cross street seemed to her to be of indestructible beauty. The window it sheltered was hollowed with sadness and shadow. She said with the same deep sadness, "I believe you." The wave of revulsion receded, sucked back under another wave – a powerful adolescent craving for something simple, such as true love.

Her face did not show this. It was set in adolescent stubbornness, and this was one of their old, secret meetings when, sullen and hurt, she had to be coaxed into life as Jack wanted it lived. It was the same voyage, at the same rate of speed. The Place seemed to her to be full of invisible traffic – first a whisper of tires, then a faint, high screeching, then a steady roar. If Jack heard anything, it could be only the blood in the veins and his loud, happy thought. To a practical romantic like Jack, dying to get Netta to bed right away, what she was hearing was only the uh-hebb and flo-ho of hormones, as Dr. Blackley said. She caught a look of amazement on his face: *Now* he knew what he had been deprived of. *Now* he remembered. It had been Netta, all along.

Their evening shadows accompanied them over the long square. "I still have a car," she remarked. "But no petrol. There's a train." She did keep on hearing a noise, as of heavy traffic rushing near and tearing away. Her own quiet voice carried across it, saying, "Not a hope." He must have heard that. Why, it was as loud as a shout. He held her arm lightly. He was as buoyant as morning. This *was* his morning – the first light on the mirror, the first cigarette. He pulled her into an archway where no one could see. What could I do, she asked her ghosts, but let my arm be held, my steps be guided?

Later, Jack said that the walk with Netta back across the Place Masséna was the happiest event of his life. Having no reliable counter-event to put in its place, she let the memory stand.

1976

Grippes and Poche

AT AN EARLY hour for the French man of letters Henri
Grippes – it was a quarter to nine, on an April morning –
he sat in a windowless, brown-painted cubicle, facing a slight,
mop-headed young man with horn-rimmed glasses and
dimples. The man wore a dark tie with a narrow knot and a
buttoned-up blazer. His signature was "O. Poche"; his title, on
the grubby, pulpy summons Grippes had read, sweating, was
"Controller." He must be freshly out of his civil-service training school, Grippes guessed. Even his aspect, of a priest hearing a confession a few yards from the guillotine, seemed newly
acquired. Before him lay open a dun-colored folder with not
much in it – a letter from Grippes, full of delaying tactics, and
copies of his correspondence with a bank in California. It was
not true that American banks protected a depositor's secrets;
anyway, this one hadn't. Another reason Grippes thought O.
Poche must be recent was the way he kept blushing. He was
not nearly as pale or as case-hardened as Grippes.

At this time, President de Gaulle had been in power five
years, two of which Grippes had spent in blithe writer-in-
residenceship in California. Returning to Paris, he had left
a bank account behind. It was forbidden, under the Fifth
Republic, for a French citizen to have a foreign account. The
government might not have cared so much about drachmas

or zlotys, but dollars were supposed to be scraped in, converted to francs at bottom rate, and, of course, counted as personal income. Grippes' unwise and furtive moves with trifling sums, his somewhat paranoid disagreements with California over exchange, had finally caught the eye of the Bank of France, as a glistening minnow might attract a dozing whale. The whale swallowed Grippes, found him too small to matter, and spat him out, straight into the path of a water ox called Public Treasury, Direct Taxation, Personal Income. That was Poche.

What Poche had to discuss – a translation of Grippes' novel, the one about the French teacher at the American university and his doomed love affair with his student, Karen-Sue – seemed to embarrass him. Observing Poche with some curiosity, Grippes saw, unreeling, scenes from the younger man's inhibited boyhood. He sensed, then discerned, the Catholic boarding school in bleakest Brittany: the unheated forty-bed dormitory, a nightly torment of unchaste dreams with astonishing partners, a daytime terror of real Hell with real fire.

"Human waywardness is hardly new," said Grippes, feeling more secure now that he had tested Poche and found him provincial. "It no longer shocks anyone."

It was not the moral content of the book he wished to talk over, said Poche, flaming. In any case, he was not qualified to do so: he had flubbed Philosophy and never taken Modern French Thought. (He must be new, Grippes decided. He was babbling.) Frankly, even though he had the figures in front of him, Poche found it hard to believe the American translation had earned its author so little. There must be another considerable sum, placed in some other bank. Perhaps M. Grippes could try to remember.

The figures were true. The translation had done poorly. Failure played to Grippes' advantage, reducing the hint of deliberate tax evasion to a simple oversight. Still, it hurt to have things put so plainly. He felt bound to tell Poche that American readers were no longer interested in the teacher-student imbroglio, though there had been some slight curiosity as to what a foreigner might wring out of the old sponge.

Poche gazed at Grippes. His eyes seemed to Grippes as helpless and eager as those of a gun dog waiting for a command in the right language. Encouraged, Grippes said more: in writing his novel, he had overlooked the essential development – the erring professor was supposed to come home at the end. He could be half dead, limping, on crutches, toothless, jobless, broke, impotent – it didn't matter. He had to be judged and shriven. As further mortification, his wife during his foolish affair would have gone on to be a world-class cellist, under her maiden name. "Wife" had not entered Grippes' cast of characters, probably because, like Poche, he did not have one. (He had noticed Poche did not wear a wedding ring.) Grippes had just left his professor driving off to an airport in blessed weather, whistling a jaunty air.

Poche shook his head. Obviously, it was not the language he was after. He began to write on a clean page of the file, taking no more notice of Grippes.

What a mistake it had been, Grippes reflected, still feeling pain beneath the scar, to have repeated the male teacher–female student pattern. He should have turned it around, identified himself with a brilliant and cynical woman teacher. Unfortunately, unlike Flaubert (his academic stalking-horse), he could not put himself in a woman's place, probably because he thought it an absolutely terrible place to be. The novel had not done well in France, either. (Poche had still to get round to that.) The critics had found Karen-Sue's sociological context obscure. She seemed at a remove from events of her time, unaware of improved literacy figures in North Korea, never once mentioned, or that since the advent of Gaullism it cost twenty-five centimes to mail a letter. The Pill was still unheard of in much of Europe; readers could not understand what it was Karen-Sue kept forgetting to take, or why Grippes had devoted a contemplative no-action chapter to the abstract essence of risk. The professor had not given Karen-Sue the cultural and political enlightenment one might expect from the graduate of a pre-eminent Paris school. It was a banal story, really, about a pair of complacently bourgeois lovers. The real victim was Grippes, seduced and abandoned by the American middle class.

It was Grippes' first outstanding debacle and, for that reason, the only one of his works he ever reread. He could still hear Karen-Sue – the true, the original – making of every avowal a poignant question: "I'm Cairn-Sioux? I know you're busy? It's just that I don't understand what you said about Flaubert and his own niece?" He recalled her with tolerance – the same tolerance that had probably weakened the book.

Grippes was wise enough to realize that the California-bank affair had been an act of folly, a con man's aberration. He had thought he would get away with it, knowing all the while he could not. There existed a deeper treasure for Poche to uncover, well below Public Treasury sights. Computers had not yet come into government use; even typewriters were rare – Poche had summoned Grippes in a cramped, almost secretive hand. It took time to strike an error, still longer to write a letter about it. In his youth, Grippes had received from an American patroness of the arts three rent-bearing apartments in Paris, which he still owned. (The patroness had been the last of a generous species, Grippes one of the last young men to benefit from her kind.) He collected the rents by devious and untraceable means, stowing the cash obtained in safe deposit. His visible way of life was stoic and plain; not even the most vigilant Controller could fault his underfurnished apartment in Montparnasse, shared with some cats he had already tried to claim as dependents. He showed none of the signs of prosperity Public Treasury seemed to like, such as membership in a golf club.

After a few minutes of speculative anguish in the airless cubicle, Grippes saw that Poche had no inkling whatever about the flats. He was chasing something different – the inexistent royalties from the Karen-Sue novel. By a sort of divine evenhandedness, Grippes was going to have to pay for imaginary earnings. He put the safe deposit out of his mind, so that it would not show on his face, and said, "What will be left for me, when you've finished adding and subtracting?"

To his surprise, Poche replied in a bold tone, pitched for reciting quotations: "'What is left? What is left? Only what remains at low tide, when small islands are revealed, emerging . . .'" He stopped quoting and flushed. Obviously, he had committed the worst sort of blunder, had been intimate, had let his own personality show. He had crossed over to his opponent's ground.

"It sounds familiar," said Grippes, enticing him further. "Although, to tell the truth, I don't remember writing it."

"It is a translation," said Poche. "The Anglo-Saxon British author, Victor Prism." He pronounced it "Prissom."

"You've read Prism?" said Grippes, pronouncing correctly the name of an old acquaintance.

"I had to. Prissom was on the preparatory program. Anglo-Saxon Commercial English."

"They stuffed you with foreign writers?" said Grippes. "With so many of us having to go to foreign lands for a living?"

That was perilous: he had just challenged Poche's training, the very foundation of his right to sit there reading Grippes' private mail. But he had suddenly recalled his dismay when as a young man he had looked at a shelf in his room and realized he had to compete with the dead – Proust, Flaubert, Balzac, Stendhal, and on into the dark. The rivalry was infinite, a Milky Way of dead stars still daring to shine. He had invented a law, a moratorium on publication that would eliminate the dead, leaving the skies clear for the living. (All the living? Grippes still couldn't decide.) Foreign writers would be deported to a remote solar system, where they could circle one another.

For Prism, there was no system sufficiently remote. Not so long ago, interviewed in *The Listener*, Prism had dragged in Grippes, saying that he used to cross the Channel to consult a seer in Half Moon Street, hurrying home to set down the prose revealed from a spirit universe. "Sometimes I actually envied him," Prism was quoted as saying. He sounded as though Grippes were dead. "I used to wish ghost voices would speak to me, too," suggesting ribbons of pure Prism running like ticker tape round the equator of a crystal ball. "Unfortunately, I had to depend on my own creative intelligence, modest though I am sure it was."

Poche did not know about this recent libel in Anglo-Saxon Commercial English. He had been trying to be nice. Grippes made a try of his own, jocular: "I only meant, you could have been reading *me*." The trouble was that he meant it, ferociously.

Poche must have heard the repressed shout. He shut the file and said, "This dossier is too complex for my level. I shall have to send it up to the Inspector." Grippes made a vow that he would never let natural pique get the better of him again.

"What will be left for me?" Grippes asked the Inspector. "When you have finished adding and subtracting?"

Mme. de Pelle did not bother to look up. She said, "Somebody should have taken this file in hand a long time ago. Let us start at the beginning. How long, in all, were you out of the country?"

When Poche said "send up," he'd meant it literally. Grippes looked out on a church where Delacroix had worked and the slow summer rain. At the far end of the square, a few dark shops displayed joyfully trashy religious goods, like the cross set with tiny seashells Mme. de Pelle wore round her neck. Grippes had been raised in an anticlerical household, in a small town where opposing factions were grouped behind the schoolmaster – Grippes' father – and the parish priest. Women, lapsed agnostics, sometimes crossed enemy lines and started going to church. One glimpsed them, all in gray, creeping along a gray-walled street.

"You are free to lodge a protest against the fine," said Mme. de Pelle. "But if you lose the contestation, your fine will be tripled. That is the law."

Grippes decided to transform Mme. de Pelle into the manager of a brothel catering to the Foreign Legion, slovenly in her habits and addicted to chloroform, but he found the idea unpromising. In due course he paid a monstrous penalty, which he did not contest, for fear of drawing attention to the apartments. (It was still believed that he had stashed away millions from the Karen-Sue book, probably in Switzerland.) A summons addressed in O. Poche's shrunken hand, the following spring, showed Grippes he had been tossed back downstairs. After that he forgot about Mme. de Pelle, except now and then.

It was at about this time that a series of novels offered themselves to Grippes – shadowy outlines behind a frosted-glass pane. He knew he must not let them crowd in all together, or keep them waiting too long. His foot against the door, he admitted, one by one, a number of shadows that turned into young men, each bringing his own name and address, his native region of France portrayed on color postcards, and an index of information about his tastes in clothes, love, food, and philosophers, his bent of character, his tics of speech, his attitudes toward God and money, his political bias, and the intimation of a crisis about to explode underfoot. "Antoine" provided a Jesuit confessor, a homosexual affinity, and loss of faith. Spiritual shilly-shallying tends to run long; Antoine's covered more than six hundred pages, making it the thickest work in the Grippes canon. Then came "Thomas," with his Spartan mother on a Provençal fruit farm, rejected in favor of a civil-service career. "Bertrand" followed, adrift in frivolous Paris, tempted by neo-Fascism in the form of a woman wearing a bedjacket trimmed with marabou. "René" cycled round France, reading Chateaubriand when he stopped to rest. One morning he set fire to the barn he had been sleeping in, leaving his books to burn. This was the shortest of the novels, and the most popular with the young. One critic scolded Grippes for using crude symbolism. Another begged him to stop hiding behind "Antoine" and "René" and to take the metaphysical risk of revealing "Henri." But Grippes had tried that once with Karen-Sue, then with a roman à clef mercifully destroyed in the confusion of May, 1968. He took these contretemps for a sign that he was to leave the subjective Grippes alone. The fact that each novel appeared even to Grippes to be a slice of French writing about life as it had been carved up and served a generation before made it seem quietly insurrectional. Nobody was doing this now; no one but Grippes. Grippes, for a time uneasy, decided to go on letting the shadows in.

The announcement of a new publication would bring a summons from Poche. When Poche leaned over the file, now, Grippes saw amid the mop of curls a coin-sized tonsure. His diffident, steely questions tried to elicit from Grippes how many copies were likely to be sold and where Grippes had already put the money. Grippes would give him a copy of the book, inscribed. Poche would turn back the cover and glance at the signature, probably to make certain Grippes had not written something compromising and friendly. He kept the novels in a metal locker, fastened together with government-issue webbing tape and a military-looking buckle. It troubled Grippes to think of his work all in a bundle, in the dark. He thought of old-fashioned milestones, half hidden by weeds, along disused roads. The volumes marked time for Poche, too. He was still a Controller. Perhaps he had to wait for the woman upstairs to retire, so he could take over her title and

office. The cubicle needed paint. There was a hole in the
brown linoleum, just inside the door. Poche now wore a wedding ring. Grippes wondered if he should congratulate him,
but decided to let Poche mention the matter first. He tried to
imagine Mme. Poche.

Grippes could swear that in his string of novels nothing had
been chipped out of his own past. Antoine, Thomas, Bertrand, and René (and, by now, Clément, Didier, Laurent,
Hugues, and Yves) had arrived as strangers, almost like histor-
ical figures. At the same time, it seemed to Grippes that their
wavering, ruffled reflection should deliver something he
alone might recognize. What did he see, bending over the
pond of his achievement? He saw a character close-mouthed,
cautious, unimaginative, ill at ease, obsessed with particulars.
Worse, he was closed against progress, afraid of reform, shut
into a literary, reactionary France. How could this be? Grippes
had always and sincerely voted left. He had proved he could be
reckless, open-minded, indulgent. He was like a father gazing
round the breakfast table and suddenly realizing that none of
the children are his. His children, if he could call them that,
did not even look like him. From Antoine to Yves, his reflected
character was small and slight, with a mop of curly hair, horn-
rimmed glasses, and dimples.

Grippes believed in the importance of errors. No political
system, no love affair, no native inclination, no life itself
would be tolerable without a wide mesh for mistakes to slip
through. It pleased him that Public Treasury had never
caught up with the three apartments – not just for the sake of
the cash piling up in safe deposit but for the black hole of
error revealed. He and Poche had been together for some
years – another blunder. Usually Controller and taxpayer
were torn apart after a meeting or two, so that the revenue
service would not start taking into consideration the client's
aged indigent aunt, his bill for dental surgery, his alimony

payments, his perennial mortgage. But possibly no one except Poche could be bothered with Grippes, always making some time-wasting claim for minute professional expenses, backed by a messy-looking certified receipt. Sometimes Grippes dared believe Poche admired him, that he hung on to the dossier out of devotion to his books. (This conceit was intensified when Poche began calling him "*Maître.*") Once, Grippes won some City of Paris award and was shown in *France-Soir* shaking hands with the mayor and simultaneously receiving a long, check-filled envelope. Immediately summoned by Poche, expecting a discreet compliment, Grippes found him interested only in the caption under the photo, which made much of the size of the check. Grippes later thought of sending a sneering letter – "Thank you for your warm congratulations" – but he decided in time it was wiser not to fool with Poche. Poche had recently given him a thirty-three-per-cent personal exemption, three per cent more than the outer limit for Grippes' category of unsalaried earners – according to Poche, a group that included, as well as authors, door-to-door salesmen and prostitutes.

The dun-colored Gaullist-era jacket on Grippes' file had worn out long ago and been replaced, in 1969, by a cover in cool banker's green. Green presently made way for a shiny black-and-white marbled effect, reflecting the mood of opulence of the early seventies. Called in for his annual springtime confession, Grippes remarked about the folder: "Culture seems to have taken a decisive turn."

Poche did not ask what culture. He continued bravely, "Food for the cats, *Maître.* We *can't.*"

"They depend on me," said Grippes. But they had already settled the cats-as-dependents question once and for all. Poche drooped over Grippes' smudged and unreadable figures. Grippes tried to count the number of times he had examined the top of Poche's head. He still knew nothing about

Poche, except for the wedding ring. Somewhere along the way, Poche had tied himself to a need for retirement pay and rich exemptions of his own. In the language of his generation, Poche was a fully structured individual. His vocabulary was sparse and to the point, centered on a single topic. His state training school, the machine that ground out Pelles and Poches all sounding alike, was in Clermont-Ferrand. Grippes was born in the same region. That might have given them something else to talk about, except that Grippes had never been back. Structured Poche probably attended class reunions, was godfather to classmates' children, jotted their birthdays in a leather-covered notebook he never mislaid. Unstructured Grippes could not even remember his own age.

Poche turned over a sheet of paper, read something Grippes could not see, and said, automatically, "We *can't*."

"Nothing is ever as it was," said Grippes, still going on about the marbled-effect folder. It was a remark that usually shut people up, leaving them nowhere to go but a change of subject. Besides, it was true. Nothing can be as it was. Poche and Grippes had just lost a terrifying number of brain cells. They were an instant closer to death. Death was of no interest to Poche. If he ever thought he might cease to exist, he would stop concentrating on other people's business and get down to reading Grippes while there was still time. Grippes wanted to ask, "Do you ever imagine your own funeral?," but it might have been taken as a threatening, gangsterish hint from taxpayer to Controller – worse, far worse, than an attempted bribe.

A folder of a pretty mottled-peach shade appeared. Poche's cubicle was painted soft beige, the torn linoleum repaired. Poche sat in a comfortable armchair resembling the wide leathery seats in smart furniture stores at the upper end of Boulevard Saint-Germain. Grippes had a new, straight metallic chair that shot him bolt upright and hurt his spine. It was the heyday of the Giscardian period, when it seemed more important to keep the buttons polished than to watch where the regiment was heading. Grippes and Poche had not advanced one inch toward each other. Except for the paint and the chairs and "*Maître*," it could have been 1963. No matter how many works were added to the bundle in the locker, no matter how often Grippes had his picture taken, no matter how many Grippes paperbacks blossomed on airport bookstalls, Grippes to Poche remained a button.

The mottled-peach jacket began to darken and fray. Poche said to Grippes, "I asked you to come here, *Maître*, because I find we have overlooked something concerning your income." Grippes' heart gave a lurch. "The other day I came across an old ruling about royalties. How much of your income do you kick back?"

"Excuse me?"

"To publishers, to bookstores," said Poche. "How much?"

"Kick back?"

"What percentage?" said Poche. "Publishers. Printers."

"You mean," said Grippes, after a time, "how much do I pay editors to edit, publishers to publish, printers to print, and booksellers to sell?" He supposed that to Poche such a scheme might sound plausible. It would fit his long view over Grippes' untidy life. Grippes knew most of the literary gossip that went round about himself; the circle was so small that it had to come back. In most stories there was a virus of possibility, but he had never heard anything as absurd as this, or as base.

Poche opened the file, concealing the moldering cover, apparently waiting for Grippes to mention a figure. The nausea Grippes felt he put down to his having come here without breakfast. One does not insult a Controller. He had shouted silently at Poche, years before, and had been sent upstairs to do penance with Mme. de Pelle. It is not good to kick over a chair and stalk out. "I have never been so insulted!" might have no meaning from Grippes, keelhauled month after month in one lumpy review or another. As his works increased from bundle to heap, so they drew intellectual abuse. He welcomed partisan ill-treatment, as warming to him as popular praise. Don't forget me, Grippes silently prayed, standing at the periodicals table in La Hune, the Left Bank bookstore, looking for his own name in those quarterlies no one ever takes home. Don't praise me. Praise is weak stuff. Praise me after I'm dead.

But even the most sour and despairing and close-printed essays were starting to mutter acclaim. The shoreline of the eighties, barely in sight, was ready to welcome Grippes, who had re-established the male as hero, whose left-wing heartbeat could be heard, loyally thumping, behind the armor of his right-wing traditional prose. His re-established hero had curly hair, soft eyes, horn-rimmed glasses, dimples, and a fully structured life. He was pleasing to both sexes and to every type of reader, except for a few thick-ribbed louts. Grippes looked back at Poche, who did not know how closely they were bound. What if he were to say, "This is a preposterous insinuation, a blot on a noble profession and on my reputation in particular," only to have Poche answer, "Too bad, *Maître* – I was trying to help"? He said, as one good-natured fellow to another, "Well, what if I own up to this crime?"

"It's no crime," said Poche. "I simply add the amount to your professional expenses."

"To my rebate?" said Grippes. "To my exemption?"

"It depends on how much."

"A third of my income?" said Grippes, insanely. "Half?"

"A reasonable figure might be twelve and a half per cent."

All this for Grippes. Poche wanted nothing. Grippes considered with awe the only uncorruptible element in a porous society. No secret message had passed between them. He could not even invite Poche to lunch. He wondered if this arrangement had ever actually existed – if there could possibly be a good dodge that he, Grippes, had never heard of. He thought of contemporary authors for whose success there could be no other explanation: it had to be celestial playfulness or twelve and a half per cent. The structure, as Grippes was already calling it, might also just be Poche's innocent, indecent idea about writers.

Poche was reading the file again, though he must have known everything in it by heart. He was as absorbed, as contented, and somehow as pure as a child with a box of paints. At any moment he would raise his tender, bewildered eyes and murmur, "Four dozen typewriter ribbons in a third of the fiscal year, *Maître*? We *can't*."

Grippes tried to compose a face for Poche to encounter, a face above reproach. But writers considered above reproach always looked moody and haggard, about to scream. "Be careful," he was telling himself. "Don't let Poche think he's doing you a favor. These people set traps." Was Poche angling for something? Was this bait? "Attempting to bribe a public servant" the accusation was called. "Bribe" wasn't the word: it was "corruption" the law mentioned – "an attempt to corrupt." All Grippes had ever offered Poche was his books, formally inscribed, as though Poche were an anonymous reader standing in line in a bookstore where Grippes, wedged behind a shaky table, sat signing away. "Your name?" "Whose name?" "How do you spell your name?" "Oh, the book isn't for me. It's for a friend of mine." His look changed to one of severity and impatience, until he remembered that Poche had never asked him to sign anything. He had never concealed his purpose, to pluck from Grippes' plumage every bright feather he could find.

"Careful," Grippes repeated. "Careful. Remember what happened to Prism."

Victor Prism, keeping pale under a parasol on the beach at Torremolinos, had made the acquaintance of a fellow-Englishman – pleasant, not well educated but eager to learn, blistered shoulders, shirt draped over his head, pages of the

Sunday Express round his red thighs. Prism lent him some-thing to read – his sunburn was keeping him awake. It was a creative essay on three émigré authors of the nineteen-thirties, in a review so obscure and ill-paying that Prism had not bothered to include the fee on his income-tax return. (Prism had got it wrong, of course, having Thomas Mann – whose plain name Prism could not spell – go to East Germany and with his wife start a theatre that presented his own plays, sending Stefan Zweig to be photographed with movie stars in California, and putting Bertolt Brecht to die a bitter man in self-imposed exile in Brazil. As it turned out, none of Prism's readers knew the difference. Chided by Grippes, Prism had been defensive, cold, said that no letters had come in. "One, surely?" said Grippes. "Yes, I thought that must be you," Prism said.)

Prism might have got off with the whole thing if his new friend had not fallen sound asleep after the first lines. Waking, refreshed, he had said to himself, "I must find out what they get paid for this stuff," a natural reflex – he was of the Inland Revenue. He'd found no trace, no record; for Inland Revenue purposes "Death and Exile" did not exist. The subsequent fine was so heavy and Prism's disgrace so acute that he fled Eng-land to spend a few days with Grippes and the cats in Montparnasse. He sat on a kitchen chair while Grippes, nose and mouth protected by a checked scarf, sprayed terror to cockroaches. Prism, weeping in the fumes and wiping his eyes, said, "I'm through with Queen and Country" – some-thing like that – "and I'm taking out French citizenship tomorrow."

"You would have to marry a Frenchwoman and have at least five male children," said Grippes, through the scarf. He was feeling the patriotic hatred of a driver on a crowded road seeing foreign license plates in the way.

"Oh, well, then," said Prism, as if to say, "I won't bother."

"Oh, well, then," said Grippes, softly, not quite to Poche.

Poche added one last thing to the file and closed it, as if something definite had taken place. He clasped his hands and placed them on the dossier; it seemed shut for all time now, like a grave. He said, "*Maître*, one never stays long in the same fiscal theatre. I have been in this one for an unusual length of time. We may not meet again. I want you to know I have enjoyed our conversations."

"So have I," said Grippes, with caution.

"Much of your autobiographical creation could apply to other lives of our time, believe me."

"So you have read them," said Grippes, an eye on the locker.

"I read those I bought," said Poche.

"But they are the same books."

"No. The books I bought belong to me. The others were gifts. I would never open a gift. I have no right to." His voice rose, and he spoke more slowly. "In one of them, when What's-His-Name struggles to prepare his civil-service tests, '. . . the desire for individual glory seemed so inapposite, suddenly, in a nature given to renunciation.'"

"I suppose it *is* a remarkable observation," said Grippes. "I was not referring to myself." He had no idea what that could be from, and he was certain he had not written it.

Poche did not send for Grippes again. Grippes became a commonplace taxpayer, filling out his forms without help. The frosted-glass door was reverting to dull white; there were fewer shadows for Grippes to let in. A fashion for having well-behaved Nazi officers shore up Western culture gave Grippes a chance to turn Poche into a tubercular poet, trapped in Paris by poverty and the Occupation. Grippes threw out the first draft, in which Poche joined a Christian-minded Resistance network and performed a few simple miracles, unaware of his own powers. He had the instinctive feeling that a new generation would not know what he was talking about. Instead, he placed Poche, sniffling and wheezing, in a squalid hotel room, cough pastilles spilled on the table, a stained blanket pinned round his shoulders. Up the fetid staircase came a handsome colonel, a Curt Jurgens type, smelling of shaving lotion, bent on saving liberal values, bringing Poche butter, cognac, and a thousand sheets of writing paper.

After that, Grippes no longer felt sure where to go. His earlier books, government tape and buckle binding them into an œuvre, had accompanied Poche to his new fiscal theatre. Perhaps, finding his career blocked by the woman upstairs, he had asked for early retirement. Poche was in a gangster-ridden Mediterranean city, occupying a shoddy boom-period apartment he'd spent twenty years paying for. He was working at black-market jobs, tax adviser to the local mayor, a small innocent cog in the regional Mafia. After lunch, Poche would sit on one of those southern balconies that hold just a deck chair, rereading in chronological order all Grippes' books. In the late afternoon, blinds drawn, Poche totted up Mafia accounts by a chink of light. Grippes was here, in Montparnasse, facing a flat-white glass door.

He continued to hand himself a forty-five-and-a-half-percent personal exemption – the astonishing thirty-three plus the unheard-of twelve and a half. No one seemed to mind. No shabby envelope holding an order for execution came in the mail. Sometimes in Grippes' mind a flicker of common sense flamed like revealed truth: the exemption was an error. Public Treasury was now tiptoeing toward computers. The computer brain was bound to wince at Grippes and stop functioning until the Grippes exemption was settled. Grippes rehearsed: "I was seriously misinformed."

He had to go farther and farther abroad to find offal for the cats. One tripe dealer had been turned into a driving school, another sold second-hand clothes. Returning on a winter evening after a long walk, carrying a parcel of sheep's lung wrapped in newspaper, he crossed Boulevard du Montparnasse just as the lights went on – the urban moonrise. The street was a dream street, faces flat white in the winter mist. It seemed to Grippes that he had crossed over to the nineteen-eighties, had only just noticed the new decade. In a recess between two glassed-in sidewalk cafés, four plainclothes cops were beating up a pair of pickpockets. Nobody had to explain the scene to Grippes; he knew what it was about. One prisoner already wore handcuffs. Customers on the far side of the glass gave no more than a glance. When they had got handcuffs on the second man, the cops pushed the two into the entrance of Grippes' apartment building to wait for the police van. Grippes shuffled into a café. He put his parcel of lights on the zinc-topped bar and started to read an article on the wrapping. Someone unknown to him, a new name, pursued an old grievance: Why don't they write about real life anymore?

Because to depict life is to attract its ill-fortune, Grippes replied.

He stood sipping coffee, staring at nothing. Four gun-bearing young men in jeans and leather jackets were not final authority; final authority was something written, the printed word, even when the word was mistaken. The simplest final authority in Grippes' life had been O. Poche and a book of rules. What must have happened was this: Poche, wishing to do honor to a category that included writers, prostitutes, and door-to-door salesmen, had read and misunderstood a note about royalties. It had been in italics, at the foot of the page. He had transformed his mistake into a regulation and had never looked at the page again.

Grippes in imagination climbed three flights of dirty wooden stairs to Mme. de Pelle's office. He observed the sea-shell crucifix and a brooch he had not noticed the first time, a silver fawn curled up as nature had never planned – a boneless fawn. Squinting, Mme. de Pelle peered at the old dun-colored Gaullist-era file. She put her hand over a page, as though Grippes were trying to read upside down. "It has all got to be paid back," she said.

"I was seriously misinformed," Grippes intended to answer, willing to see Poche disgraced, ruined, jailed. "I followed instructions. I am innocent."

But Poche had vanished, leaving Grippes with a lunatic exemption, three black-market income-bearing apartments he had recently, unsuccessfully, tried to sell, and a heavy reputation for male-oriented, left-feeling, right-thinking books. This reputation Grippes thought he could no longer sustain. A Socialist government was at last in place (hence his hurry about unloading the flats and his difficulty in finding takers). He wondered about the new file cover. Pink? Too fragile – look what had happened with the mottled peach. Strong denim blue, the shade standing for *giovinezza* and workers' overalls? It was no time for a joke, not even a private one. No one could guess what would be wanted, now, in the way of literary entertainment. The fitfulness of voters is such that, having got the government they wanted, they were now reading nothing but the right-wing press. Perhaps a steady right-wing heartbeat ought to set the cadence for a left-wing outlook, with a complex, bravely conservative heroine contained within the slippery but unyielding walls of left-wing style. He would have to come to terms with the rightist way of considering female characters. There seemed to be two methods, neither of which suited Grippes' temperament: treat her disgustingly, then cry all over the page, or admire and respect her – she is the equal at least of a horse. The only woman his imagination offered, with some insistence, was no use to him. She moved quietly on a winter evening to Saint-Nicolas-du-Chardonnet, the rebel church at the lower end of Boulevard Saint-Germain, where services were still conducted in Latin. She wore a hat ornamented with an ivory arrow, and a plain gray coat, tubular in shape, with a narrow fur collar. Kid gloves were tucked under the handle of her sturdy leather purse. She had never heard of video games, push-button telephones, dishwashers, frozen filleted sole, computer horoscopes. She entered the church and knelt down and brought out her rosary, oval pearls strung on thin gold. Nobody saw rosaries anymore. They were not even in the windows of their traditional verities, across the square from the tax bureau. Believers went in for different articles now: cherub candles, quick prayers on plastic cards. Her iron meekness resisted change. She prayed constantly into the past. Grippes knew that one's view of the past is just as misleading as speculation about the future. It was one of the few beliefs he would have gone to the stake for. She was praying to a mist, to mist-shrouded figures she persisted in seeing clear.

He could see the woman, but he could not approach her. Perhaps he could get away with dealing with her from a distance. All that was really needed for a sturdy right-wing novel was its pessimistic rhythm: and then, and then, and then, and death. Grippes had that rhythm. It was in his footsteps, coming up the stairs after the departure of the police van, turning the key in his triple-bolted front door. And then, and then, the cats padding and mewing, not giving Grippes time to take off his coat as they made for their empty dishes on the kitchen floor. Behind the gas stove, a beleaguered garrison of cockroaches got ready for the evening sortie. Grippes would be waiting, his face half veiled with a checked scarf.

In Saint-Nicolas-du-Chardonnet the woman shut her missal, got up off her knees, scorning to brush her coat; she went out to the street, proud of the dust marks, letting the world know she still prayed the old way. She escaped him. He had no idea what she had on, besides the hat and coat. Nobody else wore a hat with an ivory arrow or a tubular coat or a scarf that looked like a weasel biting its tail. He could not see what happened when she took the hat and coat off, what her hair was like, if she hung the coat in a hall closet that also contained umbrellas, a carpet sweeper, and a pile of old magazines, if she put the hat in a round box on a shelf. She moved off in a gray blur. There was a streaming window between them Grippes could not wipe clean. Probably she entered a dark dining room – fake Henri IV buffet, bottles of pills next to the oil and vinegar cruets, lace tablecloth folded over the back of a chair, just oilcloth spread for the family meal. What could he do with such a woman? He could not tell who was waiting for her or what she would eat for supper. He could not even guess at her name. She revealed nothing; would never help.

Grippes expelled the cats, shut the kitchen window, and dealt with the advance guard from behind the stove. What he needed now was despair and excitement, a new cat-and-mouse chase. What good was a computer that never caught anyone out?

After airing the kitchen and clearing it of poison, Grippes let the cats in. He swept up the bodies of his victims and sent them down the ancient cast-iron chute. He began to talk to himself, as he often did now. First he said a few sensible things, then he heard his voice with a new elderly quaver to it, virtuous and mean: "After all, it doesn't take much to keep me happy."

Now, that was untrue, and he had no reason to say it. Is that what I am going to be like, now, he wondered. Is this the new-era Grippes, pinch-mouthed? It was exactly the sort of thing that the woman in the dark dining room might say. The best thing that could happen to him would be shock, a siege of terror, a knock at the door and a registered letter with fearful news. It would sharpen his humor, strengthen his own, private, eccentric heart. It would keep him from making remarks in his solitude that were meaningless and false. He could perhaps write an anonymous letter saying that the famous author Henri Grippes was guilty of evasion of a most repulsive kind. He was, moreover, a callous landlord who had never been known to replace a doorknob. Fortunately, he saw, he was not yet that mad, nor did he really need to be scared and obsessed.

He had got the woman from church to dining room, and he would keep her there, trapped, cornered, threatened, watched, until she yielded to Grippes and told her name – as, in his several incarnations, good Poche had always done.

1982

Overhead in a Balloon

AYMERIC had a family name that Walter at first didn't catch. He had come into the art gallery as "A. Régis," which was how he signed his work. He must have been close to sixty, but only his self-confidence had kept pace with time. His eyes shone, young and expectant, in an unlined and rosy face. In spite of the face, almost downy, he was powerful-looking, with a wrestler's thrust of neck and hunched shoulders. Walter, assistant manager of the gallery, was immediately attracted to Aymeric, as to a new religion – this time, one that might work.

Painting portraits on commission had seen Aymeric through the sunnier decades, but there were fewer clients now, at least in Europe. After a brief late flowering of Moroccan princes and Pakistani generals, he had given up. Now he painted country houses. Usually he showed the front with the white shutters and all the ivy, and a stretch of lawn with white chairs and a teapot and cups, and some scattered pages of *Le Figaro* – the only newspaper, often the only anything, his patrons read. He had a hairline touch and could reproduce *Le Figaro*'s social calendar, in which he cleverly embedded his client's name and his own. Some patrons kept a large magnifying glass on a table under the picture, so that guests, peering respectfully, could appreciate their host's permanent place in art.

Unfortunately, such commissions never amounted to much. These were not the great homes of France (they had all been done long ago, and in times of uncertainty and anxious thrift the heirs and owners were not of a mind to start over) but weekend places. Aymeric was called in to immortalize a done-up village bakery, a barn refurbished and brightened with the yellow awnings "Dallas" had lately made so popular. They were not houses meant to be handed on but slabs of Paris-area real estate, to be sold and sold again, each time with a thicker garnish of improvements. Aymeric had by now worked his territory to the farthest limit of the farthest flagged terrace within a two-hour drive from Paris in any direction; it had occurred to him that a show, a sort of retrospective of lawns and *Figaros*, would bring fresh patronage, perhaps even from abroad. (As Walter was to discover, Aymeric was blankly unprofessional, with that ignorance of the trade peculiar to its fringe.) It happened that one of the Paris Sunday supplements had published a picture story on Walter's gallery, with captions that laid stress on the establishment's boldness, vitality, visibility, international connections, and financial vigor. The supplement project had cost Walter's employer a packet, and Walter was not surprised that one of the photographs showed him close to collapse, leaning for support against the wall safe in his private office. The accompanying article described mobbed openings, private viewings to which the police were summoned to keep order, and potential buyers lined up outside in below-freezing weather, bursting in the minute the doors were opened to grab everything off the walls. The name of the painter hardly mattered; the gallery's reputation was enough.

Who believes this, Walter had wondered, turning the slippery, rainbow pages. Then Aymeric had lumbered in, pink and hopeful, believing.

He had dealt with, and been dealt with by, Walter's employer, known privately to Walter as "Trout Face." Aymeric

showed courteous amazement when he heard just how much
a show of that kind would cost. The uncultured talk about
money was the gallery's way of refusing him, though a clause
in the rejection seemed to say that something might still be
feasible, in some distant off-season, provided that Aymeric
was willing to buy all his own work. He declined, politely. For
that matter, Trout Face was civil, too.

Walter, from behind his employer's back, had been letting
Aymeric know by means of winks and signs that he might be
able to help. (In the end, he was no help.) He managed to make
an appointment to meet Aymeric in a café not far away, on
Boulevard Saint-Germain. There, a few hours later, they sat
on the glass-walled sidewalk terrace – it was March, and still
cold – with Walter suddenly feeling Swiss and insufficient as
Aymeric delicately unfolded a long banner of a name. Walter
had already introduced himself, much more briefly: "Obermauer." He pointed, because the conversation could not get
going again, and said, "That's my Métro station, over there.
Solférino."

They had been through some of Aymeric's troubles and
were sliding, Walter hoped, along to his own. These were, in
order, that for nine years his employer had been exploiting
him; that he had a foot caught in the steel teeth of his native
Calvinism and was hoping to ease it free without resorting to a
knife; that the awfully nice Dominican who had been lending
books to him had brusquely advised him to try psychoanaly-
sis. Finally, the apartment building he lived in had just been
sold to a chain of health clubs, and everybody had to get out. It
seemed a great deal to set loose on a new friend, so Walter
mentioned only that he had a long underground ride to work
every day, with two changes.

Aymeric replied that from the Notre-Dame-des-Champs
station there was no change. That was how he had come,
lugging his portfolio to show Walter's employer. "I was too
soft with him, probably," Aymeric resumed. His relatives had

already turned out to be his favorite topic. "The men in my family are too tolerant. Our wives leave us for brutes."

Leaning forward the better to hear Aymeric, who had dropped to a mutter, Walter noticed that his hair was dyed, pale locks on a ruddy forehead. His voice ran like clockwork, drawling to a stop and then, wound up tight, picking up again, like a refreshed countertenor. His voice was like the signature that required a magnifying glass; what he had to say was clear, but a kind of secret.

Walter said he was astonished at the number of men willing to admit, with no false pride, that their wives had left them.

"Oh, well, they do that nowadays," said Aymeric. "They wait for the children to." To? He must have meant "to grow up, to leave home."

"Are there children?" He imagined Aymeric lingering outside the fence of a schoolyard, trying to catch a glimpse of his estranged children, ducking behind a parked car when a teacher looked his way.

"Grandchildren."

Walter continued to feel sympathy. His employer, back in the days when he had been training Walter to be a gallery instrument as silent and reliable as the lock on the office safe, had repeatedly warned him that wives were death to the art trade. Degas had remained a bachelor. Did Walter know why? Because Degas did not want to have a wife looking at his work at the end of the day and remarking, "That's pretty."

They had finally got the conversation rolling evenly. Aymeric, wound up and in good breath, revealed that he and his cousin Robert and Robert's aged mother occupied a house his family had lived in forever. Actually, it was on one floor of an apartment building, but nearly the whole story – three sides of the court. For a long time, it had been a place the women of the family could come back to when their husbands died or began showing the indifference that amounts to desertion. Now that Paris had changed so much, it was often the men who returned. (Walter noticed that Aymeric said "Paris" instead of "life," or "manners," or "people.") Probably laziness of habit had made him say they had lived forever between the Luxembourg Gardens and the Boulevard Raspail. Raspail was less than a century old, and could scarcely count as a timeless landmark. Still, when Aymeric looked down at the damp cobblestones in the court, out of his kitchen window, he could not help feeling behind him the line of ancestors who had looked out, too, wondering, like Aymeric, if it really would be a mortal sin to jump.

Robert, his cousin, owned much of the space. It was space one carved up, doled out anew, remodelled; it was space on which one was taxed. Sixty square metres had just been sold to keep the city of Paris from grabbing twice that amount for back taxes. Another piece had gone to pay their share in mending the roof. Over the years, as so many single, forsaken adults had tried to construct something nestlike, cushioning, clusters of small living quarters had evolved, almost naturally, like clusters of coral. All the apartments connected; one could walk from end to end of the floor without having to step out to a landing. They never locked their doors. Members of the same family do not steal from one another, and they have nothing to hide. Aymeric said this almost sternly. Robert's wife had died, he added, just as Walter opened his mouth to ask. Death was the same thing as desertion.

Walter did not know what to answer to all this, especially to the part about locks. A good, stout bolt seemed to him a sensible and not an unfriendly precaution. "And lead us not into temptation," he was minded to quote, but it was too soon to begin that ambiguous sort of exchange.

At that moment Walter's employer appeared across the boulevard, at the curb, trying to flag a taxi by waving his briefcase. None stopped, and he moved away, perhaps to a bus stop. Walter wondered where he was going, then remembered that he didn't care.

"I hate him," he told Aymeric. "I *hate* him. I dream he is in danger. A patrol car drives up and the execution squad takes him away. I dream he is drinking coffee after dinner and far off in the night you can hear the patrol car, coming to get him."

Aymeric wondered what bound Walter to that particular dealer. There were other employers in Paris, just as dedicated to art.

"I hate art, too," said Walter. "Oh, I don't mean that I hate what you do. That, at least, has some meaning – it lets people see how they imagine they live."

Aymeric's tongue rested on his lower lip as he considered this. Walter explained that he had to spend another eleven years working for Trout Face if he was to get the full benefit of a twenty-year pension fund. In eleven years, he would be forty-six. He hoped there was still enjoyment to be had at that age.

"When you are drawing retirement pay, I'll be working for a living," Aymeric said. He let his strong, elderly hands rest on the table – evidence, of a kind.

"At first, when I thought I could pull my funds out at any time, I used to give notice," Walter went on. "When I stopped giving notice, he turned mean. I dreamed last night that there was a bomb under the floor of the gallery. He nearly blew himself up digging it out. He was saved. He is always saved. He escapes, or the thing doesn't explode, or the chief of the execution squad changes his mind."

"Robert has a book about dreams," said Aymeric. "He can look it up. I want him to meet you."

About four weeks after this, Walter moved into two rooms, kitchen, and bathroom standing empty between Robert's quarters and his mother's. It was Robert who looked after the practical side of the household and to whom Walter paid a surprisingly hefty rent; but he was on a direct Métro line, and within reach of friendship, and, for the first time since he had left Bern to work in Paris, he felt close to France.

That spring Robert's mother had grown old. She could not always remember where she was, or the age of her two children. At night she roamed about, turning on lights, opening bedroom doors. (Walter, who felt no responsibility toward her, kept his locked.) She picked up curios and trinkets and left them anywhere. Once a month Robert and Aymeric traded back paperweights and snuffboxes.

One night she entered her son's bedroom at two in the morning, pulled open a drawer, and began throwing his shirts on the floor. She was packing to send him on a summer holiday. Halfway through (her son pretended to be asleep), she turned her mind to Aymeric. Aymeric woke up a few minutes later to find his aunt in bed beside him, with her finger in her mouth. He got up and spent the rest of the night in an armchair.

"Why don't you knock her out with pills?" Walter asked him.

"We can't do that. It might kill her."

What's the difference, said Walter's face. "Then shut her up in her own bedroom."

"She might not like that. By the way, here's your phone bill."

Walter was surprised at the abruptness of the deadlock. Aymeric did not so much change the subject as tear it up. Walter could not understand many things – the amount of his telephone bill, for instance. He did most of his calling from the gallery, dialling his parents in Bern with the warm feeling that he was putting one over on Trout Face. He had been astonished to learn that he was supposed to pay a monthly fee for using the elevator. Apparently, it was the custom of the house. Aymeric was turning out to be less of a new religion than Walter had expected. For one thing, he was seldom there. His old life moved on, in an unseen direction, and he did not offer to bring Walter along. He seemed idle yet at the same time busy. He hardly ever sat down without giving the impression that he was trying to get to his feet; barely entered a room without starting to edge his way out of it. Running his fingers through his pale, abundant hair, he said, "I've got an awful lot to do."

Reading in bed one night, Walter glanced up and had the eerie sight of a doorknob silently turning. "Let me in," Robert's mother called. Her voice was sweet and pitched to childhood. "The latch is caught, and I can't use both hands." Walter tied the sash of the Old England dressing gown his employer had given him one Christmas, when they were still getting along.

She had put on lipstick and eye-shadow. "I'm taking my children to Mass," she said, "and I thought I'd just leave this with you." She opened her fist, clenched like a baby's, and offered Walter a round gold snuffbox with a cameo portrait on its lid. He set the box down on a marble-topped table and led her through a labyrinth of low-ceilinged rooms to Robert's bedroom door, where he left her. She went straight in, turning on an overhead light.

By morning, the box had drawn in the cold of the marble, but it became warm in Walter's hand. He and his employer were barely speaking; they often used sign language to show that something had to be moved or hung up or taken down. Walter seemed to be trying to play a guessing game until he opened his hand, as Robert's mother had done.

"Just something I picked up," he said, as if he had been combing second-hand junk stores and was no fool.

"Picked up where?" said his employer, appreciating the weight and feel of the gold. He changed his spectacles for a stronger pair, ran his thumb lightly and affectionately over the cameo. "Messalina," he said. "Look at those curls." He held the box at eye level, tipping it slightly, and said, "Glued on. An amateur job. Where did you say you got it?"

"I happened to pick it up."

"Well, you'd better put it back." A bright spot moved on his bald head as he leaned into the light. "Or, wait; leave it. I'll look at it again." He wrapped the box in a paper handkerchief and locked it up in his safe.

"I brought it just to show you," said Walter.

His employer motioned as if he were pushing a curtain aside with the back of his right hand. It meant, Go away.

Robert was in charge of a small laboratory on the Rue de Vaugirard. He sat counting blood cells in a basement room. Walter imagined Robert pushing cells along the wire of an abacus, counting them off by ten. (He was gently discouraged from paying a visit. Robert explained there was no extra chair.) In the laboratory they drew and analyzed blood samples. Patients came in with their doctor's instructions, Social Security number, often a thick file of medical history they tried to get Robert to read, and blood was taken from a vein in the crook of the arm. The specimen had to be drawn before breakfast; even a cup of coffee could spoil the result. Sometimes patients fainted and were late for appointments. Robert revived them with red wine.

Each morning, Robert put on a track suit and ran in the Luxembourg Gardens, adroitly slipping past runners whose training program had them going the other way. Many of the neighborhood shopkeepers ran. The greengrocer and the Spaniard from the hardware store signalled greetings with their eyes. It was not etiquette to stop and talk, and they had to save breath.

Walter admired Robert's thinness, his clean running shoes, his close-cropped gray hair. When he was not running, he seemed becalmed. He could sit listening to Walter as if he were drifting and there was nothing but Walter in sight. Walter told him about his employer, and the nice Dominican, and how both, in their different spheres, had proved disappointing. He refrained from mentioning Aymeric, whose friendship had so quickly fallen short of Walter's. He did not need to be psychoanalyzed, he said. No analysis could resolve his wish to attain the Church of Rome, or remove the Protestant martyrs who stood barring the way.

Sometimes Robert made a controlled and quiet movement while Walter was speaking, such as moving a clean silver ashtray an inch. No one was allowed to smoke in his rooms, but they were furnished with whatever one might require. Walter confessed that he admired everything French, even the ashtrays, and Robert nodded his head, as if to say that for an outsider it was bound to be so.

Robert got up at five and cleaned his rooms. (Aymeric had someone who came in twice a week.) He ran, then came back to change and eat a light breakfast before going to work. The first thing he did at five was to put on a record of Mozart's Concerto in C Major for Flute and Harp. He opened his windows; everyone except Walter-the-Swiss slept with them tight shut. The Allegro moved in a spiral around the courtyard, climbed above the mended roof, and became thin and celestial.

Walter usually woke up in the middle of the Andantino. It was much too early to get up. He turned on his side, away from the day. The mysterious sadness he felt on waking he had until now blamed on remoteness from God. Now he was beginning to suppose that people really must be made in His image, for their true face was just as concealed and their true whereabouts as obscure. A long, dangerous trapeze swoop of friendship had borne him from Aymeric's to Robert's side of the void, but all Robert had done was make room for Walter on the platform. He was accommodating, nothing more. Walter knew that he was too old at thirty-five for those giddy, hopeful swings. One of these days he was going to lose momentum and be left dangling, without a safety net.

He could hear music, a vacuum cleaner, and sparrows. The nice Dominican had assured him that God would still be there when his analysis had run its course. From his employer he had learned that sadness was supposed to be borne with every outward sign of elegance. Walter had no idea what that was supposed to mean. It meant nothing.

By the Rondo Allegro, Robert's mother would begin shaking Aymeric awake. Aymeric guided her back to her own apartment and began to boil water and grind coffee for her breakfast. She always asked him what he was doing in her private quarters, and where he had put his wife. She owned a scratched record of "Luna Rossa" sung by Tino Rossi, to which she could listen twelve times running without losing interest. It was a record of the old, breakable kind, and Walter wondered why someone didn't crack it on the edge of a sink. He thought of Farinelli, the castrato who every evening for ten years had to sing the same four tunes to the King of Spain. Nothing had been written about the King's attendants – whether at the end of ten years there were any of them sane.

In his own kitchen, Aymeric brewed lime-flower tea. Later, an egg timer would let him know he was ready for coffee. If he drank coffee too soon, his digestive system became flooded with acid, which made him feel ill. Whenever Robert talked about redistributing the space, Aymeric would remark that he would be dead before long and they could do as they liked with his rooms. His roseate complexion concealed an ashen inner reality, he believed. Any qualified doctor looking at him saw at once that he was meant to be pale. He followed the tea with a bowl of bran (bought in a health-food store) soaked in warm water. After that, he was prepared for breakfast.

When Aymeric was paying a weekend visit to a new patron, in some remodelled village abattoir, he ate whatever they gave him. Artist-in-residence, he had no complaints. On the first evening, sipping a therapeutic Scotch (it lowered blood pressure and made arterial walls elastic), he would tactfully, gradually, drop his chain-link name: he was not only "A. Régis" but "Aymeric Something Something de Something de Saint-Régis." Like Picasso, he said, he had added his mother's maiden name. His hostess, rapidly changing her mind about dinner, would open a tin of foie gras and some bottled fruit from Fauchon's. On Monday, he would be driven home, brick-colored, his psychic image more ashen than ever. Rich food made him dream. He dreamed that someone had snubbed him. Sometimes it was the Archbishop of Paris, more often the Pope.

In a thick, thumbed volume he kept at his bedside, Robert looked up all their dreams. Employer, execution squad, patrol car, arrest combined to mean bright days ahead for someone especially dear to the dreamer. Animals denoted treachery. Walter, when not granted a vision of his employer's downfall, dreamed about dormice and moles. Treachery, Robert repeated, closing the book. The harmless creatures were messengers of betrayal.

Coming up from underground at the Chambre des Députés station (his personal stop at Solférino was closed for repair) one day, Walter looked around. On a soft May morning, this most peaceful stretch of Boulevard Saint-Germain might be the place where betrayal would strike. He crossed the road so that he would not have to walk in front of the Ministry of Defense, where men in uniform might make him say that his dreams about patrol cars were seditious. After a block or so he crossed back and made his way, with no further threats or dangers, to his place of work.

Immersion in art had kept him from spiritual knowledge. What he had mistaken for God's beckoning had been a dabbling in colors, sentiment cut loose and set afloat by the sight of a stained-glass window. Years before, when he was still training Walter, his employer had sent him to museums, with a list of things to examine and ponder. God is in art, Walter had decided; then, God *is* art. Today, he understood: art is God's enemy. God hates art, the trifling rival creation.

Aymeric, when Walter announced his revelation, closed

his eyes. Closing his eyes, he seemed to go deaf. It was odd, because last March, in the café, he had surely been listening. Robert listened. His blue gaze never wavered from a point just above Walter's head. When Walter had finished, Robert said that as a native Catholic he did not have to worry about God and art, or God and anything. All the worrying had already been done for him. Walter replied that no one had ever finished with worrying, and he offered to lend Robert books.

Robert returned Walter's books unread. He was showing the native Catholic resistance to religious history and theology. He did not want to learn more about St. Augustine and St. Thomas Aquinas than he had been told years before, in his private school. Having had the great good luck to be born into the only true faith, he saw no reason to rake the subject over. He did not go in for pounding his head on an open door. (Those were Robert's actual words.)

Robert's favorite topic was not God but the administration of the city of Paris, to which he felt bound by the ownership of so many square metres of urban space. He would look withdrawn and Gothic when anyone said, "The city does such a lot for the elderly now." The latest folderol was having old people taken up for helicopter rides, at taxpayers' expense. Robert's mother heard about the free rides while toying with a radio. Robert borrowed his sister's car and drove his mother to the helicopter field near the Porte de Versailles, where they found a group of pensioners waiting their turn. He was told he could not accompany his mother aloft: he was only forty-nine.

"I don't need anyone," his mother said. She unpinned her hat of beige straw and handed it to him. He watched strangers help her aboard, along with three other old women and a man with a limp. Robert raised his hands to his ears, hat and all, against the noise. His mother ascended rapidly. In less than twenty minutes she was back, making sure, before she would tell him about the trip, that he had not damaged her hat. The old gentleman had an arthritic leg, which he had stuck out at an awkward angle, inconveniencing one of the ladies. The pilot had spoken once, to say, "You can see Orléans." When the helicopter dipped, all the old hens screamed, she said. In her own mind, except now and then, she was about twenty-eight. She made Robert promise he would write a letter to the authorities, telling them there should be a cassette on board with a spoken travelogue and light music. She pulled on her hat, and in its lacy shadow resembled her old black-and-white snapshots, from the time before Robert.

One evening, Walter asked Aymeric if Monique de Montrepos, Robert's sister, had ever done anything, any sort of work. He met a drowsy, distant stare. Walter had blundered into a private terrain, but the fault was Aymeric's – never posted his limits. Aymeric told scandalous and demeaning stories about his relatives; Walter thought that half of them were invented, just for the purpose of teasing Walter and leading his speculations about the family astray. And yet Aymeric backed off a simple question, something like, "Does Robert's sister work?"

Finally Aymeric yielded and said Monique could infer character from handwriting. Walter's picture of a gypsy in a trailer remained imprinted even after Aymeric assured him that she worked with a team of psychotherapists, in the clean, glassy rooms of a modern office building in Montparnasse. Instead of dropping the matter, Walter wanted to know if she had undergone the proper kind of training; without that, he said, it was the same thing as analyzing handwriting by mail order.

Aymeric thought it over and said that her daughters were well educated and that one of them had travelled to Peru and got on quite well in Peruvian. This time, Walter had sense enough to keep quiet.

By June, Robert's mother had become too difficult for him to manage alone, and so his sister, Monique, who did not live with her husband, turned her apartment over to one of her daughters and moved in to help. Her name was added to the list of tenants hanging from the concierge's doorknob. Walter asked Aymeric if "Montrepos" was a Spanish name. Walter was thinking of the Empress Eugénie, born Montijo, he said.

One would need to consult her husband, Aymeric replied. Aymeric thought that Gaston de Montrepos had been born Dupuy or Dupont or Durand or Dumas. His childhood was spent in one of the weedier Paris suburbs, in a bungalow called Mon Repos. The name was painted, pale green on a rose background, on an enamel plaque just over the doorbell. Most family names had a simple, sentimental origin, if one cared to look them up. (Walter doubted that this applied to Obermauer.) Monique was a perfect specimen of the paratroop aristocracy, Aymeric went on. He was referring not to a regiment of grandees about to jump in formation but to a recognizable upper-class physical type, stumping along on unbreakable legs. Aymeric represented a more perishable race; the mother with the spun-out surname had left him bones that crumbled, teeth that dissolved in the gum, fine, unbiddable hair. (There was no doubt that Aymeric was haunted by the subject of hair. He combed his own with his fingers all the while he was speaking. The pale tint Walter had observed last March had since been deepened to the yellow of high summer.) Monique's husband had also carried a look of impermanence, in spite of his unassuming background. Monique's father had at first minded about the name. Some simple names he would not have objected to – Rothschild, for instance. He would have let his only daughter be buried as "Monique de Rothschild" any day. Even though. Yes, even though. Gaston had some sort of patronage appointment in the Senate, checking stationery supplies. He had spent most of his working life reading in the Luxembourg when it was fine, and eating coffee éclairs in Pons on rainy afternoons.

After Gaston Dumas or Dupuy had asked for Monique's hand and been turned down, and after Monique had tried to kill herself by taking port wine and four aspirin tablets, Gaston had come back with the news that he was called Montrepos. He showed them something scribbled in his own hand on a leaf torn off a Senate memo pad.

Well, said her father, if Monique wanted that.

Walter soon saw that it was not true about Monique's stumpy legs. For the rest, she was something like Aymeric – blooming, sound. Unlike him, she made free with friendly slaps and punches. Her pat on the back was enough to send one across the room; a knuckle ground into one's arm was a sign of great good spirits. She kissed easily – noisy peasant smacks on both cheeks. She kissed the concierge for bringing good tidings with the morning mail (a check from Gaston, now retired and living in Antibes); kissed Aymeric's cleaning woman for unpaid favors, such as washing her underclothes. The concierge and the cleaning woman were no more familiar with Monique than with Robert or Aymeric. If anything, they showed a faint, cautious reserve. Women who joke and embrace too easily are often quick to mount a high horse. Of Walter they took the barest notice, in spite of the size of his tips.

Monique soon overflowed two rooms and a third belonging to Robert. She shared her mother's bathroom and Robert's kitchen, striding through Walter's apartment without asking if her perpetual trespassing suited him. In Robert's kitchen she left supper dishes to soak until morning. Robert could not stand that, and he washed and dried them before going to bed. Soon after he had fallen asleep, his mother would come in and ask him what time it was.

"He was her favorite," Monique told Walter. "Poor Robert.

He's paying for it now. It's a bad idea to be a mother's favorite. It costs too much later on."

Entering without knocking, Monique let herself fall into one of Walter's cretonne-covered armchairs. She crossed her legs and asked if anyone ever bought the stuff one saw in windows of art galleries. Walter hardly knew how to begin his reply. It would have encouraged him if Monique had worn clothes that rustled. Rustle in women's dress, the settling of a skirt as a woman sat down, smoothing it with both hands, suggested feminine expectancy. Do explain, the taffeta hiss said. Tell about spies, interest rates, the Americans, Elizabeth Taylor. Is Hitler somewhere, still alive? But all that was the far past – his boyhood. He had grown adult in a world where clothes told one nothing. As soon as he thought of an answer, Monique shouted at him, "What? What did you say?" When she made a move, it was to knock something over. In Walter's sitting room she upset a cut-glass decanter, breaking the stopper; another time it was a mahogany plant stand and a Chinese pot holding a rare kind of fern. He offered sponge cakes and watched in distress as she swept the crumbs onto the floor.

"You've got the best space in the house," she said, looking around.

Soon after that remark, after giving himself time to think about it, Walter started locking all his doors.

Monique and Robert began by discussing Walter's apartment, and moved along to the edge of a quarrel.

"In any case," said Robert, "you should be under your husband's roof. That is the law. You should never have left him."

"Nobody left. It's been like this for years." Monique did not ·mention that she had come here to help; he knew that. He did not say that he was grateful.

"The law is the law," Robert said.

"Not anymore."

"It was a law when you got married," he said. "The husband is head of the family, he chooses the domicile, the wife is obliged to live under his roof, and he is obliged to receive her there. Under his roof."

"That's finished. If you still bothered to go to weddings, you'd know."

"It was still binding when you married him. He should be offering you a roof."

"He can't," said Monique, flinging out her arm and hitting Robert's record-player, which resisted the shock. "It's about to cave in from the weight of the mortgage."

"Well," said Robert, forgetting Gaston for a moment, "he has a lease and he pays his rent regularly. And I am still paying for mending *my* roof." After a pause he said, "Aymeric says Gaston has a rich woman in Antibes."

"I was said to have been a rich young one."

"There is space for you here, always," said Robert instantly. There would be even more, later on. When the time came, they would knock all the flats into one and divide up the new space obtained.

"Look up 'harp' in your dream book," she said. "I dreamed I was giving a concert."

Robert usually got the dream book out on Sundays. The others saved up their weeknight dreams. Aymeric continued to dream he had been slighted. It was a dream of contradiction, and meant that in real life he was deeply appreciated. Robert's mother dreamed she was polishing furniture, which prophesied good luck with the opposite sex. Monique played tennis in a downpour: her affections would be returned. Robert went to answer the doorbell – the sign of a happy surprise. They began each new week reassured and smiling – all but Walter. He had been dreaming about moles and dormice again.

As the summer weather settled in, and with Monique there

to care for their mother, Robert began spending weekends out of town. He took the Dijon train at the Gare de Lyon and got off at Tonnerre. Monique found cancelled railway tickets in wastepaper baskets. Walter had a sudden illumination: Robert must be attending weekend retreats in a monastery. That thin, quiet face belonged to a world of silence. Then, one day, Robert mentioned that there was a ballooning club in Tonnerre. Balloons were quieter than helicopters. Swaying in silence, between the clouds and the Burgundy Canal, he had been able to reach a decision. He did not say what about.

He accepted books from Walter to read in the train. They piled up at his bedside as he kept forgetting to give them back. Some he owned up to having lost. Walter could see them overhead, St. Augustine and St. Thomas Aquinas, drifting and swaying. He had no wish to ascend in a balloon. He had seen enough balloons in engravings. Virtually anything portrayed as art turned his stomach. There was hardly anything he could look at without feeling sick. In any case, Robert did not invite him.

Sometimes they watched television together. Aymeric had an old black-and-white set with only two channels. Monique had a Japanese portable, but the screen was too small for her mother to enjoy. They all liked Walter's set, which had a large screen and more buttons than there would ever be channels in France. One Saturday when Robert was not ballooning, he suddenly said he was getting married. It was just in the middle of "Dallas." They were about a year behind Switzerland, and Monique had been asking Walter, whose occasional trips to Bern kept him up-to-date, to tell them how it would all turn out. Aymeric switched off the sound, upon which Robert's mother went straight to sleep.

Robert said only that his first marriage had been so happy that he could hardly wait to start over. The others sat staring at him. Walter had a crazy idea, which he kept to himself: Would Robert get married overhead in a balloon? "I am happy,"

Robert said, once or twice. Walter fixed his eyes on the bright, silent screen.

Monique prepared their mother's meals and carried them from Robert's kitchen on a tray. She had to make a wide detour around Walter's locked apartment. Everything was stone cold by the time the old lady had been coaxed to sit down. Their mother had her own kitchen, but she filled the oven with whatever came to hand when she was tidying – towels, a shoe-box full of old Bic pens. Once, Monique found a bolster folded in two, looking like a bloated loaf. She disconnected the stove, so that her mother could not turn on the gas and start a fire.

Robert showed them a picture of his bride-to-be. She and Robert stood smiling, with arms linked, both wearing track suits. "Does she run as well as float?" said Aymeric. He turned the snapshot over and read a date and the initial "B."

"Brigitte," said Robert.

"Brigitte what?"

"I don't want anyone driving to Tonnerre for long talks," said Robert. He did say that she taught French grammar to semi-delinquents in a technical high school. She was trying to obtain a transfer to a Paris suburb. There could be no question of the Capital itself: one had to know someone, and there was a waiting list ten years long.

Monique's arrival was followed closely by a new shock from the administrative authorities of Paris: a telephone number old people could call in the summertime, free of charge, in case their families were away and they felt lonely. Robert's mother dialled the number on Aymeric's phone. The woman at the other end – young, from the sound of her – seemed surprised to hear that Robert's mother lived with a son, a daughter, and a nephew, all attentive; had the use of a large television set with plenty of buttons and dials; and still suffered from feelings of neglect and despair. She was afraid of dying alone in the dark. All night long, she tried to stay on her feet.

The young voice reminded her about old people who had absolutely no one, who lived at the top of six steep flights of stairs, who did not dare go down to buy a packet of macaroni for fear of the long climb back. Robert's mother replied that the lives of such people were at the next-to-final stage of hopelessness and terror. Her own meals were brought to her on a tray. She was not claiming more for her sentiments than blind panic.

Aymeric took the telephone out of her hand, said a few words into it, and hung up. His aunt gave him her sweet, steady smile before remarking, "Your poor mother, Aymeric, was nothing much to look at."

Walter, trying to find a place to go for his summer holiday where there would be no reminders of art, fell back on Switzerland and his mother and father. He scrubbed and vacuumed his rooms and put plastic dust sheets over the furniture. Just before calling for a taxi to take him to the airport, he asked Robert if he could have a word with him. He was more than usually nervous, and kept flexing his hands. Terrible things had been said at the gallery that day; Walter had threatened his employer with the police. Robert could not understand the story – something incoherent to do with the office safe. He removed a bundle of clothes fresh from the launderette (he did his own ironing) and invited Walter to sit down. Walter wanted to know if the imminent change in Robert's life and Monique's constant hints about the best space in the house meant that Walter's apartment was coveted. "Coveted" was a heavy word, but Robert finally answered, "You've got your lease."

"According to the law," said Walter, more and more fussed, "you can throw me out if you can prove you need the space." Robert sat quietly, and seemed to be waiting for something else. "I've got to be sure I have a home to come back to – a home I can keep for a long time. This time I really intend to give notice. I don't care about the pension. He's making me an accomplice in crime. I'll stay just until he can train a replacement for me. If he sees I am worried about something else as well, it will give him the upper hand. And then, I'm like you and Aymeric. I feel as if my own family had been living here forever." Robert at this looked at him with a terrible politeness. Walter rushed on, mentioning a matter that other tenants, he thought, would have brought up first. Since moving in, he had painted the kitchen, paved the bathroom with imported tiles, and hung custom-made curtains on rods designed to fit the windows. All this, he said, constituted an embellishment of space.

"Your vacation will do you good," said Robert.

Walter gave Robert his house keys and said he hoped Monique would feel free to use his apartment as a passageway while he was gone. Handing them over, he was reminded of another gesture – his hand, outstretched, opening to reveal the snuffbox.

Their mother had begun polishing furniture, as in some of her dreams. A table in Walter's sitting room was like a pond. Everything else was dusty. The plastic sheets lay like crumpled parachutes in a corner. On Aymeric's birthday, late in August, he and Robert and Monique sat at the polished table eating pastries out of a box. Robert picked out a few of the kind his mother liked and put them aside for her on a plate. They could hear her, in Walter's bedroom, telling City Hall that they had disconnected her stove.

Perhaps because there was an empty chair, Robert suddenly said that Brigitte was immensely sociable and liked to entertain. She played first-class bridge. She had somehow managed to obtain a transfer to Paris after all. They would be getting married in October.

"How did she do it?" Aymeric asked.

"She knows someone."

They fell silent, admiring the empty chair.

"Who wants the last strawberry tart?" said Monique. When no one answered, she cut it in three.

"We will have to rearrange the space," said Robert. He traced lines with his finger on the polished table and, with the palm of his hand, wiped something out.

Aymeric said, "Try to find out what she did with that snuffbox. I wanted to give it to you as a wedding present."

"I'll look again in the oven," Monique said.

"Ask her carefully," said Aymeric. "Don't frighten her. Sometimes she remembers."

Robert went on tracing invisible lines.

Walter came back in September to find his kitchen under occupation, full of rusted sieves and food mills and old graters. On the stove was a saucepan of strained soup for the old woman's supper; a bowl of pureed apricots stood uncovered in the sink. He removed everything to the old woman's kitchen.

I was brought up so soundly, he said to himself. He had respected his parents; now he admired them. At home, nothing had made him feel worried or tense, and he hadn't minded his father's habit of reading the newspaper aloud while Walter tried to watch television. When his father answered the telephone, his mother called, "What do they want?" from the kitchen. His father always repeated everything the caller said, so that his mother would not miss a word of the conversation. There were no secrets, no mysteries. What Walter saw of his parents was probably all there was.

After cleaning his rooms and unpacking his suitcase, Walter called on Robert. He had meant to ask how they had spent their holidays, if in spite of the old lady they had managed to get away, but instead he found himself telling about a remarkable dream he'd had in Switzerland: A large badger had burst into the gallery and taken Walter's employer hostage.

Trout Face had said, "You're not getting away with this. I'm not having anybody running around here with automatic weapons." It was not a nightmare, said Walter. He had seen himself, aloof and nonchalant, enjoying the incident.

Robert said he would look it up. That night he made a neat stack of the books Walter had lent him – all that he could still find – and left it outside his locked front door. He wrote on the back of a page torn off a calendar, "Dream of badger taking man hostage means a change of residence, for which the dreamer should be prepared. R." He rewrote this several times, changing a word here and there. In the morning, after starting the record and opening all the windows, he sat down and read his message again. He kept running his finger over the note, as he had traced new boundaries on Walter's table, and seemed to be wondering if there was any point in trying to say the same thing some other way.

1984

Afterword

BY MORDECAI RICHLER

I first met Mavis Gallant in Montreal in 1950. We were introduced by John Sutherland, the editor of *Northern Review*, the pioneering Canadian "little magazine" where one of her earliest short stories was published. At the time, there were no more than fifty bookshops from coast to coast in Canada, and most of them were really no more than glorified stationery stores. Notable exceptions to that rule were Burton's and Classics in Montreal and Britnell's in Toronto. The indigenous writers we knew of and respected were Morley Callaghan, Robertson Davies, Roger Lemelin, Hugh MacLennan, and Gabrielle Roy, and beyond them there seemed to be only thousands of miles of wheat and cultural indifference. The commonly asked questions put to those of us who were starting out were, "Under what name do you write?" as if the act itself was suspect, or, "Yes, but what do you do for a living?" or, "Good grief, you mean to say you are going to become a *Canadian* writer?"

In these cornucopia days of Canadian best-sellers, Canada Council grants, reading tours, prizes, and at least some newspaper book pages that are not an embarrassment, it is worth remembering that there was a time when any serious writer who sold more than a thousand copies in Canada of his or her novel or short story collection was doing amazingly well. Back in those days S. Morgan-Powell, the resident critic of the Montreal *Star*, denounced both *The Naked and the Dead* and, later, *The Catcher in the Rye* as "dirty books," which seems charming in retrospect, and William Arthur Deacon, the more influential critic of the Toronto *Globe and Mail*, was equally picayune. Changes were in the wind. The audacious Jack McClelland, back from the war, had just inherited the reins at McClelland and Stewart, and the admirable Robert Weaver was beginning to establish himself at the CBC. Between the two of them, they contrived to sponsor writers who would yank Canlit into the twentieth century, but we had no way of knowing that yet.

John Sutherland, a dedicated but fierce man, set the type for *Northern Review*, circulation 400 or so, on a flat-bed press in his basement. I first encountered the short stories of Ethel Wilson in its pages, and – once Sutherland had veered sharply to the right – the poetry of Roy Campbell, who had supported Franco in the Spanish Civil War. Patrick Anderson was a regular fixture at *Northern Review* parties, as were an unhappy Stephen Leacock Jr., F.R. Scott, and, on occasion, Irving Layton, who was seldom without a briefcase stuffed with copies of his most recent poetry collection for sale. But I did not meet Mavis at one of those rambunctious, hard-drinking evenings that often ended in a brawl. When Sutherland discovered that both Mavis and I were bound for Paris, he arranged for the three of us to get together for lunch. Mavis was already a local journalist of repute, a glamorous figure, and I was still a college student, ostensibly cocksure but actually awash in printed rejection slips. In my mind's eye, I can still see Mavis's photograph on top of her column in the Montreal *Standard*, as the Saturday edition of the *Star* was then called. Mavis, looking decidedly saucy in her beret. The first of what would become an increasingly brilliant flow of her short stories had already been accepted by *The New Yorker*.

We met regularly in Paris, going to dinner or the theatre, Mavis tolerant of my foolish, wispy beard. Then I drifted on to Ibiza and London, and years would pass before we managed to get together again in Paris, New York, or Montreal.

It amazed me that Canadian recognition of Mavis Gallant as one of our most gifted writers was so long in coming, most likely because, to her credit, she never ran with the Canlit hounds, but instead chose "exile, cunning." Once, during the '70s, Mavis, who had come to Canada on a university reading tour, phoned me in Montreal. She had been astonished by the hostility of Canadian cultural nationalists who demanded to know why she wrote stories about damn foreigners and why she continued to live abroad, as if that were an act of treachery.

There is a story I cherish about Mavis. Once, I'm told, a naive young Canadian reporter asked her, "Why do you live in Paris?"

To which Mavis replied, "Have you ever been to Paris?"

Mavis Gallant's prose is impeccable, her intelligence daunting, but what is most impressive to me is the ease with which she assumes so many diverse identities in her stories, getting the social nuances and inner-life details exactly right, settling for nothing less than a character's tap-root. Possibly it should come as no surprise that in "The Ice Wagon Going Down the Street" she should faultlessly render a feckless international civil servant, the butt-end of a once prosperous Presbyterian family, adrift in Geneva, filing photographs for an obscure UNESCO agency – Peter Frazier of the Ontario Fraziers. After all, she must have endured more than one such emotionally frozen bore in her formative Canadian years, never mind obligatory expatriate dinner parties in Paris. "If he had been European he would have ridden to work on a bicycle, in the uniform of his class and condition. He would have worn a tight coat, a turned collar, and a dirty tie. He wondered then if coming here had been a mistake, and if he should not, after all, still be in a place where his name meant something." Instead, oh dear oh dear, one day he finds himself reduced to working "for a woman – a girl," Agnes Brusen, a Norwegian out of small-town Saskatchewan, who hangs her university degree on a wall of their shared office that contains two desks, filing cabinets, and a map of the world as it was in 1945. "It was one of the gritty, prideful gestures that stand for push, toil, and family sacrifice." Eventually, Peter of the Ontario Fraziers is liberated. He leaves for a job in Ceylon after "somebody read the right letter, passed it on for the right initials . . ."

Given that Mavis is a first-rate storyteller, I suppose it might also be expected of her that, writing in the first-person in "An Autobiography," she should so movingly portray a Parisian woman who teaches botany to the children of the newly rich in a Swiss school in the immediate postwar years. Two of her pupils are German, and in one damning, typically understated paragraph Mavis tells us more about the new Germany than most writers can manage in a chapter of flat statement. The girls' "parents certainly speak English, because it was needed a few years ago in Frankfurt, but the children may not remember. They are ignorant and new. Everything they see and touch at home is new. Home is built on the top layer of Ur. It is no good excavating; the fragments would be without meaning. Everything within the walls was inlaid or woven or cast or put together fifteen years ago at the very earliest."

What is truly remarkable is that in "The Latehomecomer," writing again in the first person, Mavis can so convincingly imagine young Thomas Bestermann, a German soldier, returning to his forlorn mother's house in a ravaged Berlin, after having been detained overlong as a prisoner of war in France.

Years ago, V.S. Naipaul complained that he could not write any more novels set in England because he did not know what an Englishman did when he went home at night. But in this superb story, Mavis, seemingly without effort, never striking a false note, appears to convey precisely how people talked, and what they felt, in a working-class home in Berlin, circa 1950.

Mavis is an astute, unsentimental observer of the expatriate life. Never guilty of an unnecessary sentence, or redundant adjective for that matter, her beautifully composed stories can also be read for the considerable pleasure of their incidental observations. In "The Moslem Wife," a tale of two British hotel-keepers on the Riviera, she notes: "The Riviera was no place for Americans. They could not sit all day waiting for mail and the daily papers and for the clock to show a respectable drinking time. They made the best of things when they were caught with a house they'd been rash enough to rent unseen."

She is also blessed with a sure grasp of Ontario. In "In Youth Is Pleasure," a charming story about a young woman returning from school in New York to the Montreal where she was born, she writes: "The first time I ever heard people laughing in a cinema was there [in New York]. I can still remember the wonder and excitement and amazement I felt. I was just under fourteen and I had never heard people expressing their feelings in a public place in my life. The easy reactions, the way a poignant moment caught them, held them still – all that was new. I had come there straight from Ontario, where the reaction to a love scene was a kind of unhappy giggling, while the image of a kitten or a baby induced a long flat 'Aaaah,' followed by shamed silence. You could imagine them blushing in the dark for having said that – just that 'Aaaah.'" In this story, incidentally, she conveys how dreadfully easy it is for an intelligent, young single woman to be dismissed and, on occasion, importuned in a man's world, and she manages this without once stooping to flat statement or feminist cant.

*

"The Moslem Wife" and the other stories in this volume present some of the many fictional worlds of Mavis Gallant. But, remember, this collection, rich and far-ranging as it is, should count as no more than an introduction to the work of one of our wisest and most gifted writers.

BY MAVIS GALLANT

DRAMA
What Is To Be Done? (1983)

ESSAYS
Paris Notebooks: Essays and Reviews (1986)

FICTION
The Other Paris (1956)
Green Water, Green Sky (1959)
My Heart Is Broken: Eight Stories and a Short Novel (1964)
A Fairly Good Time (1970)
The Pegnitz Junction: A Novella and Five Short Stories (1973)
The End of the World and Other Stories (1974)
From the Fifteenth District:
A Novella and Eight Short Stories (1979)
Home Truths: Selected Canadian Stories (1981)
Overhead in a Balloon: Stories of Paris (1985)
In Transit (1988)
Across the Bridge: New Stories (1993)
The Moslem Wife and Other Stories (1994)

New Canadian Library
The Best of Canadian Writing

NCL — A Series Worth Collecting

New Canadian Library
The Best of Canadian Writing   *NCL*

NCL — A Series Worth Collecting

New Canadian Library
The Best of Canadian Writing

NCL — A Series Worth Collecting